COURT
of
LIONS

Also by Somaiya Daud

Mirage

SOMAIYA DAUD

COURT
of
LIONS

HODDER

First published in Great Britain in 2020 by Hodder & Stoughton
An Hachette UK company

This paperback edition published in 2021

1

A CIP catalogue record for this title is available from the British Library

Paperback ISBN 978 1 473 65177 7

Typeset in Plantin Light

Printed and bound in Great Britain by Clays Ltd, Elcograf S.p.A.

Hodder & Stoughton policy is to use papers that are natural,
renewable and recyclable products and made from wood grown in
sustainable forests. The logging and manufacturing processes are expected
to conform to the environmental regulations of the country of origin.

Hodder & Stoughton Ltd
Carmelite House
50 Victoria Embankment
London EC4Y 0DZ

www.hodder.co.uk

For those who pray for wanting and wish to be seen.

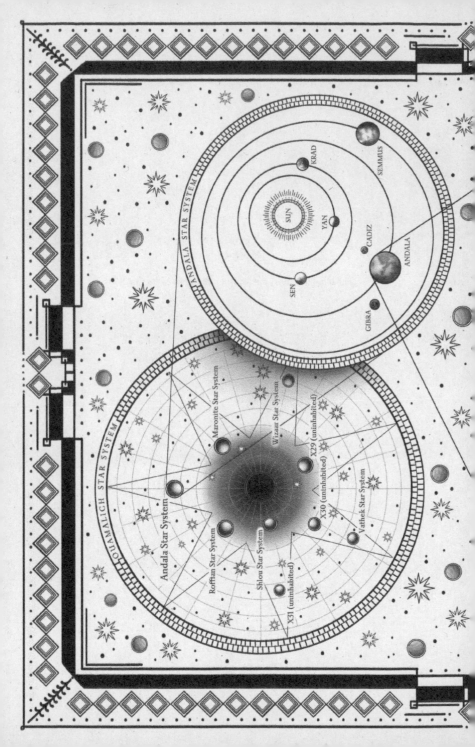

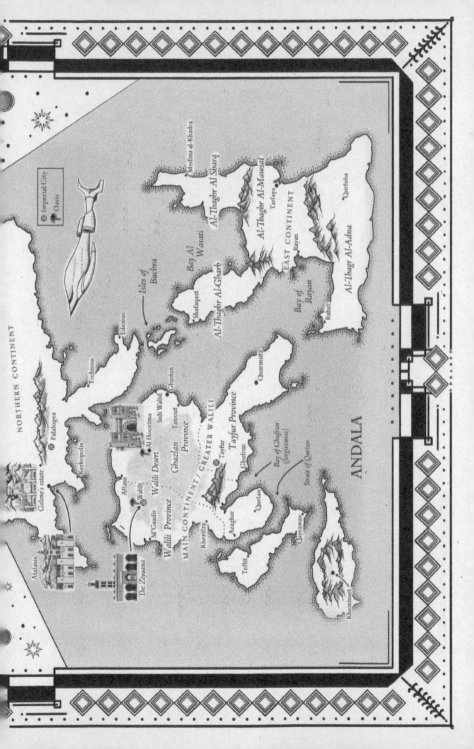

DRAMATIS PERSONAE

KUSHAILA

Amani bint Tariq: a young village girl from Cadiz kidnapped to the imperial palace. The body double to the Imperial Heir, Maram, and temporarily a rebel.

Maram vak Mathis: the half-Kushaila, half-Vathek daughter of King Mathis and Queen Najat, and the Imperial Heir to Andala and the Vathek empire.

Idris ibn Salih: the scion of the Banu Salih and Maram's fiancé.

Tala: Amani's handmaiden and confidante.

'Imad Mas'udi: one half of the ruling pair of the Banu Mas'ud; I'timad's twin brother.

I'timad Mas'udi: one half of the ruling pair of the Banu Mas'ud; 'Imad's twin sister.

Khulood al-Nasiriyya: the ruler of the Banu Nasir.

Tariq: Khulood's younger brother and heir.

Itou al Ziyadia: the exiled Dowager Sultana of Andala and former Ziyadi queen. Maram's grandmother.

Najat al Ziyadia: Maram's deceased mother, the last Ziyadi queen of Andala. Brokered the peace between Andala and the Vath.

ZIDANE

Rabi'a bint Ifran: the newly risen ruler of the Banu Ifran.

Buchra bint Ifran: Rabi'a's younger sister.

Furat al Wattasia: the last living Wattasi, living largely in exile with the dowager sultana. Maram's distant cousin.

TAZALGHIT

Arinaas: Massinia reborn and the leader of the rebellion.

Tinit al-Hurra: Massinia's mother, and the queen of the Tazalghit.

THE VATH

King Mathis: king of the Vath, committed patricide to gain control of the empire. Father to Maram and her elder half sister, Galene.

Nadine cagir Elon: the high stewardess of the Ziyaana and Maram's caretaker.

Galene vak Mathis: Maram's half sister and aspirant to the Vathek crown.

Ofal vak Miranous: Maram's cousin and one of the only family members she gets along with.

One

NASIB: PRELUDE

PROLOGUE

Once upon a time, there was a girl—a nestling—and she was a glorious creature. Born of sacred fire, cloaked in jeweled feathers, she could pass from one realm to another, could cross the space between stars as easy as breathing. She was raised in a crystalline palace wreathed in sacred flame.

When the nestling was a child, long before she'd ever been sent out into the world, her mother told her the story of her long-ago ancestor, Tayreet.

Fi youm minal ayaam . . .

Once upon a time . . .

Like the nestling, Tayreet had grown to strength in the heart of their sacred city, and like the nestling, she'd been sent down to their lost kin as a symbol of strength and war. High above a battlefield an arrow pierced Tayreet's breast and knocked her from the sky. When the prince hunting her found her, her body had loosed its natural bird shape and taken on a human one.

The prince loved her from the first, and Tayreet him.

The nestling was always astonished that anyone might fall in love with their hunter, and her cousin had scoffed and tugged on a white braid.

"Not a *real* arrow, nestling," her cousin said. "Love. Love knocked her from her lofty perch."

How awful, the nestling remembered thinking.

In the center of the palace was a room with nothing but windows and mirrors. From there the nestling could see everything. They showed her life far away, across galaxies and in places hidden away by star dust. In the far corner of the room, wreathed in shadow, was a great mirror, many times as tall as she was. Consigned to shadows but for the great crack that ran through its center, she nonetheless sat in front of it for hours. Its gilt frame was carved with images of birds and lions and spears, and any time she stepped close she felt a pulse of life.

Until at last, one day, it woke and showed her the image of another girl. A princess.

She was young and stone-faced, cloaked in black. Around her forehead was a gold coronet, studded with a single green gem. Her small hand was engulfed by an elder woman's larger one, and she didn't move—she seemed to not breathe at all. A moment later, a procession passed in front of her bearing a coffin draped in green.

She didn't see the princess again, not for many years, though she went to the mirror nearly every day. It showed her other things: the cost of war on the princess's planet, loss of life, rebellion and the rebellion's end. The nestling thought that, perhaps, the stone-faced girl had died. And then one day the nestling returned to the mirror, a woman grown, and found that the princess had grown too, and that she had a twin. Somehow, she knew which was the princess she'd seen all those years ago at the funeral and which was her double.

Please, the double said. *Let me explain.*

Nothing you say will fix this, the princess said, and though her expression was as stone-faced as it had been at the funeral, the nestling could hear a world of grief buried in that single sentence.

I was sincere, the double said.

A viper is never sincere.

Please, Maram. I took your place and risked my life for you.

Maram, the nestling repeated softly to herself, tasting the name for the first time.

And then a woman with silver hair entered.

She saved a rebel, the woman said, and laid her hand on the princess's shoulder. *A person hired to kill you.*

Her heart skipped a beat, startled at the idea that the princess might have died, and she never would have known. Would the mirror have shown her? Would it have revealed a second funeral procession?

Fate intervened as it always did, and for the first time the nestling was commanded from her sacred city and into the war-ravaged world below. It should have surprised her that she was directed to the double she'd seen instead of Maram herself—it didn't. Despite her fascination, there was something about the double—even as she'd begged she'd seemed regal.

The double had saved someone's life. She'd taken the princess's place in the line of fire.

Sacred fire only ever came to the brave and courageous. Hope was given to a person who might reshape the world. The nestling watched it take root in the double, watched the way light returned slowly and chased out the shadows that lived in her now. Saw the double draw in the heat that was a matter of course for someone like her, saw it give strength to her spine and speed to her will.

And from His first creatures He made stars, glowing hot with their fire and warmth.

All may see the stars, but few will see their forbears. And those whose eyes see golden fire We say heed Us and listen.

For We have sent unto you a Sign. See it and take heed.

The nestling's wings unfurled and the double gasped as she cried out and launched herself up and into the sky.

She was meant to return to her sacred city.

She did not.

I

In a city in the heart of the world, in a palace in its very center, was a slave—a *girl*. Once upon a time the girl had borne ancestral markings on her face and danced happily among family and friends. She'd been kidnapped, as all girls in stories were, and brought against her will to the royal palace to serve as body double to a princess. Once upon a time, the girl—*I*—had been a rebel, and forced to make a choice between the rebellion and a princess who had undergone a spell of transformation herself. I'd chosen the princess and saved her life. The price had been high—my family was beaten, and I was threatened with their lives.

On ancient maps of Andala, Walili was the center of the world— all the world on the map was oriented to it, and all roads led to it. The palace had once been its exact center. The "center" was, of course, relative. The world was a globe, and unless Walili had once lived in its core, it was no more central than Shafaqaat or Al Hoceima. And yet it had become the center of my world, cut off as I was from the rest of it. Six weeks had passed in the center of the world. Six weeks of being cut off from the rest of it, being cut off from news, from everyone and everything, save Tala. Tala, my first friend, who even now in the shadow of my greatest mistake, remained with me. Remained *kind*.

A near impossible feat in a place like the Ziyaana.

In my isolation I'd requested a loom and wool to weave. I'd missed the old comforts of my village, and though as a child I'd resented turning wool to yarn, and yarn into tapestry, my days in the Ziyaana were empty unless I was called upon to serve. Tala obliged me and sometimes joined me when I offered to teach her.

In Tanajir, the village of my childhood, I would have made the loom myself, would have heckled my brothers Husnain and Aziz as they attempted to shear sheep the next village over, would have helped in spinning and dying it. Here, all those steps were taken care of by someone else, so I could begin designing the tapestry almost immediately. In the last six weeks I'd managed to produce a tapestry of Massinia, the prophet of Dihya, with her tesleet companion behind her. It was a poor replica of the mural on Ouzdad, but I'd done the best rendering I could.

If I could, I would have worked on the tapestry all day. But the third bell of the morning roused me from my reverie, and despite the enclosure of this wing, the desert chill still managed to seep in early in the morning and late at night. The autumn months were finally here. On Cadiz the first frost would be appearing, coating windows and whatever was left in the orchards and rose fields. I would be darning my winter cloaks, and likely arguing with Husnain over whether we wanted to risk poaching the small foxes that lived at the foot of the mountains. A small crime that I would have gladly gone along with in the past, but with the burning of the orchards before my abduction, would have seemed foolhardy—tempting the Vath soldiers for more trouble.

A small smile stole across my features, then faded. I was lucky he yet lived—Aziz had likely had to tie him up to keep him from reaching out to the rebels the Vath suspected of hiding on our small moon.

I was still thinking of him and the rest of my family when Tala came to collect me.

"The high stewardess has commanded your presence," she said softly. I set the loom down, throat dry.

"Now?" I asked. She nodded.

"Come. Let's get you dressed quickly."

I dressed, and once done, Tala draped a hooded mantle over my shoulders and drew the hood over my hair. Our walk was short and quiet, and at last we returned to the aviary where I'd held my first audience with Nadine. The high stewardess sat on a chair as she had on our first meeting, flanked by four droids and with Maram to her right. Maram didn't acknowledge our entrance, but the droids came to attention and Nadine smiled.

All these weeks I'd dreaded my next meeting with Nadine. She was the shadow cast over my internment, my jailer and kidnapper, determined to break me by any means. I expected to feel small and afraid as I sank to my knees before her.

I didn't.

A hot anger sat in the pit of my belly, churning. Anger at the stewardess and everything she represented, and anger at myself for my ignorance. She was an adversary I'd never accounted for, the hand on Maram's cradle, the snake in the grass, the whisper in her ear. If not for Nadine, perhaps, I might have convinced Maram of the truth: that I was her friend, her sister. Nadine's arrogance and hatred had stolen my home, hurt my family, and finally turned my friend away from me.

"How penitent you seem," she drawled, coming to stand over me.

"My lady," I murmured, then raised my head a little. "Your Highness."

Maram did not meet my gaze. There was a dazed look to her, as if she had slipped somewhere deep inside herself. She had no desire to be here, I realized with a start. Did she not want to see me? What had transpired in the six weeks since we'd seen each other last? I knew her, though Nadine, I was sure, wished I didn't. I knew greatness and kindness lay in her. I *knew* that if given the chance, she would be a great queen. That if given the strength, she would stand up for what was right. Maram understood the weight of her mother's legacy, as much as she had shied from it in the end. If she were out of Nadine's shadow, I *knew*—

"Do you know why you are alive?" Nadine said.

"I am Maram's only twin," I said, rather than hold my tongue.

"The penitence was a ruse, then?" Nadine said. The droids raised their arms as one. "Some contrition would be worth your while, girl."

"I have done my duty," I replied, still looking at Maram. "She is alive."

Maram stared at me, her eyes blank, her chin propped up on the heel of her hand. She looked as a traumatized child might—she had endured this particular horror before, and today she had shut down and refused to engage.

"She's right," she said dully and made a gesture with her hand. The droids retracted their weapons and returned to standing attention. "Get on with it, Nadine."

I frowned in confusion. *It?*

"In a week," Nadine said—was that *glee?*—and returned to her seat, "Her Highness will be getting married. The wedding is a public affair. You will take her place."

My eyes widened in horror. Never would I have imagined that I would have to go through her marriage on her behalf.

I had given Idris up after seeing what Nadine would do to my family. Like my connection to the rebels, the cost of our relationship was too high. I loved him—Dihya knew how much I loved him—but there was no world in which we could be together.

"It's a sacred rite," I gasped out. "For the Vath and the Kushaila. You cannot mean to have me proxy for you?"

Proxy marriages were an old and antiquated tradition. In the past they were the product of distance and necessity. In some places, parents proxied for their children. But we all of us understood that regardless of who went through the ritual, it was the people on whose behalf we enacted those rituals that were married. And so, though it would be me standing there, Maram and Idris would be the ones who were wed.

She raised an eyebrow, and the Maram I'd known at the beginning of my sojourn in the Ziyaana appeared.

"Yes," she drawled. "It is entirely reasonable that I should allow Idris, my political shield among your people, to marry my shield, a *farmer's daughter.*"

I struggled to not lower my gaze, even as I flushed hot with embarrassment. "Then why?" I whispered.

"Sending a proxy in place is perfectly legal. It will not take away from its sanctity and legitimacy. He will still be married to me." Her face was now entirely blank, her voice flat. I was in the grip of a panic, my chest tight with anxiety. I did not want to see him again, to watch those feelings rise up, to have a hand in giving him to someone else.

"But—" I started.

"It is public," Nadine repeated. "And this is *why* you yet live. If you will shirk your duty, then I will march you to the executioner."

I almost reached for Maram, almost begged. The intervening weeks had healed the wound of letting him go, of tearing him out of my heart. This—going through the motions of a marriage to him for someone else—would undo it all.

Maram stood from her chair as silent as a ghost and walked to me. The hems of her skirts brushed over my knees.

"Is there a problem?" she asked softly. "Or are all your words hollow?"

I drew in a shuddering breath and closed my eyes.

"No, Your Highness," I said. "I am capable of fulfilling my duty."

Her hand came beneath my chin, the hold gentle, as if she were cradling a child. As if the look in her eye—that she might take my head at any moment—was not there.

"Understand, Amani," she said softly, "I would do anything just to spite you."

And then her hand was gone, and she swept out of the room, an orchestra of fluttering skirts and the chime of jewelry following in her wake.

❧ 2 ❧

The weeks passed in a blur of fittings and preparation. I had taken in some crucial part of Maram in our time of knowing each other, so falling back into her mannerisms and speech felt like slipping into an old gown. The day of the wedding dawned like any other—I was in the center of the world, but I was not *its* center. No one cared that my world was about to collapse. No one cared that I was about to go through an unimaginably cruel thing in the name of a sovereign nation that had colonized mine.

I sat in a stone tub, its surface covered in flowers. Tala stood in the entryway, hands folded in front of her, an eyebrow raised. Serving girls waited quietly in the dressing chamber just beyond the entryway.

"Daydreaming?" she asked, voice mild.

"No," I said softly. "Just . . . preparing for the inevitable."

"Come, Your Highness," she said. "We have much to do today, and not very much time to do it."

I climbed out of the bath and into the towel waiting for me and dried off efficiently.

The room was quiet as I dressed, with Tala taking lead on guiding the other serving girls. The qaftan was tea and dark gold in color, made of a luxurious velvet, its skirts slashed with silk panels. The bodice was embroidered in ivory thread, a spill of feathers from my shoulders and over my chest, and there was a slender gold belt that went around the waist. The back along my shoulders and down to my hips was made of delicate lace, dyed a pale, tea-like gold, and so too were the insides of the qaftan's sleeves. My hair was smoothed back, the ends braided and threaded with strands of pearls then wound into a bun. From my throat hung several silver strands studded with gleaming red stones, and around my forehead was a silver coronet, with the same stone at its center. I hadn't missed wearing Maram's elegant finery during my time of seclusion. Plain and comfortable qaftans suited me, and I'd liked the way I'd slowly returned to myself in the last month and a half. I was not Maram, and a part of me resented that I would have to be her again, and under such circumstances.

Tala bade me stand and circled me for a moment before producing two hairpieces, a collection of a dozen thin pearl strands. She pinned one on the hair behind each ear. Then came the Vathek crown. Nestled in my curls was a gold wreath that wrapped around the crown of my head. Different flowers, all alien to Andalaan soil, all representative of the wishes of the Vath for their newly married brides. Health, longevity, endurance, fertility: not so foreign, and yet entirely foreign at the same time.

Maram's wedding ceremony would likely be the first of its kind. When her parents, Najat, queen of Andala, and Mathis, her conqueror, married, Najat conceded to a wholly Vathek ceremony. I imagined in part because none of the Kushaila would be able to feign the joy inherent in our rites for such a marriage. But a marriage between Maram and Idris would be—or at least was meant to represent—a marriage between nations and cultures. The ceremony would have to reflect that. A part of me was glad. It would make it easier to live in the reality: this was not my wedding. I was not the one marrying Idris.

It was easy to forget when I was with Idris, but he—and all the children of makhzen families—were hostages. There was little they did—little that Idris did—that was not monitored. There were few choices available to him. And hanging over every choice he made, just as it hung over mine, was the safety of his family.

He had never been mine. We'd only been skilled in creating the illusion that we could belong to each other instead of the Vath.

If this were my wedding, if I were back in Cadiz, if I'd had the freedom to choose, to marry—all of this would be different. I would have worn henna for more than a day so that its stain was as close to black as I could get it, a complement to the sharp, geometric lines of daan that would still be on my face. My clothes would be heavier, brighter, in green or gold or blue. I would be surrounded by women: my mother, Khadija, all of the khaltous of my village.

I would not have been alone, reflecting on my impending marriage rites. My heart would not be filled with dread nor my fingers stiff with fear. If I'd been marrying Idris in truth—

Tala bade me stand and at last deemed my transformation complete. I stared in the mirror, my mind carefully blank lest I give myself away to the other serving girls. The woman who stared back was neither Amani nor Maram, but a princess who resembled neither. She was aloof and remote, without the great rage that characterized Maram or the innocence that had characterized me for a time. "Are you ready, Your Highness?" she asked.

I turned away from the mirror. "Yes."

"You have done well," Tala said. She lowered her voice and squeezed my hand, out of earshot of the others. "Your family remains safe."

"For how long?" I said quietly, then shook my head. This was not the time or place. Whatever Dihya's plans for me, they'd not yet revealed themselves. And in the meantime, I had to pacify both Nadine and Maram.

"I know this is difficult," Tala began.

"It is inevitable," I interrupted. "The dream is over, and the story finished, Tala."

She looked, remarkably, as upset as I was. I covered her hand, which lay on my shoulder, with mine.

"There are worse endings," I said, as much to myself as to her.

She smiled sadly. "There are better ones, too."

There were many outside waiting to witness Maram's purification, her ascent from adolescent girl into a woman willing to enter a savage's home in the name of her empire. Nadine stood in the doorway, her silver hair gleaming in the bright sunlight. There were no embellishments on the dark gray gown she wore, and from her neck hung a pendant signifying her class: High Vathek, and stewardess to the king.

"The water is ready," she said.

Beyond the preparation chamber was a flat open-air pavilion hung with lightweight scarves, all in white, and lined with creamy marble columns. Cut through the middle of the pavilion was a pool of still, crystalline water. And standing all around were women of the highest echelons of Vathek and Andalaan nobility. Beyond the pavilion, in the open air, were high-ranking city folk—merchants, magistrates, and so on. People high enough to warrant an invitation, but too low to merit a front-row seat.

I stepped into the water, no more than an inch deep. As I walked, Vathek and Andalaan alike flicked sanctified oil toward me.

Finally, I reached the end of the pool. I stepped out and knelt on the waiting cushion as Nadine and Maram's elder half sister, Galene, came to stand over me.

"Be blessed," they said, as Galene tipped a small vase of oil over my hair.

Be blessed echoed back from the crowd, reverberating and out of sync. I felt a chill rush up and down my spine. Sometimes it was easy to forget that the Vath were aliens to our world. And the soft, rising murmur, like wind ripping through grass, so different than any wedding celebration I'd ever attended, reminded me. No crying out, no expressions of joy, no singing. Only stately whispers.

Be blessed.

I didn't think, no matter how much all those attending believed in those words, that it was possible.

A pair of serving girls came forward with a great blue veil of sheer cloth, its edges stitched in the Kushaila style with gold thread. In the Vathek style it would have been white and not so sheer, and as a compromise it was as large as a Vathek veil. The two held it carefully over the gold wreath atop my head and draped it just so, as another serving girl came forward with a pair of gold slippers for me to put on.

I rose to my feet and caught a glimpse of my reflection—of a woman preparing to face a planet that hated her to marry a prince they loved. I loved—we all had loved—stories of clever girls of little means who'd risen high above their rank to marry a prince. Khadija and I had spent hours telling and retelling them to each other, imagining a world where it was possible. I'd imagined—

The dream was over, the story done.

I was grateful for the veil. For the first time in many months, I felt as I had during my first days in the Ziyaana. Not even Tala's presence beside me carrying the trail of my gown could alleviate the loneliness. The crowd was silent and hushed, though I heard the whir of camera probes and the soft murmur of journalists narrating to their liaisons across the galaxy.

The first words of a Kushaila wedding song rang out over the crowd and at last my tears fell as the whole city seemed to echo in song.

I didn't remember the ceremony. I was conscious of the fact that Idris never let go of my hand. That we knelt side by side as the ceremony progressed. That at some point the wreath was drawn from my head and set on a pyre. I knew that I looked up at him and recited Vathek

and Kushaila vows and that he repeated them gravely. I knew that I
saw the same pain at this final separation in his eyes that I felt in my
heart. Neither Vathek nor Kushaila custom demanded a kiss, and for
that I was grateful. I could not have endured it.

But at last the applause and cheer of Vathek and Andalaan nobility both pierced my mind, and I looked up as if waking from a dream.

The next I knew, the veil was lifted and at last I could breathe. I
was alone with Tala as she touched up the kohl around my eyes and
replaced the pins on my shoulders with Kushaila brooches, preparing
me for the feast.

She was straightening the folds in my gown when the doors opened.
Mathis, *King* Mathis, stood framed in the doorway, his tall and broad
form blocking out the light of the other room. Tala dropped to her
knees instantly, and I joined her a little more slowly, as Maram would.

"Your Eminence," I murmured.

He flicked his hand at Tala, who shot me a quick glance before all
but fleeing the room. I couldn't blame her. There was a malignance to
the Vathek king's presence, as if terror spawned in his wake. I didn't
know if he'd been informed I would be taking Maram's place, and I
would not risk the discovery of a plot that would anger him. Instead,
I remained perfectly still, waiting for his leave to rise.

Instead, he came in front of me and slid a gloved hand beneath
my chin.

"You are the image of your mother," he said, his voice low. "Without her softness or her doubt."

Nothing he said was a threat, and yet I felt the threat of violence
in the single movement, in his refusing to give me leave to stand, in
the way he spoke of the late queen. And I feared, viscerally, what he
would do if he realized that I was not his daughter.

"You will suffer a Kushaila spouse as I suffered a Kushaila spouse
in order to do what is necessary," he said quietly. I felt a spark of rage
rise up in me on Maram and Najat's behalf. If anyone had suffered
it had been Najat, whose marriage had robbed her of her life. She'd
survived the civil war that predated our conquest, and all the ills and

difficulties that came with it. She'd survived the war of conquest, the occupation, the siege of Walili. Her marriage had sapped the life out of her, or so public opinion believed.

How would Maram have reacted to the maligning of her mother, who she—we—so closely resembled? In all likelihood as she had suffered everything from her father. In dignified silence.

"Come along," he said. I moved as if I were a droid reduced to its base programming. My hand slipped into the crook of his elbow, and his large hand in turn first adjusted my veil so that it fell correctly. I could hear Tala falling in line behind us, straightening out the folds of my gown so that they trailed behind me just so.

The doors to the hall boomed open, and somewhere a herald announced our entrance.

The reception hall was a grand ballroom, with a high glass ceiling, and fortified glass walls all around. This, I knew, was the center of the center of the world. The light refracted off white clouds, so that everything had a pink, orange, and red cast to it. The sun would be entirely gone from this side of the planet soon, and in its place would be a hundred shining orbs of light, and many strung over the ceiling, to mimic the stars.

The king guided me to the center of the room, and I sat demurely on the divan. A moment later his fatherly hands lifted the veil from my face and crown and pinned it to my shoulder.

"Feast," he said softly, "for tomorrow is a new world."

3

Up until the ceremony, I'd been surrounded only by women. And during the ceremony itself, I could not focus on anything but Idris—on avoiding his eyes, on trying to make sure he did not see me, realize that it was not Maram who stood across from him. But now, I was aware of all the Vathek and Andalaan men who were present. Those who'd been denied Maram's hand and access to the throne, and those who mourned the loss of the last heir of the Banu Salih, at last absorbed into the Vathek family structure. By Vathek and Kushaila law, Maram had been absorbed into Idris's household. But in practice, Idris was more tightly bound than ever to the Vathek throne and their aims. Every now and then I would look out at the crowd feasting and laughing and singing and I would find more than one pair of eyes fixed on me, contemplative and hostile.

It was no wonder Maram didn't want to attend her own wedding.

Mathis stood behind me with a few other dignitaries and directors. Ambassadors from planets conquered by the Vath, generals in his imperial war, high-level representatives from the galactic senate. Maram's inheritance of the planet, and therefore Mathis's hold on it, relied on her marriage to Idris, or so I understood. Here Mathis could survey the work of the last twenty years: his daughter, born of a marriage to a savage he had *stomached* in the name of the state. The makhzen who, in another life, might have supported her against him now suitably afraid of him and the cost of dissent. Their children firmly in the grip of empire, hostages in all but name, raised in the Ziyaana against their will. The Vathek aristocrats vying for his favor. All the wealth of the worlds laid out at his feet, carousing at his daughter's wedding.

I could barely stand to look out at their faces, to see evidence of his triumph. It was a twofold triumph: Najat's marriage to Mathis all those years ago, and now Maram's marriage to Idris. The Vath and Andalaans were now more tightly bound than ever.

I hated these people. Even those who had suffered in the war of conquest, even those who had no choice about the people they'd become. Few had known the hunger and disease of a siege, much less understood the terror of the sudden appearance of the Imperial Garda. Here they were, wreathed in finery and jewels, celebrating the seal of our doom. And here *I* was, a slave, alone, trotted out as a shield. I was in the center of the world and I was alone.

The doors opened again and a herald announced Idris. Maram's husband.

He was haloed by the brilliant light shining in through the windows like some sort of prince out of legend. His hair was shorter than I remembered, his face clean-shaven. He wore black trousers and a black jacket embroidered in gold, with a tea-gold shirt beneath it. I remained perfectly still and drank him in as if I were a woman denied water all her life. He was as I remembered—tall and broad-shouldered, his face gentle, his mouth tilted into a half smile. I saw the moment his smile faltered when our eyes met—how quickly he recognized me. Electricity zipped along my skin as he took my hand and bent over it, as his mouth brushed over my knuckles.

"Lady wife," he murmured.

I had forgotten and not forgotten, thought and not thought about Idris and this moment.

I lowered my gaze and folded my ringed hands against my skirt. I was a fool—I'd spent no time preparing for this eventuality, for having to see him again like this. The stakes of our separation were real; I could not risk the safety of my family, nor he his. But it made it no less a bitter pill to swallow, no easier to watch him play the part of a man happily wed to someone else. I'd never felt as if I needed to flee his presence, but today the air seemed to suffocate me, and the reality of my situation came to bear down on my shoulders.

He leaned forward and pressed a gentle kiss to my forehead. My eyes closed and I inhaled, savoring this one moment in time. The reception continued around us, but for this half heartbeat he was mine and I was his. We had duties to perform and our families depended on our success. I could not wallow or weep or linger. So I steeled my spine and committed this sliver of a moment to memory.

"We have ministers to greet," I said softly.

His eyes met mine again for a moment, and then he took up his spot beside me.

The light filtering through the glass was now red—the sun was setting, the day was ending, and the orbs of light strung up high across the ceiling were flickering to life like distant stars. Idris and I had sat through a receiving line of ministers, dignitaries, and directors, then passed a circle through the room, greeting his cousins and friends. Mathis had taken the time to announce with a great deal of gravity that the Salihis would host continuing wedding festivities at M'Gaadir. I had never been, but now my mind was occupied by images of quiet rest at a seaside city.

A chime sounded through the air and Tala tapped my arm gently.

"Wardrobe change," she said softly. I squeezed Idris's hand in warning and departed with her a moment later. She led me to a small parlor stocked with a mirrored vanity and a wardrobe filled with clothes for this occasion.

"How do you feel?" she asked as I slid out of my slippers.

"Stretched too tightly," I said, watching her reflection as she unbuttoned the back of my gown.

She hummed in response. "We have some time before dinner begins. Once you are in your new gown, the orchard is through that door. You can rest."

I closed my eyes. "Thank you, Tala."

I shrugged the tea-gold gown off and stood still as she drew a black undergown over my head. Its sleeves were cinched tightly at my wrists, but the rest of it flowed down to my feet. When I shifted this way and that, thin threads of gold glittered in the light. Over it went a gown of ivory lace, studded with tiny champagne-colored beads and silver thread. Its sleeves were wide and its neck was low, so that one saw the black-and-gold gown beneath it. Around my waist was a leather belt, a hand wide, stitched with a tesleet, its wings spread to wrap around my waist.

"There," Tala said. "I will collect you when it's time."

The garden was an orange orchard. I recognized the trees—their fruit was perennial and its scent was sharp in the air. It reminded me of my majority night. There were lights strung through these trees and somewhere in the garden a fountain flowed, babbling cheerily into the silence. There were no birds—no animals at all, and it gave the orchard a still, hushed feeling. I breathed deep and lifted my face to the sky.

When I lowered my face, there stood Idris, framed by the trees and the light of the setting sun. I knew it was only my heart that made him appear more than he was—not just a prince for this moment, but a prince out of legend and antiquity. A man who belonged at the immortal center of the world.

"Amani," he said softly. He'd crossed the orchard without my hearing, and now slid a hand beneath my chin and raised my face so that he might look at me. The breath I took lodged itself beneath my breastbone like a knife and I couldn't stop myself from covering the hand now pressed against my cheek with my own.

"You look well," I said at last, meeting his eyes.

"As do you," he replied.

A thousand words lodged in my throat. What did I say to him? That I loved him? That I thought of him always? That of all the possible futures I would have chosen—

"You're safe," he said, and it was as if some spell had broken. His arms came around me and drew me against his chest. I laid my head against his shoulder, and my hands clung to the back of his jacket. "Dihya—I'd thought—Nadine is a terror, she would not have balked at killing you for so small a slight."

I choked out a laugh. "I think she considered, before realizing that my family was a better target."

He drew back, his eyes wide. "Are they safe?"

"I don't know," I said and hated the waver in my voice. "I've had no news since the coronation. This is the first time I've been allowed out. Nadine says . . . she says that so long as I perform as I'm expected no harm will come to them."

"Do you trust her?"

Another laugh that sounded too much like a sob. "I don't have a choice."

"Amani—"

I shook my head and leaned away from him. He was resplendent in his wedding finery, a vision of Kushaila grace and dignity. Dihya, he was married. I pressed a hand over his heart.

"I did not expect this day to come so quickly," I said, voice thick with tears. "Even though—"

He laid his hand over mine and squeezed. "Nor did I," he said. "I thought we might have more time. One more meeting before—"

"Before you were married," I whispered. "I wish we'd run away when you asked."

The sound he let out was half laughter, half grief. "You don't mean that."

His mouth was curled into a half smile, but grief lay heavy over his eyes. He was right, of course—I didn't mean it. I couldn't mean it, not with everything at stake. And yet, Kushaila legend was filled with lovers who cared nothing for the consequences and everything for each other.

"I—"

"Our families would pay too high a price," he said, giving voice to my thoughts. "And we would neither of us be able to live with that. We both have family being held hostage by the state. Neither of us would take that risk."

"No," I replied softly. "And yet, I dreamed of it."

His expression sobered. "You don't dream of it anymore?"

I blinked back my tears. "How can I? You are someone else's husband now."

His thumb stroked my cheek and I closed my eyes as a shiver rolled through me.

"You are always in my mind, Amani. And in my heart."

"As you are in mine."

He pressed one last kiss against my forehead, squeezed my hands, and then we parted. He walked to his dressing parlor, and I to mine. Our paths would not cross in this—in *love*—ever again.

01. Maram

Maram's grip tightened in the folds of her gown as ocean winds buffeted the cruiser for the hundredth time in the four-hour flight. It was only wind, she reminded herself. Not an assassin, not a gravity beam meant to reel her ship in. Powerful late-summer winds were the norm in this part of Andala, and so close to the surface of the water there was bound to be turbulence.

She had not left the Ziyaana in the weeks following the attempt on her life. She'd made appearances among the makhzen and Vathek courtiers, smiled as if nothing were wrong, and expected a knife in the dark every moment. Eventually, she'd had enough and, without warning or permission, packed her bags.

The cruiser shuddered again, but for once this shudder was welcome. Outside she saw the ground rushing up to meet them. She came to her feet, smoothed her hands down the folds of her qaftan, and took a deep breath.

This place, this estate, was safe. It was well guarded, and no one made it past its boundaries without passing through a bioscan. The wall to her left hissed and detached, then lowered into a ramp.

Waiting for her beneath a linen canopy were twelve servants all dressed in green and white, the Ziyadi crest embroidered on their right sleeves. Heading them up was an elderly Kushaila woman.

As a group they knelt. Maram made a quick motion with her hand and the woman—Fatiha—stood.

"Welcome, Your Highness, to Dar at-Tuyyur."

"The last stone was set almost a month ago," Fatiha said as they strolled down the path. The cruiser had landed in one of the flower meadows east of the main estate. "All the flowers you requested have been imported, and half the fields have been planted."

"The orchards?"

"Coming along," Fatiha replied.

"It looks so different," Maram breathed.

Twenty years ago, the estate and the surrounding lands had been rubble. Bombed out of existence by air raids during the Vathek conquest of Andala, almost nothing had survived. But Maram had pictures—holos of her mother's visitation to the falconing retreat, recordings of hunts from the years before the Vath ever darkened Andalaan skies. And in the six months since Maram had decided to rehabilitate it and rebuild, it was transformed into something close to what it might have been in antiquity.

The first time she'd set foot here there'd been green, but it'd been the wild untamed greenery that sprung up after wildfire. Now, in the distance, she could see the aviary tower, gleaming in the early-morning sunlight, and the flags with her mother's crest, whipping in the wind.

"Yes," Fatiha said with a smile. "We have come a long way toward your vision. And we are all quite proud of the result, Your Highness."

"What remains to be done?"

"The aviary is empty," she said, her voice clipped and efficient. "We'll need to hire a falconer, which I'm working on, and implement a breeding program."

Maram wandered from the beaten path and into the fields. She'd seen pictures of what this part of the estate looked like prior to the work she'd ordered. It was chaotic—beautiful but unordered. The grass was knee-high, but a few feet away from where she stood the dirt was overturned, and stacked neatly on small benches were flower bulbs. The world was in chaos and on the brink of civil war. Maram couldn't fix that—she couldn't fix the world. But she could do this, she could instill a little peace and beauty in these twenty square miles.

When she turned around, Fatiha was watching her, her dark eyes soft, as if she didn't see Maram when she looked at her. No one looked at her as Fatiha did, not on purpose.

"What is it?"

She'd expected her to avert her eyes or look embarrassed, but the old woman met her eyes. She forgot, ofttimes, that Fatiha had been nursemaid to queens. She'd raised her mother Najat and served her grandmother Itou. There was very little that cowed her.

"You look very much like your mother, Your Highness," she said when Maram returned to the path. "You remind me of her."

Her gut twisted, half pleasure, half unease. "Children often resemble their parents."

"Few could emulate a will such as your mother's," Fatiha replied, and then began to walk again. "Shall I show you the main palace?"

Maram watched as the great iron doors to the palace groaned open on their own power. The walls of the palace were high and sturdy, the stone a pale gold. She followed Fatiha inside and they in turn were followed by the twelve servants who'd greeted Maram at her landing. The walls were hung with thick tapestries; the floor a brilliant white stone.

"The palace is almost an exact replica of its pre-conquest predecessor,"

Fatiha said. "Your assistance in providing holos and film from your mother's cultural archive were a great asset, Your Highness."

Maram fought the feeling of pride that unwound in her belly. This project— she loved and hated it with equal measure. It was her respite, as it had been her mother's, and yet it was wholly alien to everything Vathek in her life. She should not have come, she should not have built it, and yet she followed Fatiha through the palace as if a string were tied to her breastbone and drew her through its bright and high-ceilinged halls.

"The courtyard," Fatiha continued, leading Maram out into sunlight, "is the crown jewel of the palace."

Her eyes widened as she took in the verdant center of the palace. It seemed to go on forever—nearly the full length of the palace. They were on a rise—several steps would take them down to the floor level—and from the rise she could see the tops of orange trees, the gleam of water winding its way through. A sharp cry echoed through the air.

"You've introduced peacocks?" she said, trying to hide the delight in her voice.

"Your mother loved them," Fatiha said. "I imagined you might like them too."

"Should I be on the lookout for other wildlife?" she drawled.

"A small family of gazelles," Fatiha said.

Maram stared at her, eyes wide. "You can't be serious."

"Of course I am," Fatiha said, her voice perfunctory. "Now come along."

Maram followed quietly as if she were a young child and not the Vathek heir. Her eyes remained wide as they swept over vegetation and wildlife— aside from the peacocks and gazelles she saw pheasants, and the air was filled with birdsong. Every few minutes she'd see a brilliant flash of jewel-toned feathers as a small bird darted from one branch to the next.

"And here is my favorite part of the estate," Fatiha said, her voice laced with warmth. "The Ziyadi triptych—the artist did it in the classical style."

Maram's breath punched out of her on a quiet gasp as she looked up. The image was threefold: her grandmother, her mother, and Maram herself. Her grandmother was resplendent in a Kushaila hunting outfit, astride a horse, with a great golden eagle on her fist. The Golden Punishment—the eagle was legend for having taken down a deer on its own and lifting it into the air for several minutes. On the right was a good likeness of Maram herself, turned away from the viewer, bow in one hand, arrow in the other. Hovering over her head was a small falcon, a freedom falcon, its wings outstretched as if it were ready to pierce the vault of heaven at any moment. Like her grandmother, she wore a green Kushaila hunting jacket, but she'd explicitly asked the artist to have her turn away so that the absence of daan on her face would not be so clear to the viewer.

Maram almost walked away before looking at her mother's image. But there was an inexorable pull to her, as in life so too in death. This was the greatest departure of the painting—elsewhere in the palace generations of Ziyadi women hunted on horseback and with falcons and spears, but here Najat bint al-Ziyad stood in ivory and black, with a tesleet on her fist, its crown of feathers a brilliant white. Though Mathis had scoured Najat's Kushaila daan from her face as a stipulation of the peace and marriage treaties, here they were depicted on her brow and cheeks, and clutched in her left fist were gold-tipped arrows.

This version of her mother was one Maram seldom saw—when she was a child, Najat had only ever looked so when they'd emerged out of the shadow of her father. In holos she caught glimpses of her—the vibrant woman who'd inherited a kingdom recovering from civil war, who'd been equal to the task of its many problems. People in the Ziyaana remembered Najat's last days, bedridden, hollowed out by sickness and disease.

Maram remembered the woman in front of her, back straight, gaze fierce. Forged in fire and made of steel.

"Your Highness." Fatiha's voice held a faint note of doubt, as if she worried she'd made a mistake in showing the triptych to Maram. The princess schooled her features and tried to return herself to the present. Fatiha stood beside her, gesturing to a pathway leading further into the palace.

"We have set out a light repast for you, if you wish to rest before touring the rest of the grounds."

She bodily turned herself away from the painting. Her stomach turned with unease—this was a bad idea. There was no escaping the past in a place meant to replicate it. There was no holding on to her Vathek roots in a place where she pretended they didn't exist.

"Yes," she said, her voice even. "Let's."

The palace, aviary, and surrounding lands all made up a large estate for Ziyadi heirs called Dar al-Zahra', the house of flowers. Maram had wanted, more than anything, when she began this project, to have a place without worry. A place she could go outside without needing guards or droids. She didn't trust the locals any more than she trusted the people who lived in the imperial palace—the estate borders had an airtight security grid that prevented anyone from passing through. Those who wanted to leave had to go through a complicated exit process, and security codes were changed every four hours. It was expensive and far-reaching and complicated, but it meant that Maram could mount a horse and ride out onto the grounds on her own, without escort or worry.

But now, as she rode out into the late-afternoon air, wrapped in a heavy velvet mantle, she shivered. There were times when all she could hear was the first shot, when all she could see was sunlight glinting off the metal of the blaster. This place was safe, she'd made it so, and she would not let some nameless, faceless boy take it from her.

Maram was good at not thinking, at ignoring the great things that her conscience required her to see. And so it was with practiced ease that she turned away from the facts: she had not stood on that stage, she was not the one who'd faced a child turned killer. Amani, her body double, had. It was easy to settle into the selfish fear and anger that cared only about herself—the child had been trying to kill Maram, not Amani, after all. And so it was easy to shed the difficult feelings of being afraid for another person, of fearing for them, of caring about them. She did not think about the risk Amani took for her, or the complicated situation they now found themselves in. She did not think about how desperately she missed Amani's friendship or the gulf that now stood between them because of her betrayal.

She thought of the horse beneath her, and the sky above, and the cry of a ghazal falcon. Nothing else.

Maram's heart beat a staccato rhythm behind her ribs. The woman stood in the open field between four hills. She was well into the estate, but she didn't creep the way Maram expected someone who had trespassed on royal property to creep. She stood tall, her broad shoulders straight. She was beautiful, her skin a dark copper, her black hair bound into hundreds of braids and held in place with a silver clip. Her cheekbones were sharp, her mouth wide, her face stoic. On each arm was a silver vambrace nearly the length of her forearm; she held her left arm aloft, and as Maram watched, a small young falcon alit on her wrist.

Maram's grip tightened on her horse's reins as she realized the impossible: it was a wild falcon, without bells or leash or hood. It had come to the woman of its own volition and settled on her wrist without bait or prompt. It remained there, its wings outstretched for balance, and when she lifted a hand and stroked its breast, it cooed, as if it were a tame nestling.

Wild falcons had no tolerance for people, less tolerance for being treated like pets. Maram's grip tightened on the reins further, sure the falcon would attack the woman at any moment, and the horse neighed and shook its head in protest. The falcon startled—it gave out an angry, sharp cry, and launched itself into the air in a flurry of wings and talons. The woman watched it climb in the sky, her expression bemused, seemingly unharmed. In truth, the woman's encounter with the falcon should have left her with several large wounds, and perhaps even a missing eye or finger.

For long moments Maram stared at her as if what she was—who she was—might resolve itself in her mind. She'd never seen her before on the estate. Certainly, she'd never seen someone at such ease and in such harmony with a wild hawk. Part of her wondered if she'd wandered into a dream.

At last the woman turned her gaze from the sky to Maram, and the princess flinched at the directness of her stare. Her eyes were so dark they were nearly black, and Maram felt them cut through her like a scythe through wheat. When the woman bowed she didn't lower her eyes, and the bemused, half-cocked smile did not leave her features.

"Your Highness," she said, then straightened.

Something like lightning rushed up Maram's spine and she didn't know if it was fear. She was on her estate alone, with nothing but a horse for protection, with a stranger who should not have been able to make it onto the grounds.

"Who are you?" she said at last. "And what are you doing on my estate?"

"I am Aghraas, a master falconer."

Fatiha had hired her.

"It's been twenty years since humans have disturbed this ecosystem," Aghraas said. Maram had at last descended from her horse only to find that Aghraas was a head taller than her. "Your stewardess—"

Maram startled, frightened that her secret might have escaped her already. "My stewardess?"

"Fatiha," Aghraas said patiently.

Of course. Nadine was no longer her only stewardess.

"Your stewardess," Aghraas continued, "wanted the whole of the estate mapped, including potential hunting and nesting grounds. She was quite insistent that I attempt to calendar breeding cycles, which is a bit harder."

"Why was I not informed that you were hired?"

"I only started yesterday," she said and then smiled. "You must not scold Fatiha too harshly. I was eager to start as soon as possible, and I took advantage of her divided attention."

Maram turned her face away sharply. "Well?"

"Well?" Aghraas repeated.

"The falcons—how are they?"

The falconer smiled at her and Maram felt that rush of lightning again. Her fists clenched in anger.

"Come here at dawn and I'll show you."

4

I thought with the wedding over and my part finished I might be given a reprieve. I returned to my chambers in the early hours of the morning free of the weight of Maram's jewelry and heavy wedding regalia. I bathed and broke my fast, then settled down to work on my tapestry. I had only just picked up my loom when Tala arrived.

"Her Highness has summoned you to her chambers," she said, holding out a cloak and veil.

I frowned, startled. "What for?" She had done this once before, in the days just after my return to Gibra. Then it had been boredom, but what a new bride could be bored *of* was beyond me.

"She would not tell me, Amani," Tala said, and shook the cloak at me. "But she was insistent both that I retrieve you and that I do so with all possible secrecy and haste."

My eyebrows rose. "Secrecy?"

"*Amani*," Tala snapped, and my eyebrows rose higher. She was never short with me. "Please. I did not like how insistent she was, and you know how she is."

"I'm sorry," I said, standing. "You're right. I just—what could she possibly want?"

"I cannot imagine," Tala replied as she draped the mantle over my shoulders. "You know her better than I do."

Maram stood as she had that long-ago day, one hand braced on the stone balustrade of her balcony, the other twisted in the folds of her skirt, robed in finery and gold. She was limned by the golden afternoon light, her body framed by the out-of-season greenery of her garden's treetops rising into the air behind her. Her body was as still as a statue, her expression stoic and regal as if she'd stepped out of a painting of antiquity. She wore a mask, when she rarely needed to with me. Her rage or her happiness—what I saw was of little consequence, for I could relay it to no one, nor could I use it against her.

I sank to my knees, mind racing. It had seemed to me the last time I'd seen her that she wanted nothing to do with me. But here she was now, without her stewardess, and quick on her heels was an air of secrecy.

"Your Highness," I greeted her as I came to my feet. "Is anything amiss?"

"Why should anything be the matter?" she said.

I would have agreed except for the hollow ring of her voice.

"Have I displeased you in some way, Your Highness?"

"I do not think of you enough for you to displease me, Amani," she said, voice cool. "I have summoned you to give you another assignment."

My eyebrows rose. "Assignment?"

"You are to take my place tonight," she said, turning away from me.

"Tonight?"

"Are you a parrot?" she snapped. "Yes. The wedding procession into the marriage bed."

I could not stop the surprised laugh that came out of me. "You can't be serious."

"I didn't think your duty was a laughing matter."

I stared at her, bewildered. The wedding procession to the marriage bed was the consummation night. It was not a festival or a dinner or any other engagement for which I was prepared to take her place. It was a private family affair—the bride waited for her husband as he was escorted to their new and shared bedchamber. There was no risk of harm—certainly not enough to invoke her shield. And she had come here alone, without Nadine.

Something clicked into place. Nadine did not *know*.

Regardless, I wouldn't. I couldn't.

"No."

"You are refusing a royal command—"

"I am a *shield*, not a doll," I said.

"Amani—" I ignored the way her face had drained of color, the way my name came out of her mouth: small and frightened. I'd rarely felt rage as I did then, but my grief had given way to it, at long last. Had I become so small in Maram's mind that she might barter my body for her own peace of mind on her wedding night? She didn't know that I loved him—and even if she had, the marriage was done. The marriage bed belonged to Maram, and I would not enter it.

"Idris is *your* husband," I said, forcing my voice to be even. "It is *your* duty to consummate the marriage."

"You don't understand—!"

"Explain it to me then." I was dangerously close to yelling. "You are asking me to be you on a night you are expected to bed him. Have I fallen so low in your mind that you would prostitute me?"

My rage had at last eclipsed my sense.

Her eyes glimmered in the light of her room and searched my face as if she might find softness or weakness. She would find neither.

She stepped back. Her shoulders sagged as if strings that held her up had been cut, and she sank down onto a bench on the balcony.

My rage did not disappear entirely, but I felt fatigue take its place. I sighed as I sat down beside her.

"Why don't you want to go to your wedding night?"

She huffed a nervous laugh. "I just . . . I can't explain it. All my life I've known I would have to lie with a man." She rubbed her hands up and down her arms. "I can't do it."

My eyebrows rose. "Idris is widely regarded as one of the best-looking young men on the planet," I said. "More importantly for you, he is kind and cares about you. He would never harm you."

"You don't understand," she whispered and shook her head. I watched her hands, twined around one another, white knuckled in their grip. "I can't. Just . . . until I talk myself into it."

Talk herself into it?

"Even if I wanted to," I told her, "Idris would know the difference between us immediately. You delay the inevitable. You've known you would marry him most of your life, Maram."

"Then don't sleep with him," she said. "I don't even care if you tell him you aren't me. Just. Take my place in the bed."

"Wait." I raised a hand. "Your Highness—"

"You had no problem helping me—" she burst out.

"Before my family was beaten in your name?" I asked.

Her mouth hung agape in shock for a moment, and then to my horror I saw a glimmer of tears. None of them fell, but I remembered a different girl who had come to me, desperate to do right by her mother's legacy. Who had been terrified of all the things that were expected of her, of the two worlds she had to straddle to avoid death.

She swallowed. "I didn't do that."

"Someone did."

"And so I should pay the price?"

"Someone should," I snapped, then took a deep breath.

"I liked things before," she said softly. Here again was the girl I'd come to know in the last days before her coronation, peeking out at me again. Not gentle-hearted, but frightened and in need of an ally.

"Before I made things difficult with my split loyalties?"

"Yes."

"But they aren't split at all," I told her. If the girl I'd known for an instant would come back. If she would trust me again. "I risked my life for you, Maram. *That* is where my loyalty lies."

"If that's true, why won't you do this for me?" She looked so frightened, and I knew it wasn't of the marriage bed. I *knew* her, though she wanted to pretend I didn't. Something else was at play here. If this had been about her marital duties, she would have sent Nadine in her place—what an easy thing it would have been to do, and for Maram in particular. *I will not bed down with savages.*

I took another breath and closed my eyes. It was an unfair thing she asked of me, but she didn't know the half of it. But I knew *her* well enough to know that she would not show this side of herself to me unless her need were truly dire. What that need could be, I could not begin to imagine. But Maram showed the softest, most vulnerable parts of herself to no one.

"I will not sleep with him. Not even for you," I said to her. "And if he asks me why you are missing, I shall send him to you."

Relief washed away her fear and doubt and brought forth the girl I'd known briefly, bright-eyed, beautiful, and *happy.* Her head dropped and she braced her hands against the bench as if to get herself under control. When she came to her feet she didn't look at me. Instead she walked to the glittering outfit hanging off the wardrobe. She raised a ringed hand to it and trailed a touch down its center.

"What would your wedding have been like, Amani?" she said. Her voice was blank, even—there was none of the emotion I'd heard only moments ago. Not even the cool, slightly amused charm that normally preceded her anger. It was as if she'd wiped it all away in an attempt to return us to what we were—master and slave. As if she abhorred that she'd had to ask me anything at all and wanted to erase the moment.

"I won't have a wedding, Your Highness," I said, struggling to control the sharp spike of anger.

"Oh?" she said without turning around.

"Unless you are in the habit of allowing your body double the luxury of a personal and private life," I said, my voice at last even and flat. "No, I will not."

I rose just as she turned away from the gown. I imagined we were mirror images of each other, faces carefully blank, bodies held in tension.

"No," she said at last. "I suppose you won't."

She gestured to the vanity.

"I'll have the gown sent to you. And this, too." She lifted a necklace from her jewelry box and laid it against my neck. "It was my mother's."

It was beautiful and more complicated than any of the jewelry I had worn to date. Eight strands of pearls gathered on each side of the necklace with a gold nugget studded with emeralds and met at the center behind a circular brooch that just barely fit in the palm of my hand, it was so large. The brooch itself was several discs of gold layered over one another, etched with Kushaila designs ringing a large emerald.

"It matches you," she said softly, fastening it behind my neck. Her mask slipped. "Us."

I examined her carefully, though she avoided my gaze now. There were dark circles under her eyes, and a strange, haunted look about them. If I knew less about Maram, I would have guessed she was in the grip of some illness.

"Are you alright?" I asked.

The mask dropped back into place and the necklace went back into the jewelry box.

"Tala will collect you when it's time," she said coolly. Her eyes met mine in the mirror briefly, then skittered away. "Go."

I rose to my feet, then paused in the doorway. The urge to comfort her for some invisible thing lay over me like a weight. It was absurd—I was the one being forced into an impossible position. But I could not help but wonder how *much* we mirrored each other—what impossible position was Maram being put in, that she would ask this of me? And how much of a fool was I that I had agreed to it?

But whatever Maram thought of me, I was her friend, and loyal to her besides. And I knew something she would never admit: I was the stronger of the two of us. I could bear up under this single night. I was not brittle, like she was. And I knew, soon enough, she would come to understand that. To understand why she had come to me first and not Idris with this fear.

5

The royal bedchamber was beautiful. Lushly carpeted, dark wood paneling, tapestries depicting moments from the Book and from history. The bed was wide and large, stacked with pillows, and hung with light curtains that lifted on the ocean breeze. I sat in the center of it, my eyes fixed on the window open to the ocean, and waited. Brass lanterns hung from the ceiling, and two more sat on the floor on either side of the bed.

I'd entered the bedchamber from the side door that led to the dressing room, flanked by three serving girls, including Tala. A hand held mine as I climbed the few steps from the floor and up to the mattress, and was settled in its center. The trail of my gown and mantle were arranged around me just so, and I was bid to fold my legs beneath me, instead of pulling my knees up to my chest as I wanted.

"It will be easier," Tala said to me gently, "for the Salihi tradition."

My eyes widened in alarm. "Salihi tradition?"

"Be calm," she said. "A rosewater ceremony."

I stared at her bewildered, but she didn't expand and so I waited with my hands in my lap. The lamplight glinted off the rings on my fingers and the bracelets on my wrists.

Earlier, Tala had ringed my eyes with kohl and arranged my hair so that my curls hung over my shoulders and down my back, threaded with gold chain. I wore heavy earrings with green stones, rings, a necklace, and several bracelets of Kushaila design. I tried not to think about why I wore them—to be taken off—so late in the evening. I wore a simple, flowing red gown, belted at the waist, and an even lighter black mantle, stitched with gold.

It's just a play, I told myself as voices singing Kushaila song rose up outside the door. *You're just an actor. It's not real.*

Two of the serving girls walked to the double doors of the suite and pulled them open. Sound flooded in—they were singing unaccompanied by instruments, though many clapped their hands in time to the song. The sea of people—no more than a dozen, though they sounded louder—parted and there was Idris in their center.

He wore a white djellaba, and his hair was loose and curled beneath his ears. He looked as haunted as I felt and did not manage the smile of a groom elated to at last meet his bride. I watched him carefully, my heart thundering in my chest, as he clambered onto the bed and sat across from me, his legs folded beneath him as mine were.

His family circled us, and one of his cousins came forward with a silver bowl filled with rosewater.

"That had better not be for the bed," I said, and his cousin grinned. I recognized him—one of the few who had been allowed to grow up in Al Hoceima: Fouad.

"Don't worry, cousin," he said cheerfully. "It's to purify mouths and hearts."

I stared at him, uncomprehending.

"To drink," Idris said gently. It was over quickly—Idris dipped a cup into the bowl and held it for me to drink, and I in turn dipped a second cup into the bowl and held it for him to drink. His hand wrapped around my wrist and his grip tightened when his eyes fixed on my face.

He knows.

I drew the cup away and Fouad pulled it from my fingers. I heard a roar in my ears as the Salihis recited a short prayer over us, and then filed out of the room. The serving girls, including Tala, filed out after them, the doors clicked shut, and we were alone.

For long moments we sat in the center of the bed, neither one looking at the other. His hand reached forward and he linked his fingers through mine.

"She sent you in her place," he said softly.

"Yes," I replied and at last moved.

"Is she . . . she's alright, isn't she?"

"Yes."

"Then why—"

"She's afraid," I said. Afraid, and carrying a secret, I thought. But I couldn't say so to Idris. I wouldn't betray her trust.

"Of me?" he asked, bewildered.

"Of marriage."

"Oh. Do you—"

"I'm fine," I said, sliding off the edge. A moment later I stumbled but managed to right myself easily.

"Amani."

I didn't respond. There was a vanity at the far end of the room, and it was there I went. The process of removing my jewelry was a slow one. None of the bracelets were large enough to pull off—each required that a link be undone. I worked methodically and single-mindedly, as if no one else were in the room. So focused was I on my work that I didn't hear Idris climb off the bed and walk up behind me. His hand covered mine where it worked on the last bracelet.

"Let me help," he said. I couldn't meet his eyes but held up my wrist for him to finish. The bracelet came off, and I turned away and lifted my hair. There were four latches to the pearl and emerald necklace

Maram had sat around my neck. I watched Idris in the mirror as he began undoing them.

He was so far from me now—further than I'd ever imagined him being while being in the same room. The first latch came undone, and the necklace sagged. I dropped my hair over my shoulder and began to work the rings off my shoulder. The second and third latch came undone. Maram, it seemed, had never done up the fourth one, so the necklace slid down my chest and hit the vanity dresser with a loud crash.

I ignored it—Idris's thumb pressed against the exposed skin of my neck, the knobs of my spine as they disappeared beneath the collar of my gown. He pressed his face into my hair.

"Amani," he said hoarsely. I was afraid to move, as if I might dislodge him, or worse, might turn to him and press myself into his arms. "I'm haunted by you—by us."

I forced myself to turn around and raised my hand to his cheek. "I was told to reveal my identity to you—to protect myself. Tell her you don't wish to see me anymore," I said.

His forehead lay against mine. "That's the problem, isn't it? You are the only one I want to see."

It was that, for some reason, that broke whatever held back my tears. I disliked tears—they seemed to me at this juncture a waste of time. What was done was done—our story was over. And yet there was no clean end, no avoiding Idris or my heart. I pressed my face against his shoulder and clung to him as he put his arms around me.

"It isn't fair," I rasped through my tears.

"No," he said into my hair. "It isn't."

My fingers tightened in the folds of his shirt, and at last I forced myself to pull away.

"Idris," I said, "I'm serious. You must tell her—I can't keep doing this. *Please.*"

"This is all we have, Amani," he said and brushed a thumb over my cheek.

"It's not *enough*," I cried, pulling away. "Can you keep doing this? Stuck in limbo like this? You have a *wife.*"

"Amani—"

"You have a wife," I repeated, voice softer. "Think about how painful that is for me. To be made party to your marriage. To be forced into its intimate spaces."

"She won't listen to me," he said at last. "She never has."

I dropped into the vanity seat and covered my face. I wondered if this was what Maram had felt—sick and caught adrift, unable to wrangle her destiny into place. A moment later Idris joined me and took one of my hands in both of his.

"Before—before we were ever this, we were friends," he said softly. "Allies. We can be allies in this, too, Amani. I would not see you come to harm—I would not see you in so much pain."

"You think an alliance would be less painful?" I asked hollowly. "It's a new word for the same situation."

"With a new goal: survival. It's all we have ever been able to do," he replied.

It's not enough, I wanted to scream. Nothing under the Vath was ever enough.

But I closed my eyes and nodded, turned my hand under his and linked our fingers.

"We have both survived worse," he reminded me when my eyes opened. "And we have the scars to prove it."

"Friends, then," I said softly.

"Always," he replied, then stood. "Take the bed. I'll sleep on the divan."

We were quiet as we readied for bed properly. I'd never really thought about the sounds one made when one settled into bed. The shift of clothes, the ripple of the duvet as it was lifted, the quiet sigh of pillows and body both as one reclined. But now the sounds filled my ears as I climbed into bed. Idris's breath seemed loud as he blew out the last few lanterns—manually lit in what I can only imagine was a fit of romantic nostalgia.

At last it was dark and quiet, and I curled in on myself and tried to block out the world.

Friends, I thought, and squeezed my eyes shut. I had been friends with Idris before. We had *always* been friends. That was the problem, wasn't it? We were one heart and one mind. We had been drawn inexorably together, against all odds, despite the threat that loomed over us from the very start.

In Kushaila there were degrees of love: *gharaam, 'ishq, najoua, la'wa, hoyaam.* Attachment, passion, communion, anguish, madness. It felt as if we had passed through all of them. And it seemed to me there was no de-escalation. The old stories that invoked such words ended in union or death. Nothing would bring Idris and I together, and I could not submit to death. So what else was there for us? Submission and grief? *Khula?* Deep friendship? Could one go back from the pain of love to its serene origins?

There was no choice for me, I supposed. I would find out.

⇥ 6 ⇤

I slept fitfully that night, burrowed under the covers, my body cramped and tormented by an uncomfortable sleep. I'd been aware of every noise—the skitter of servants' footsteps before dawn, the scrape of tree branches against the balcony. Now, the sun's rays peeked in through the wooden slats at the far end of the room. In my grogginess the bedroom seemed as another world—dust motes floated in the air, and the room seemed to glow, as if drenched in the light of the sacred fire of the tesleet.

Idris frowned in his sleep, and slept on his back, one arm beneath a pillow, the other outstretched toward me, as if he were searching for me. Now, I slipped from the bed as quietly as I was able and made my way to the bathing chamber. It was empty, save for Tala, who had filled the stone tub in the center of the colorful chamber with steaming water.

"I am blessed by your friendship," I said to her gratefully, gripping her hands.

She smiled. "I imagined you would want to flee as fast as possible. But you cannot afford to shirk her morning routine—so, quickly. Into the tub."

We were well practiced at this routine by now. I scrubbed as she washed and oiled my hair. In under an hour I was out of the tub, dried, dressed in a blue qaftan, with my hair braided in Maram's preferred style.

I hesitated for a moment in the dressing room. It was cowardly of me to flee Idris after our conversation last night, but I hadn't lied. This—being forced into this part of his life—was painful. I did not want to know what he looked like when he woke in the morning. So I fled and returned with Tala, veiled and hidden, to the double's suite. It was time for this part of the farce to end and for Maram to take up her spot beside Idris.

I found her in my parlor, seated on a divan, her hair hanging loose around her shoulders. She was facing my in-progress tapestry of Massinia with a heavy mantle wrapped around her and a steaming glass of tea cradled between her hands. Tala left us alone, and the sound of the door clicking shut behind her drew Maram's attention away from the tapestry and to me. She examined me as she had examined the tapestry before finally gesturing to a seat across from her.

"So," she said, tucking her hair behind her ear. "What happened?"

I hated the sting that appeared behind my eyes. I wanted to keep our conversation private, the trials of the night to myself. But I couldn't, not with Maram's eyes on me waiting for some answer. Nor could I risk a lie.

"He knew I wasn't you," I said at last and took the glass she offered me gratefully. "He said—"

"Yes?"

I shook my head. If I told her we'd agreed to be friends it would raise more questions.

"He slept on the divan," I said. "I left before he woke."

"How chivalric of him," she said and, setting the glass down on the table between us, came to her feet. "Now that he knows who you are, the next few weeks should be easier for you."

I flinched as if she'd struck me. "What?"

"You will take my place beside him during the celebrations at M'Gaadir."

"*No!*" The word burst out of me without thought. My whole soul rebelled at such a thing.

"No?" she repeated, her voice dangerously flat.

"I cannot play-act you for the duration of the celebration—that's *two months*," I choked out.

"Why?"

There was a dangerous tenor to her voice, and yet I could not heed it, raw from last night, reeling from the shock of such a request.

"This may come as a shock to you," I said, fighting back my anger. "But I do not enjoy being you."

Something like a shudder went through Maram, as if she were trying to rein herself in.

"You are admirably steel-spined for someone who has committed treason." Her face seemed to go through as many emotions as I was feeling. Rage. Fear. Grief. Did she mourn what we had been before this as I did?

I tried to take hold of my emotions. Maram was not a girl to be manipulated, but she didn't trust me and I *needed* her to, for both of our sakes.

You are stronger than her. You can bear more.

"I don't know what I expected—why would anyone want to be the focus of a rebellion's assassination plot? Better to side against her and eliminate the problem entirely."

I didn't close my eyes as I wanted to. This was not a problem I could look away from. This was not a belief I could allow to endure. I set aside my pain and came to stand next to her. Against my better judgment, I laid a hand on her arm. She flinched.

"You *joined* them," she said without looking at me. "You said that we were sisters, and then you joined them. And now—"

"Before I was kidnapped—"

"I didn't order your kidnapping," she interrupted, and I squeezed her arm.

"I know," I said softly. "But I *was* kidnapped. And before I was kidnapped, the Imperial Garda burned down my village's only source of food. Half the village is either dead of starvation or has moved on to experience poverty in another city. During my kidnapping my best friend was shot. And when I arrived in the Ziyaana I was beaten, isolated, and attacked by a hunting raptor. My joining the rebels was not about you. It was about the Vath. About your father."

Still, she wouldn't look at me.

"And despite that—when the time came to choose between my life and yours, I chose your life, Maram."

Her gaze was hollow and disconnected. "Why?"

"Because you are our only hope," I said. "Because I saw something tremendous in you."

Her head jerked up and her eyes widened. "What?"

"You have the makings of a great queen, Maram," I said. "And I did what I could to save that."

"Really?" she said hoarsely. She blinked rapidly. "Do you still think that?"

"Yes." And the truth was that I did. Whatever Maram and my personal quibbles, in moments like these I saw a version of her that must have always existed. Vulnerable and soft and honest—whatever her father had tried to make her into, he hadn't been wholly success-ful. There existed in her a woman who could lead our planet to pros-perity, who cared about justice—she only needed to be coaxed out.

Something in the flash of her eyes, the reflection of light on un-shed tears, reminded me of the tesleet. It had come to me after I'd thought I'd lost everything—my family beaten, my friendship with Maram in tatters, and alongside it the future of everything I'd envi-sioned. The tesleet had come to me in my lowest moment and brought hope with it. It was a sign from Dihya, a calling to do what was necessary. It meant, I knew, that I had to *help* Maram since I could not and would not depose her. That I *could*, despite my current circumstance.

"I'm sorry—" she began, and I was so unprepared a laugh slipped out. "Why are you laughing? I was serious!"

"I just don't think I've ever heard you apologize," I said, smiling. "For anything."

"I have," she protested. "I think."

My smile widened.

"You're impossible," she said, but there was a hint of a smile at the corner of her mouth.

I sighed. "I will take your place at M'Gaadir. But I truly can't do it forever. The longer I play at being you, the more of a disadvantage you will have. This is the time to build relationships, Your Highness. You will have to face your destiny sometime."

"My destiny as someone's wife?" she asked dryly.

"As someone's future queen," I corrected.

Maram and I parted on tenuous but hopeful ground. She returned to take up her spot beside Idris, and I remained in the double's suite to help Tala pack for our trip to M'Gaadir. Now that I had agreed, all that was left was to do it.

"You are very brave," Tala said as she hung up a qaftan. "And very strong."

I huffed out a quiet laugh. "I am pragmatic," I said. "Which is what happens when you are the only daughter with a foolhardy brother. When there is something to do, the only answer is to do it."

She smiled. "You never talk about them."

I rubbed at the rib-space over my heart. "It's easier not to."

A bell sounded then, signaling a visitor's arrival. Maram had already gone, which meant the only other possibility was Nadine. Tala and I exchanged a look and I gestured for her to leave.

"I'll handle it," I said softly, and went out.

Nadine stood in the center of the courtyard attended by a single Garda droid. I sank to my knees demurely and bowed my head.

"My lady," I greeted her.

"It is good to see the Kushaila can take a lesson," she said. "Though I wonder if this is simply more of your excellent acting."

I said nothing and kept my eyes on the ground.

"You did well enough at the wedding and feast," she continued. "Well enough, at least, to convince the princess that you are a necessary and reliable security measure to bring along to M'Gaadir."

Still I remained silent, but my mind raced. So, she *had* kept the wedding night a secret from Nadine. What was she hiding that even the high stewardess could not know?

"The princess has not returned to the foolish state of mind you instilled in her months ago," Nadine continued. "She knows your kind are not to be trusted. So, you will be the shield that anticipates the knife, the wrist upturned for the viper. Understand?"

"Yes, my lady," I said.

"The celebration is a honeymoon hosted by the Salihis," she went on. "In light of that, the families present will be Andalaan, though that should be small comfort to you. Most of them will ape at being Vathek. You will tour the city, host these families, and be ready and willing to die in her place. You will behave *as Maram* at all times. Am I clear?"

"Yes, my lady."

"Sending you with Maram is not an act of trust," she said at last. "It is an unfortunate necessity."

"Yes, my lady," I said again.

"'Yes, my lady,'" she repeated. "How sweet you are."

Her hand gripped my chin. I was sure when she released me there would a trail of four small crescent moons indented in my skin.

"Understand this," she said, her voice hard, and jerked my chin. "Your family's survival depends on your cooperation. Misbehave, and they will begin to lose both limb and life."

A chill settled at the pit of my stomach. Nothing would erase the image of my brother being beaten by the Imperial Garda.

But Nadine's omission of the bedding ceremony had revealed something to me. She did not control Maram as she thought she did. More importantly, this visit revealed that she knew it and feared it. Feared *me*. Feared what sway I had over Maram, and the pull her kin would exert when she was surrounded by them. Perhaps even encouraged to love them.

I bowed my head when she released my chin. "Yes, my lady."

Two

TARD: THE HUNT

7

M'Gaadir had been the seat of Kushaila power in antiquity. When the Ziyadis unified the planet, it became the seat of their first rulership, and thereafter the heir to the planet ruled from the estate. It was the birthplace of the first Kushaila, Houwa, and the place she'd built after being crowned queen of the Kushaila.

It was also our beginning.

Millennia ago, on the edge of our continent where sand met sea, a few miles from where the first stones would be laid for M'Gaadir, a clutch of tesleet eggs washed ashore. The clutch had been lost and wandered through space far from its celestial nest, or so the stories say. When at last they landed on our planet and hatched, the first of mankind came from their hallowed shells. And because they were far from the sacred flames of their city, they never became what they ought, and remained mortal. And it was from these people that Houwa came and

nursed the kernel of magic in her blood. And it was from this legacy
that they chose their name—Kushaila, "those among the noble."

The queen's estate rested where many people believed Houwa had
stood after the slaying of her conqueror husband, a crown on a hill
that overlooked the city and the sea. It was a two-story structure,
ringed by a wall, and with two towers, one rising out of its southern
end, the other from its eastern side. I sat in the southern tower now,
hidden by the shadow cast over its balcony, looking down at the city.
The estate was surrounded by palm trees, and I could hear the roar
of the ocean as it threw itself over and over against the cliffs. A herd
of goats bleated as someone shepherded them around the walls of
the estate and down the hillside. The city extended around us like a
skirt draped over the hillside. White and sandstone, green and blue,
everywhere I looked there was a flash of color like jewels stitched into
fabric.

I wondered if Maram's mother, Najat, had drawn strength from
the memory of our first queen after she'd married Mathis. She had no
family to plot with, no magic to support her. Only her wits and her
will and her determination. My fingers were wrapped in the strand
of prayer beads as my mind bounced between thoughts of one queen
to another and the vision spread out before me. The two-month-long
festivities celebrating Idris and Maram's marriage would take place
here, and it would be more Kushaila than the festivities thus far.

I wondered if *Maram* thought of her mother in this place and all
the things she'd endured at the hands of her father.

The chambers I was allotted at M'Gaadir were nearly as run-
down as my quarters in the Ziyaana. Instead of a single room and
a garden, I'd been given a two-level suite with its own courtyard.
A strange excess, but one I was grateful for even if I would rarely
be allowed to use them. I drew in a breath, then stepped away. I'd
been given a small reprieve since Maram had arrived as herself, but
at any moment I could be expected to take her place. If the sound of
footsteps echoing off the steps was any indication, Tala had at last
come to collect me.

The estate was already in an uproar. In true Kushaila fashion, two of the families sworn to the Salihis had arrived ahead of schedule. The Mas'udis and Nasiris were makhzen who controlled less land but commanded as much respect as any of the old families. They had to be greeted by both Maram—*myself*—and Idris. I dressed quickly in a blue brocade qaftan with black stitching—it had a high collar and epaulets on each shoulder besides. I was not much one for armor, but it made me feel stronger to be so robed in Maram's clothes as I entered a situation I very much did not want to.

The courtyard where the Salihi guests gathered opened out into an orchard that sloped down toward the city. Its trees were tall and thick enough that you could not see the city of M'Gaadir at all, and if we so wished it, we might raise the shield and block out its sounds as well. The stone walls were old, and so clean I thought their age had been made to show purposely, so that those who sat in their shadow would never forget where they stood.

There were tables and gazebos littered through the courtyard, and though the walls were old, the tiled floors—green and white and gold—gleamed in the early-afternoon sunlight. The courtiers played games and chatted, while Idris and I sat in a white and blue–tiled bower waiting to greet his cousins. Its wall faced the sea, with a great glassless window that framed where we sat. I could only imagine the image Idris and I made, though I was sure a moment later that it made no impression on the cousins.

There were only four of them and yet they entered with the sound of a dozen Kushaila cousins come to carouse and make merry. Idris was on his feet before any of them had greeted us properly, pulled into one bear hug and then another with the two young men. The young women were more sedate for their part and kissed his cheeks, once on the left and twice on the right.

"Maram," he said, grinning, one hand still on one of his cousin's arms, "may I introduce the scions of the Mas'udi and Nasiri tribes. Khulood has been head of the Nasiri tribe for a year now. 'Imad and I'timad are twins and ascended two months ago."

Khulood was a slender woman a few years older than me, of a height with me, with dark hair threaded with gold. When she moved her head just so and the light struck it, I could see undertones of red. Her eyes were wide and dark, but there was a shrewdness to her expression that belied my instinct to mark her as innocent as the eyes would suggest. The twins, 'Imad and I'timad, were almost mirror images of each other. Brown skin darkened by many hours spent in the sun and curling brown hair that stopped just beneath 'Imad's ears, and tumbled, untamed, down I'timad's back.

I frowned as my eyes fixed on the youngest of them, a boy. He had the same coloring as Khulood, though his hair was heavy and thick. "I know you," I said. "We've met." He'd been among the makhzen attendants in the Ziyaana.

He grinned and bowed. "Tariq bin Nasir, Your Highness. I yet reside in the Ziyaana."

"Though we hope," Khulood said softly, "that the king will be kind and allow him to return to us."

That, I thought, was unlikely. Mathis kept the makhzen in check by keeping their children. And no matter the length of the occupation, he trusted none of them regardless of their apparent docility.

"How are you finding M'Gaadir?" I asked.

I'timad grinned. "It is much as we remember it." Her brother elbowed her in the side, and she sobered. "It is a beautiful estate, Your Highness."

I allowed a little of my amusement to seep into my voice. "Thank you, I'timad. It was designed with care."

After we were finished with introductions, everyone settled into a spot in the orchard. Khulood and her brother Tariq found a friend who had arrived earlier, while the Mas'udi twins joined us in the bower to show Idris holovids of the horses they'd brought.

As if summoned by talk of horses, 'Adil, Idris's much younger cousin, came barreling through the courtyard with a shout. He was covered in hay, and his fine clothes were dirty. I did not need the disapproving eye of his minder to know he'd been in the stables, and without permission. Still, I thought with a smile, it seemed not even her aggravation could overshadow his glee. He was nine or ten, caught in that awkward stage of growth where he was both gangly and small. His family had arrived even before Idris and me, part of the Salihi contingent straight from Al Hoceima.

He climbed onto the seat beside Idris and pressed close to get a better look at the horses on the holo they were watching. A less kind cousin might have wrinkled his nose or demand he wash, but Idris lifted his arm and drew him close, then angled the holo to make sure he could see. Idris hadn't raised him, but it was easy to see how he would have looked after him at home. He had no fear that the prince of Andalaa would turn him away or scold him. 'Adil talked quite quickly, and more than once I heard his voice flow from Vathekaar into Kushaila. He spoke too quickly for any of the others to follow what he said, but I understood and was hard put not to smile or laugh at his excitement. More than once he looked over Idris's arm at me, his eyes shrewd but joyful still.

Eventually, I tired of feigning interest in horses and wandered off to one of the large glassless windows that overlooked the orchard. Though I might have been a farm girl, we'd never had enough money to afford horses, and those who did used them as beasts of burden, not for racing as the makhzen did. Husnain, I thought with a pang, would have enjoyed the conversation.

"Your Highness?"

I'timad had come away from her brother and Idris to join me. She was dressed in a dove-gray qaftan that crept toward silver. There was something almost military about the high collar of her qaftan and the mantle falling from her shoulders. But the effect was wholly Kushaila—there was nothing Vathek about her, which was perhaps why she and her brother had been chosen as hostages.

"Did we bore you?" she said, and gave me a bright smile. I couldn't tell if it was sincere.

"I find myself less riveted by horseflesh than my husband," I replied, softening Maram's customary tart tone.

She joined me at the window and eyed me sidelong for a moment. "You know, you are not what I expected."

Maram had never met I'timad, I knew; though she and 'Imad had been raised in the Ziyaana, Maram had not returned until she was older, and by then they would have traveled back and forth between their stronghold and the capital. Maram had always kept her circle small, and there were enough young Vathek courtiers that she would not have consorted with many of the makhzen families outside of Idris.

I raised an eyebrow. "What did you picture?"

She grinned. "I don't know. For you to look less like one of us?"

My eyes widened in surprise. I hadn't expected that much honesty from her.

"Have I given offense?"

I didn't know. Maram's resemblance to her mother, to the Kushaila, was a sore topic. I didn't know if she would be offended, if she would lash out. I didn't want to presume. And it felt almost like a crime to pretend to understand the strange, violent line she straddled between her mother's people and her father's.

"I—I'm surprised," I managed at last. "No one talks about it."

"You will find I am not one who cares for the rules of polite conversation."

"That must have served you very well in your time at the Ziyaana," I drawled sarcastically.

She grinned again. "I survived. We all do."

By tacit agreement we returned to the bower together. I'timad surprised me a second time by looping her arm with mine, and when I looked at her, startled, she flashed me a grin again. Tariq rose from my seat when we reentered the bower, but I waved him down and found a seat opposite him, Idris, and 'Adil. 'Adil and Idris were currently deep in negotiations. From what I could gather, 'Adil thought he was old enough to ride the horses. Idris disagreed.

A servant brought over a steaming glass of tea just as Idris turned to me, a gleam in his eye.

"Whatever it is," I said, cradling the glass, "the answer is no."

His eyes widened. "You don't even know what it is."

"And yet," I drawled, "I recognize that look."

He grinned slyly, then turned back to his cousin. "The truth is, dear cousin, you're negotiating with the wrong person."

'Adil frowned. "The horses belong to you."

"They belong to *us*," he said. "They are a wedding gift, you see. And my lady wife—"

"Idris," I warned.

"I'm only telling the truth," he replied, all innocence. "My wife is the higher rank. So, in truth, the decision falls to her."

"Absolutely not," I said coolly. "This is a family affair. I recuse myself from this negotiation."

I'timad's eyes widened. "But aren't you family now?" she said. "You have married my cousin."

"Yes, Maram," Idris said. "Is my family not your family as well?"

I did not answer the question. I had no idea how Maram would answer the question. Instead, I did as she would do and deflected. I set the glass down on the ceramic tabletop with a sharp *clink* and raised an eyebrow at the young boy, my expression cool.

"So, what is it you want, then?"

'Adil's posture straightened immediately. "To ride one of the stallions, cousin."

"Absolutely not," I said, watching his mouth tighten angrily. "You aren't tall enough."

"I could be!"

"This is not an argument of hypotheticals," I replied. "It is a negotiation. You will have to make a concession."

He frowned thoughtfully while Idris watched, bemused. "I will ride . . . under supervision."

"And on an already broken stallion," I added. He opened his mouth to complain and I raised an eyebrow in Maram's fashion. "Unless you would like to not ride at all."

His shoulders sagged. "I'm old enough," he muttered.

"My lord husband is barely old enough," I said, voice dry. "That he is older than us both is the only reason he gets away with it."

Idris cried out in protest as 'Imad and I'timad burst into peals of laughter. Tariq clapped him on the shoulder.

"You will be making up for that the entirety of our visit, khouya," Tariq said. "Honor demands it."

'Adil for his part seemed pleased with the sacrifice of Idris's pride on the altar of his needing supervision. I felt some of the tension in my spine ease. Not for a moment had any of the cousins paused to wonder at my negotiation with their small cousin. I had walked the line between Maram and diplomacy well. Amid the revelry Idris caught my eye and gave me a small secret smile, and I felt my mouth twitch in answer.

So the day went. Eventually, the air cooled, and the orchard emptied. Idris and I retired to the royal chambers, and I found myself in the tower connected to the central courtyard. From there I could see both the flowering skirt of the city and the sea. The sun was dipping below the horizon, and sea and city both were awash in pinks and reds. It was a vision I had not thought to see ever. I shivered as a wind blew through the tower, and the fire in the bier flickered.

I rubbed my hands over my arms as I thought. I'timad's invocation of family had been deliberate, I knew. A push to see what I—what Maram—would do. I'd handled it well, I thought. I hadn't agreed to her assertion of family, but neither had I dismissed 'Adil out of hand. A difficult dance. It had been too long since I'd had to manage so many people against my natural reactions and Maram's.

A heavy mantle dropped over my shoulders and I jumped.

Idris had come up beside me without my hearing him. "You did well today," he said. I looked up. "I'timad is . . . well, she's intimidating."

"She's lovely," I protested.

"She's testing you," he replied. "I don't know that Maram would have passed the test."

I felt a small kernel of pride at that and a shy smile emerged. He smiled back—the sort of smile he'd given me before his marriage. I expected him to look away, but he didn't, and the longer I stared the more flushed I felt. It was moments like these, where I remembered what we were, what we'd been not so long ago, that were dangerous. That sparked along my skin like flecks of ember ready to turn to flame.

A log in the fire popped, and we jumped, our stare broken.

"How was the game?" I asked, remembering I'timad had challenged him to a game of shatranj before I retired.

"Tch," he said, and I grinned.

"Did she beat you?"

"She did not." He paused. "It was a stalemate."

"How injurious to your pride."

"I just didn't expect it," he grumbled.

"It seemed too obvious to warn you," I laughed.

"It wasn't obvious at all! She has none of the patience required for the game."

He seemed so put out by it—not even a loss, but a deadlock with a competent rival.

"You've gone too long unchallenged," I said and drew the mantle closer around me. "You must play her again—maybe she will take the board."

"She will absolutely not. My honor is at stake now—my wife thinks I will be beat by a Mas'udi."

I grinned again. "Did you come here to protest your competence or for some other purpose?"

"Come for a ride with me?" he asked.

I hesitated. It was a bad idea to be alone with him, so early in his marriage.

"As friends," he said, voice low. Insistent. I swallowed against the sudden rush of electricity over my skin.

"As friends," I repeated, and took his outstretched hand.

Idris led our horses down to the beach and they picked their way easily along the coast. The roar of the ocean and the sound of it battering itself along the cliff made it easy to talk without worrying anyone would overhear. There were drones far in the water, bobbing with the waves, watching us, and more guardsmen on the cliffs.

"Where are we going?"

"We're almost there." The beach didn't end, but the cliff seemed to fold in on itself. We had ridden down the hillside of the city and then all the way down to reach the beach. The cave seemed to be directly below the city itself.

Idris disembarked from his horse then came around to my side to help me down. It was colder so much closer to the water, so late in the year. That was what I told myself as I looked up at him and shivered. His hands lay against my ribs and seemed to burn through the layers of clothes I wore.

Idris caught my hand in his and drew me close as we walked. He seemed to know this place as well as I did, which was to say not at all. Eventually what little sun's light we had was swallowed up by the dark, and Idris drew several small orbs from his cloak. One sharp whistle and they all began to glow and lifted up into the air, lighting the path for us.

"Here we are," he said, and led me out into a smaller cave with an opening facing the sea. But that, I knew immediately, was not why he'd brought me here. A vast mural sat inside.

"Dihya," I breathed, walking toward it. It was twice or three times as high as I was and took up the entire wall. It was ancient, too, I could tell, and yet well preserved. A woman sat atop the promontory outside M'Gaadir, the ocean behind her. She was robed in Kushaila clothes, a deep, arresting green stitched with gold and white. At her shoulders were brooches in the shape of half diamonds, etched with Kushaila design. Her hair was threaded with pearls—white and coral and gray—and from her neck hung what looked like half a hundred strings of white pearls. Her daan was a sharp pictograph of a feather, its end situated perfectly between her eyebrows. She cast no shadow.

"Tala said you would know her name," Idris said, coming up behind me.

"Houwa," I said without looking away.

Houwa was prized among the Kushaila before they were ever called such, for she was clever and beautiful, and she had just a little magic in her blood that the tesleet taught her to use. And when her people were under siege by a conqueror king, she and her brothers plotted how to defeat him: she would marry the king and learn all the secrets of his army.

Each night Houwa suffered the advances of the king, and each night after he fell asleep, she would unstitch her shadow from her shoulders and her feet and loose it into the world to gather his secrets. Bit by bit, her brothers destroyed her husband's armies with the information she and her shadow provided, until only a few of his generals remained. And on the eve of the final battle Houwa's shadow led her brothers through the king's war camp and into his royal tent where Houwa waited.

Together the brothers killed him and declared victory.

For most storytellers, the tale ended there. But my mother had told me a different ending. That with her service done, the shadow asked for a boon: to be made real so that she might live separate from Houwa's demand and have her own life. Houwa used the last of her magic to free her shadow.

"The first of the Kushaila. Every royal family tracks their lineage to Kansa, but they forget that Kansa tracked her lineage from Houwa. We are in her birthplace."

"Do you like it?" he asked.

I laughed in disbelief and looked up at him.

"Did you draw it to ask?"

"No." He grinned.

My gaze returned to the mural. It brought me great joy to see it, but it was a sharp reminder, too. I was not Houwa. I was her shadow, sent out into the world to gather information only to be returned, stitched to Maram's feet.

Idris's voice pierced my melancholy. "But I remembered you had a liking for historic murals. Come," he said, and took my hand. "We have some time yet. We can sit, away from the eyes of the court and the servants."

A half-hearted protest came to and died on my lips.

We sat against a wall without cushions or blankets, facing the mural.

"I've only been here once before," he said. "To this cave, I mean. Before my parents died. Before Najat died."

"Oh?" He so rarely talked of his family, and I found myself leaning closer without meaning to.

"My father took me down into the city after." He gave me a lop-sided grin. "We saw a fortune-teller."

I could not control the laugh of disbelief. "You don't strike me as the superstitious type."

His grin widened. "I'm not. But her predictions were—well, none of them came true. I was a child, I took heart in what she said."

"Did she cast bones?" I found myself a little intrigued. There were no soothsayers in our village. They gravitated to the larger cities where their trade was more tolerated.

"She read my palm," he said. "She terrified me, you understand. She was old, and her eyes glitter in my memory. But she told me I would be happy, and that's all a boy really wants to hear."

"What did she tell your father?" I asked, curious.

"Nothing—he refused to have his future read."

"Smart man," I said.

Idris raised his eyebrows. "How so? Don't tell me you believe in fortune-tellers?"

I huffed another incredulous laugh. "It's not about the teller," I said. "But the fortune. Good or ill, true or false, it haunts the listener. What?"

"I don't know . . ." He shook his head as if shaking away the cob-
webs of a dream. "You know, I still remember some of what she told
me."

"Your fortune?"

"No," he smiled slyly. "She told me what certain lines on your palm
might signify."

I eyed him suspiciously as he took my hand into his and drew a
thumb down its center.

"Shall we try?"

I said nothing, which he took as my acceptance. He bent his
head over my hand and I waited, heart in my throat. Something had
changed in the air in the heartbeat between taking my hand and now.
His eyes were fixed on the palm of my hand, and his index finger hovered just a breadth above skin, tracing the lines in my palm. I found
myself leaning closer, leaning my head forward so that my hair joined
his in forming a curtain around my hand.

"The fortune-teller looks for four lines: happiness, fortune, passion, and love," he said softly. "For some passion and love are separate,
but for you they run parallel along your heart line."

His finger swept from the upper left corner of my palm, over the
curve, and to the upper right. I shivered and my hand twitched at the
barely there touch.

"What does that mean?" I asked before I could think better of it.

His finger swept from the tip of my middle finger, skimmed across
my palm, and stopped at my wrist.

His eyes met mine as he spoke. "I think for you, it is impossible to
have one without the other."

It was not a unique insight, but one born out of knowledge. For
who else had I loved but Idris, and how passionately did I love him. I
curled my hand so that my palm was hidden from him. Heat unfurled
in my belly as my chest tightened around my lungs and thinned my
breath.

For a moment, I allowed myself to wish that my lines for love
and happiness were linked. Because what good was a passionate love

without the ability to be with the object of that love and passion? It was a thought I had had many a time when it came to Idris, but a fruitless one.

"We should go back," I said, pulling away. "The sun is gone. They will come looking."

He watched me silently for a moment, then nodded and helped me to my feet.

"Amani," he said softly. I paused as he leaned his forehead against mine and wound his fingers in my hair.

I wrapped my fingers around his wrists, as if to pull him away, but could not bring myself to it. *Friends.* I'd known what an impossible thing it would be, to smother my heart. I remembered being in a carriage with Idris and his low laugh. *Just friends,* he'd asked. No. Never *just.* Never for two hearts made one. And yet, despite that, here we were.

"I just wanted to say your name," he sighed. "Before we went back."

02. Maram

The sky was still lit with stars. Dawn was coming, but the air was still chill, the grass frosted with ice, the stars suspended in heaven. Maram stood in front of the balcony, one hand on its engraved railing, the other clutching a string of red beads. They'd belonged to her mother and were meant to be used for religious remembrance. Maram was not Dihyan—she wasn't really anything. She only ever thought of Dihya when she thought of the dead. But the beads were her mother's and she couldn't wear them, couldn't hold them at court, in the Ziyaana, anywhere her father's people and Nadine might see them. Weakness or treason—they were the same, weren't they? There was no room for grief. There never had been.

She'd risen early, before the first cry of birdsong, and bathed and dressed. Around her, Dar at-Tuyyur was waking up—servants lit sconces, the kitchen was accepting food deliveries, the gardeners and arborists were making their way through the estate. In the wan lantern light of her room she'd nearly broken her mirror looking at herself. Did she look Kushaila? She'd bound her hair away from her face, and the bulk of it hung down her back in a thick braided rope. There were no gold pieces in her hair, no fabric woven through it. It was just her, her eyes lined with kohl, her face stark and plain.

She looked like Najat, but was that enough? Did she *want* to look Kushaila?

Her hand tightened around the beads.

The door to the office opened, but Maram didn't turn around. She knew Fatiha's gait, that she would first set a tray down on the table by the door, then turn on an extra lantern.

"When were you going to tell me you'd hired a falconer?" she said quietly.

Fatiha paused, then joined her at the balcony. "It's in today's dossier as I continue to hire and delegate staff, Your Highness. How did you find out about the falconer?"

"I ran into her on the property," Maram said dryly, and turned away from her view of the garden. Fatiha was old, she thought suddenly. Old enough to have been her wet nurse—old enough to have raised her, in another world where her mother yet lived. Perhaps she shouldn't have hired her to be stewardess of a hidden retreat. Perhaps she should have given her a pension and let her retire.

Fatiha rolled her eyes, a move that elicited a surprise grin from Maram, and gestured toward the food.

"I told her to tread lightly until you'd overseen her approval," she said as Maram sat. "But she was eager—apparently there are some species of raptor on this part of the continent that don't breed anywhere else."

Maram was quiet as she stared at the plate of food. It was all Kushaila fare—she wondered briefly if Amani knew how to cook this. It was bread—something she'd handled with ease the last time they'd been in a kitchen together. Cheese, some jam—Amani probably knew how to make those things from scratch.

Her traitorous heart wondered if Amani would like this place—would she approve of the paintings and the gardens and the fountains? Would she love the open air and the Kushaila arches and the honeycombed stone?

Amani is a traitor, she told herself angrily. *She does not love or care about you.*

"Your Highness?"

Her head jerked up to look at Fatiha.

"I can terminate her employment if it displeases you."

Maram's eyes widened. "No! Why should you terminate her?"

Fatiha fought back a smile. "You looked quite displeased, Your Highness."

"She just caught me unawares," she said. "She was . . . arrogant."

And she had been—arrogant and defiant and unafraid. Only Amani had ever looked her in the eye like that. Even Fatiha and the staff deferred to her—she was their future queen, not their friend or equal. A strange frisson worked its way over her skin—she didn't know if she was unsettled or excited. How many equals did she have? Idris, sometimes, when it wouldn't cost him anything.

A knock at the door interrupted their breakfast, and a moment later a page walked in and bowed.

"Your Highness. Stewardess. The falconer is here."

Fatiha started to rise to her feet. "I'll deal with her."

"Pardon, stewardess," the page interrupted. "She is here for Her Highness."

Maram blinked, uncomprehending. "For me?"

"Yes, Your Highness."

As protected as the grounds were, Maram was not foolish enough to go traipsing around the property with Aghraas alone. They took three guards with them and Maram brought a small blaster, strapped at her hip beneath her jacket besides. The falconer seemed even grander on her horse, her seat comfortable and easy. Her body swayed with the horse's easy gait, and she held the reins in one hand, the other braced against her thigh. She wore black and gray, her sleeves long and the vambraces Maram saw yesterday gone. Her many braids spilled down her back instead of being bound up by a single clip. There was a collection of braids that sprouted from her crown that were a shocking white, as if someone had terrified her once, and only a sliver of her had aged.

Maram watched her from the corner of her eye as she led them through the estate as if it were her own.

"Where are you from, Lady Falconer?" she asked.

"Aghraas will do, Your Highness," she replied.

Maram's mouth twisted, just a little. She did not like the familiarity of calling a person by their name if she could help it.

"You did not answer the question," she said instead.

The falconer shot her a half smile. "My family traveled a great deal, Your Highness."

"Is that your way of saying you're not Kushaila?" Maram knew the Kushaila were not the only people who wore daan on their faces, but Aghraas's were quite distinct. They looked like feathers, and she'd seen such markings in some Kushaila art, but never on a person's face. Perhaps she had never met quite as dedicated a falconer as Aghraas.

Aghraas lifted a shoulder, a gesture she would have found both intolerable and profoundly rude on anyone else.

"I'm as Kushaila as you are, Your Highness," she said at last.

Maram bristled. "What does that mean?"

She smiled. "I was not raised among them. I might have been born here, but as I said: my family are interstellar travelers. We do not stay one place for very long. We love the stars too much."

"What brought you back?" she asked before she could think to pretend indifference. "It's hardly a vacation destination."

"Isn't it?" Aghraas countered.

Maram couldn't stop the sharp laughter from bursting from her mouth. "It's a planet on the brink of civil war and has been for the last twenty years," she said, her words equally sharp. "No one with any sense ventures here or chooses to stay."

"Sometimes," she said contemplatively, "all the paths lead where we would rather not go. Sometimes you can't outrun home or destiny."

For once, Maram resisted the urge to mock. "What destiny could possibly be waiting for you here?"

"That remains to be seen," Aghraas said, and smiled. "And in the mean-time, there is my work."

"Your work?"

"I'm an ornithologist," she said. Maram stared at her blankly. "I study birds," she clarified.

"So you're not a falconer."

Again, that half-amused smile. "I *am* a falconer."

"You have just told me that you're an ornithologist."

"We are far past the times of antiquity, Your Highness," she said. "It be-hooves a falconer not just to train the birds, but to study and understand them."

Maram drew her horse to a stop and stared at Aghraas. Had she ever had a conversation like this? With Amani, perhaps—few dared correct her. Idris did it betimes when she was relaxed and not on guard. For the first time she wondered if her future husband was afraid of her? She had never seen evidence of it, but now—

"Your Highness? Have I said something amiss?"

"Are you not frightened of me, Lady Falconer?"

Aghraas's eyes widened in surprise. "Have you given me cause to fear you?"

"Surely you jest?" Her horse pranced beneath her, as if it scented her banked anger. "You may not have been raised here, but—"

"But I should give credence to every rumor and whisper I hear?" Aghraas said, raising an eyebrow.

"They are not *just* rumors—"

"Are you determined that I dislike you?"

"You have interrupted me *twice*," Maram snapped. "Do not do it a third time."

Aghraas brought her horse forward so that they were facing one another.

"I must tell you," she said calmly, "that if you wish for someone weaker or more susceptible to rumor, you will not find her in me."

"And if I demand it?" Maram said dully.

"You may demand all you like, Your Highness," she said. "That is your right, after all."

"Most people would endeavor to please me, Lady Falconer."

"You will find, Your Highness," she said, moving her horse so that they were side by side, "that I am not most people."

Maram felt as if there were an iron hand around her throat. She struggled to say *something* in the face of Aghraas's calm but could not. *I am not afraid*—if she was not afraid, then what else was there?

"We are nearly there," Aghraas said, and Maram blinked as if coming out of a dream. "We can walk, if you like?"

She barked out a half-deranged laugh. "Certainly. Why not?"

She watched as Aghraas climbed from her horse, swung her leg over, and then froze as the falconer helped her down from her stallion, hands around her waist. She remained perfectly still as her feet touched the ground, and it was only fear of being labeled a coward that forced her to raise her head to look up. Aghraas's eyes were serious when she met them, her mouth a flat, stoic line.

She liked it better when she smiled but had given her few reasons to do so in the last few minutes. She felt adrift, as if she were caught in a wave rapidly approaching a cliff and she had no recourse.

"Are all ornithologists as brazen as you are?" she said at last.

She did not like the small spark of light in her chest when Aghraas grinned.

"No, Your Highness. I am singular in that respect."

They walked through heather and tall grass in silence. Their horses and guards remained on a hill from where both of them could be seen, but enough about the morning was strange that in a fit of madness Maram instructed them to remain behind. They had crested a second rise that sat atop a cliff. Its descending slope was gentle, and rolled down into a wide valley, hedged in by high hills. In its center was a brilliant blue lake that caught the early-morning sun's rays.

"If you deign to lie down in the grass, Your Highness?"

Maram said nothing as she sank into the grass beside her and laid on her stomach. Aghraas produced a pair of binoculars; Maram watched as she scanned the valley and then stiffened, their lenses focused up above.

"See there," she said, handing them over to her.

It was a single bird, its wingspan nearly eight feet long. It hovered high in the air, gave one great push of its wings, and soared higher.

"Is that . . ." she started breathlessly.

"A golden eagle," Aghraas confirmed. "There are twenty-seven in the northwestern steppes. Likely the descendants of eagles freed or lost during the initial wave of conquest. None of them native to the area. But that—"

"Is a descendant of my grandmother's famous hunting eagles?"

"A descendant of her *most* famous hunting eagle, Your Highness," Aghraas said. "The Golden Punishment."

Maram didn't return the binoculars, but instead watched as the eagle dropped into a sharp dive and slammed bodily into another bird. She wished she could bring just one in—she loved hunting with larger raptors. But Maram knew, without Aghraas asking her, that she would not capture any of the eagles here—there were too few to risk breeding experiments. And yet to have a descendant of her grandmother's Golden Punishment in her mother's favorite retreat . . .

"Have they bred?"

"Not in enough numbers," Aghraas said, taking the binoculars back. "Maybe in another five years. She's magnificent, isn't she?"

"Yes," Maram breathed.

"People can't cross into your estate, Your Highness. But the eagles do not have the same limitation. I worry—"

"About the birds?"

"Should I worry about something else?" she said. "They need official protection."

Maram sat up in the grass.

"Don't you wish to protect your family's legacy?" Aghraas said, sitting up as well. "For as long as your grandmother had that eagle it was as symbolic of her as the tesleet."

Maram looked out over the valley, its pristine emerald glow, the way the sun slanted over hills and grass, and seemed to halo the single eagle below. Perhaps she was overthinking it. Mathis—the Vath—would think nothing of a measure that at its heart was about natural conservation and not familial ties.

Except, for the Vath, everything came down to the blood. And Maram knew if the question were put forth to Mathis he would say, "Let her symbol die."

"It depends," she murmured, "on which family legacy you're talking about."

8

"Did you know," I said a few days later, "the M'Gaadiri stewardess is terrifying."

Maram's eyes widened. "Aicha? She's not frightening at all."

"You've never had to review rooming assignments with her," I replied with a smile. "I didn't know the answer to a question, and I thought her glare was going to melt the flesh from my face."

Maram laughed but, as I'd expected, did not offer to take her place back. Truth be told, I was surprised she'd even summoned me for this. We were reviewing the estate ledger, along with the aforementioned rooming assignments and meal plans. When I'd said as much, she'd scoffed. *You're not a princess*, she'd said. *Unless you know how to run an estate on your own?*

Now, her eyes moved from mine to the doorway behind me.

"I take it you've come looking for your wife," Maram said. I moved aside—Idris stood in the doorway watching both of us. It was the first time, I realized, that he'd seen us side by side.

"My wife has been absent since the wedding," he replied smoothly. "I've wondered if she lives. Maram—"

She raised a hand to forestall him. "A conversation for another time."

I resisted the urge to fist my hands in my skirt as she approached him. The two of them watched each other as if waiting for the one to strike. It seemed almost as if they were strangers, seeing one another for the first time. I felt as if I'd disappeared from the room. They'd known each other so long, certainly long enough to have a conversation without speaking.

"Maram—" he started. Something in his voice made me come to attention, and when I looked at him more closely, I felt something in my stomach drop.

"What's wrong?" I asked without thinking.

Maram whipped herself around, her expression torn between surprise and frustration. But Idris raised his gaze to me, and I knew what he would say before he said it and felt my fingers clench in the folds of my skirt.

"'Adil has been taken by the garda," he said, voice flat.

I took a step back and closed my eyes. *Dihya*—he was so young. *Innocent.*

"What happened?" I said when I opened my eyes. Maram had moved to the side, as if to clear the space between us. "Who told you?"

"A messenger arrived from his parents' quarters a little while ago," he said. "He took one of the horses out after dark, beyond the city limits. Someone met him and offered him money for it and he agreed. A garda droid caught the interaction—the buyer was on a dissident list. 'Adil never made it back to the estate."

People disappeared or were taken under the shadow of the Vath regularly, among both the makhzen and the very poor. None of us were safe from random raids or abductions. But 'Adil was *ten*—a boy with no power to make change and certainly no inclination. He'd been brought up in a cruel world, but he understood the rules. He would not have sold the horse to a rebel willingly—not after growing up in Al Hoceima, in the shadow of the Purge.

"Idris—" My voice caught in my throat. Whether or not 'Adil knew they were rebels, that he had met them, spoken to one, *sold him* a horse. He was lost. There was no hope of getting him back.

He closed the space between us, despite Maram's presence, and made an aborted move to take my hand. My hands pressed against my ribs, as if I might relieve the dual pressures of grief and fear. Maram stood off to the side, but for a moment, with Idris standing over me, I forgot her.

"I'm sorry," I said, shaking my head. "I know that's not enough—"

"It's plenty," he said softly.

"No one said anything." We both turned to see Maram, her fingers wound in the fabric of her skirts so tightly that her knuckles gleamed white. Her eyes were wide and panicked. "This is my estate, Amani. I—you—would have been notified unless they specifically didn't want me to know. No one will believe it wasn't on my command—"

Her whole body shuddered. "What are we going to do?"

"Do?" I said blankly as Idris dropped down onto the divan. I had paid less attention to Maram in the last ten minutes than I ought; her mask had disintegrated. The half smirk that was her customary shield, the easy stance of her hands, were all gone. Her brown face was leeched of color, and her grip on her skirts had tightened.

She was afraid.

"They will turn against me," she whispered. "They will start to plot."

"They will rightly direct their anger at the Vath," Idris said, and both of us turned to look at him in surprise. "Are you the Vath?"

"I am *Vathek*," she snapped.

"Was it you who gave 'Adil to the Imperial Garda, then?" he replied. There was a stillness in his voice that worried me—grief and a need to channel it. Maram flinched back as if struck and raised her hand to her throat.

"How *dare* you suggest such a thing."

I laid a hand on Idris's shoulder before he could reply. I had never seen him so close to losing control, and I worried whatever he said he would regret and have to live with for however long Maram wanted to hold a grudge.

"If you do not want them to suspect you and you are innocent—" Maram opened her mouth to interrupt me and I raised a hand to forestall her. "If you are innocent, then protect them. Are you not their future sovereign? Does not their protection fall to your hands?"

I could see her struggle. All her life she had hated her mother's people for how they'd turned their backs on her. All her life she'd strived to be Mathis's perfect daughter, and that perfection included deriding one half of her. But she did not live on Luna-Vaxor, she lived here, and she would continue to live here all her life.

Idris's shoulder tensed beneath my hand. Even without looking at him, I could feel him struggle between his ever-present diplomacy and the desire to speak plainly.

"Amani is right," he said at last. His head was bowed, and his hair shadowed his eyes. Perhaps he could not bear to look at either one of us. "If you wish everyone to know you would never do such a thing, prove it."

"How . . . how would I even do that?"

"Demonstrate to them and the people that you are invested in their safety and care," I said. "No one trusts you because they believe you see them as your father sees them: a resource to be mined and pillaged and left for dead. Make friends with them."

If anything, Maram looked more distressed, not less. Her back had straightened, and if not for the divan between her and the wall, I think she might have backed up against it for strength.

"I don't—Amani, I wouldn't even know where to begin."

I squeezed Idris's shoulder. "Lucky for both of us, one of the makhzen is in this very room."

A few hours later, Idris scrubbed his hand through his hair and sighed. He'd retrieved a map of the planet and spread it out over a low table. I, for my part, had retrieved a tray laden with a teapot, glasses, and a plate of briouat drizzled with honey. Maram's eyes had widened just slightly when I'd appeared with it, and so I set the plate of pastries to my left, closer to her.

The tea was nearly done now. We'd spent the last hours discussing which makhzen families would make good allies—who would side with Maram, support her, *trust her* enough that she could build a network that would prevent what had happened to 'Adil from happening again. What would cement her as a queen of the people that could be loved instead of assassinated.

"Alright," Idris said. In his right hand were a handful of shatranj pieces. He didn't look any less grieved, only determined to be distracted by this new goal. "The trick of the map is you don't need *everyone*—if the larger houses fall in line, those allied with them will follow."

Maram had a briouat in hand, but her eyes turned to the map, her face grave. "You say that so surely."

"I am sure," he replied. "The only time that ceases to be true is when the threat posed by the liege lord overrides any loyalty to the larger house."

He said it matter-of-factly and without affect, but he might as well have thrown something at Maram. Her face drained of color and she set the pastry down.

"Like me," she said softly.

"That is up to you, Maram."

"It is not *up to me*. My reputation has already been cemented thanks to my lineage."

"That is where Amani comes in," he said, setting a shatranj piece on the map.

Maram's eyes gleamed, as if she might shed a tear at any moment. "The implication being that I cannot be loved on my own."

"Do you know what your weakness is, Maram?"

I nearly laid a hand over Idris's—the flat affect of his voice receded and in its place was a kernel of grief. I expected Maram to rise to her feet and leave, and instead she lifted her chin angrily.

"I suspect you will tell me."

"You are quick to anger, and quicker to act on that anger. Your world is large and your view of it very small—you do not think on consequences or the future, only your personal vengeance and its satisfaction."

"You have *no* idea—" Maram began, her hands pressed against the table.

"You are not the only one," Idris roared, and at that I did lay my hand over his. I did not think he'd ever raised his voice to Maram, for her face was colorless but for two angry red spots high on her cheeks.

"Idris—" I started, and he jerked his hand from under mine.

"You are *not* the only one," he said again, still angry but quieter. "All of us have suffered one loss or another. All of us live in the shadow of that. And those losses do not absolve us of the choices we make."

We sat in silence, Idris's eyes now fixed on the map, Maram's eyes fixed on a point over his shoulder. Her chest rose and fell as if she struggled for air, and her mouth, which had been firm with rage, now trembled as if she were afraid.

At last, she spoke. "Amani thinks—"

Idris's eyes jerked up, first to her and then to me. "What does Amani think?" he said.

"I want to live up to what she thinks of me," she said softly, as if I weren't there. "But the people do not love me as she does."

"The people think you are against them," I interjected softly. "Prove to them that you are not."

She drew in a trembling breath. "Do you know the cost of siding with them—it isn't neutral. I am either with the Vath or against them." She came to her feet and began to pace. "There are no half measures. I can't have both . . . Can I?"

I didn't know what went through her mind, but she paused in her pacing and frowned.

"What about the Banu Ifran?" she said, looking at Idris.

He scoffed. "They collaborated with the Vath during the conquest, why would you want to . . ." he said, and then his expression cleared. "Oh."

"They could be the line, couldn't they?" she said, eager.

"Collaborators?" I said with a frown. "Truly?"

"They're the closest Andalaan allies the Vath have on the planet," Maram said, excited.

"The Ifrani matriarch was a Vathek loyalist, but she passed recently—the new one, Rabi'a, is a little older than us. If she can be made loyal to Maram—" Idris said.

"Instead of her father," I continued, and looked over at Maram. She looked so hopeful, I couldn't help but smile. My mind whirled with possibilities.

"Amani," Maram snapped and I looked up. "You will do it, won't you?"

I stared at her blankly. "Do what?"

"Cajole her into friendship."

I was so startled by the idea that I laughed. "You can't be serious," I said. "Dihya, you're serious. I am not a magician, Your Highness. I—"

"You have done well with the Vathek aristocrats," Idris said quietly. "The makhzen should be easy."

"I cannot use any of my knowledge to help you, because Maram doesn't have that knowledge. I would be harming you in the long run," I protested.

"It's not your knowledge I need," Maram said, coming to sit beside me. "You are . . . you have a clarity of sight that I lack. Please."

"Is this your plan?" I asked her. "For the rest of your life?"

The idea felt like a yoke round my neck.

"I had not thought—"

"Of the rest of your life?" I interrupted. "Or the rest of mine?"

At that, she seemed to feel some shame and lowered her eyes.

"Not forever," she said at last. "I promise."

I drew in a breath. This was what I'd wanted, wasn't it? For Maram to take an active interest in not simply being a Vathek scion, but a good queen. One who *cared*. If I could help—and I knew that I could; I had done well the last few days—wasn't it my duty to try? I'd seen the beginnings of greatness in her. I'd told her so myself.

"She is right," Idris added. "You would do well. You *have* done well."

I gave Maram a weary smile. "Of course," I said, and squeezed her hand. "Sisters support each other, don't they?"

Her face blossomed into a bright smile. "Thank you."

We spent a few more hours discussing the landscape, the families. In the end we decided on the Banu Ifran, who as reward for their collaboration with the regime were gifted Furat's family's ancestral seat, Tayfur province. In addition, we picked two families I'd already met: the Banu Nasir, who ruled from Khenitra and were one of the largest families in Greater Walili, second only to the Ziyadis; and the Banu Mas'ud, who ruled from Azaghar within Ghazlan province, second only to the Salihis.

The pastries and tea were both gone by the time our discussion wound down. 'Adil's disappearance worried at my mind like a thorn caught beneath my skin. I knew that the best I could hope for him was a quick death. The Vath did not return those they took. But I felt some hope, too—Maram had come awake. Something had shaken her enough to push her into action. And I could see a world under her rule where children were not taken from their parents. Where law and justice were ordinary, instead of a luxury meted out to invaders.

Maram had not set me an easy task: persuading the makhzen that she was on their side, that she was worthy of their trust, was a crucible I hadn't anticipated. But I had an unexpected ally this time: Maram herself. And that in itself was remarkable enough that I could look toward the task with some optimism, even if it was peppered with fear.

9

I was getting used to the bustle of dressing in the royal suite as a new bride. Prior to her marriage, Maram had only ever had a single serving girl with her. As a married woman she had a true household, and that included a cluster of serving girls who moved around the large dressing chamber, laying out clothes, jewelry, and perfume. Most mornings, I internally reviewed names and politics, preoccupied with preparing myself to face the world as Maram, but today, I examined the face of each servant. I didn't recognize any of the girls excepting Tala, and as Maram had not occupied her marriage suite for very long I doubt she would recognize them either. I wondered, suddenly, who had brought them on.

My last encounter with Nadine rose up in my mind. She was so meticulous in all she did; she would do no less in ensuring Maram remained under her sway. It was not out of the realm of possibility that she had hired these girls herself and ensured their loyalty to her in any way possible.

I'd chosen a simple blue qaftan made of velvet, with gold trim along the hem and sleeves. Pinned to my right shoulder was a fall of white chiffon that spilled down my back and trailed to the floor. My hair was slicked back, the excess braided and pinned to the back of my head, and in lieu of a coronet or crown I wore a gold filigree cap, shaped like a tesleet, its wings wrapped around either side of my head. The effect was simple, but striking.

Thus dressed, I was escorted by the serving girls from the dressing room to the main parlor, where Idris waited. The serving girls continued to the breakfast salon without me. He looked both better and worse—he hadn't shaved this morning, which might have made another man look unkempt. But Idris simply looked more Kushaila, as if he belonged in a djellaba more than a Vathek military suit. There were shadows beneath his eyes, and when he looked at me he seemed tired, his shoulders stooped.

I reached for his hand when the last serving girl disappeared.

"I'm sorry," I said, and wished I had something better. "How did you sleep?"

"Not well," he admitted. "But better with you there. Thank you. With Maram especially."

I raised my eyebrows, surprised. "I did nothing."

"You do not give yourself due credit," he said. "I was not inclined to be diplomatic or kind."

"You are grieving—"

"There is no place for grief here," he said softly. "I know that. We both do."

I shook my head. "There is no thanks necessary for what is freely given."

He did not smile, not exactly, but there was a sense of relief in him.

"Do you think it will work? The alliance—that it will protect us?"

"You are the master shatranj player," I replied.

"We've tried before . . . it never works."

"You've never had a queen on your side," I said softly. Children could not plot together, could not stand together, without a protector. And though the hostages of the Vath were children no more, they were still distinctly at a disadvantage.

Idris watched my face closely, as though he could divine some secret without my knowing.

"Maram is too clever to entertain opposing the empire, even for a moment," he said at last.

"She need not oppose an empire—just her father."

I knew that neither Idris nor Maram would ever entertain rebellion, but the truth of the matter was that even if Maram took hold of the government prior to her father's death, the presence of the Vathek imperial machine would make real change impossible. It was erected to mine our resources and steal our wealth—it had to be eradicated. We couldn't wait for Mathis to die—the planet would not outlast him.

"Her father *is* the empire," he replied.

I looked away. Anything I said would be too close to rebellion, and I dared not even breathe it. Idris had no idea I'd ever spoken with the rebels, let alone worked alongside them, and I knew how he felt about dissidence entirely. It had cost him his family.

"Amani," he said, softly, dangerously. "Those more powerful than you have suffered for thinking less."

"I only want to protect us."

"Who is *us?*"

The world, I wanted to say, but refrained.

"I have lost enough loved ones to the Vath, Amani," he said instead of leaving. "I cannot bear to lose any more."

"Your Highness?"

Tala stood in the doorway, a small smile on her face.

"I apologize for intruding, but breakfast is ready."

Idris placed my hand in the crook of his elbow and together we entered the salon. The serving girls lined up against the wall as the two of us sat, and Tala poured tea and uncovered dishes. Idris was quiet as he tucked into his food, and as he ate I thought and watched. One of the girls watched the two of us closely, and I felt a shiver run down my spine. Did Maram always feel thus—as if someone in her house had, or would in the future, turn against her? If I lived under such suspicions all the time, Dihya only knew what sort of person I might have become. There were so many sides to the problem of Maram's rule. Securing the government was one thing, but she would not be able to do it without securing her own house. 'Adil had been taken without her knowing.

I wondered again if Nadine had hired these girls. How much control over her own house had Maram passed off to Mathis's loyal servant without realizing? I'd not thought much of it, but now it seemed the easiest way for Nadine to watch and control Maram. I waved the serving girls out of the room but held back Tala.

Maram needed allies, and she needed a household that served her. She had no friends, no supporters. The women who did her hair and changed her clothes and laid out her jewelry—these were the core of a household. On Cadiz I would not have such luxuries, but I would have my mother and my friends—when I got married, when I bore my first child, in hardship and in doubt. These women would buoy me up through it all. And so, I had to make sure that such a network existed for Maram, even if I had to forge it from nothing.

"Who among the servants here do you like best, Tala?" I asked, picking up my tea glass.

She raised an eyebrow at me.

"That bad?"

"They all gossip," she said. "Nonstop. None of them take the work seriously."

"So none of them are Nadine's?"

"I didn't say that," she replied dryly. "They need not be Nadine's— only susceptible to gifts. That's how she operates."

"Can any of them be trained?" I said. "Or turned?"

"Two. Perhaps." She said it with a touch of disdain that made me smile. Tala was good at her job—she had to be. And well trusted by the Vath at that to be entrusted with my care. I would take her word for the other handmaidens.

"I can ask Her Highness if we can interview more to replace them. But I think two or three need to be made permanent members of the household."

"Are you already shifting things around?" Idris's question suggested a challenge, but there was an approving smile in his eyes.

I turned to Tala. "Start interviewing," I said. It could not help Maram's security that every time she traveled the people who went with her were strangers. "We need a household whose loyalty is to us and us alone."

"I will bring a dossier of eligible candidates by tomorrow," Tala said, inclining her head.

"Thank you. And Tala?" She paused. "Keep a watch over them. I don't trust them."

The local diwan—ministry—met several days a week in a long, multi-level gallery on the estate. They were, if the stewardess was any proof, likely a well-oiled machine. But I knew it would help to have Maram seen at these events, and to eventually have her participate. So it was to the gallery that Idris and I went early that morning.

"Have you ever sat in on these meetings?" I asked him, my hand tucked into the crook of his elbow.

"When I'm at Al Hoceima, if the diwan is in session, yes," he said. "They are not interesting."

I smiled. "Perhaps. But they are useful."

The gallery was a traditional diwan—a council chamber. There was the main floor, with lush, low-backed couches lining either wall, divided by a pathway that led to a dais on which sat a Kushaila-style throne. Rising up on all sides of the circular chamber were three more levels, each with ornately carved pale wood railings and columns, behind which were rows of backless couches. This was where the ruling magistrate or the sovereign themself would receive complaints from locals and run government. It was at the northern end of the estate, close to one of the main gates to receive the local populations on the visiting day.

The gallery was already filling up with various magistrates and officials. It took only a moment for them to realize that Idris and I were among them, and as ripples moved through water they sank to their knees one by one. When they came to their feet a nervous air took hold. The cloud of conversation disappeared entirely, and instead they looked nervously at one another.

If this was the way Maram was greeted any time she entered such a setting, no wonder she was always ready to bite.

"Please," I drawled in Maram's customary tone, "pretend I am not here."

Idris and I made our way not to the throne, but up a level where the dowager queen or the sovereign's extended family might take a seat. There was a trellis, hiding us from view, but a small monitor at the railing's level. With us out of sight, though perhaps not out of mind, the diwan resumed its quiet air of conversation.

I'd intended only for Maram to be seen—if she truly wanted to be what I thought she was capable of being then she needed not only the makhzen but the wizaraa' as well. Without the ministers on her side, there was no one to govern effectively—it was the wizaraa' who'd kept us as afloat as we were. But the longer I listened to their discussions, the clearer it was how ineffective they were. And it was not their fault; they did their best with the resources they had. The problem, of course, was what they had was *nothing*. They could settle petty disputes, they could ameliorate some suffering, but M'Gaadir and its surrounding lands' largest problems could not be solved by them. The Vath had taken, claimed, and ruined almost everything.

The longer the diwan went on, the more it confirmed what I'd thought but had resisted saying to Idris. He believed that there was a world where he could bend the Vathek system to his will but would go no further. What he wouldn't acknowledge was that the imperial machine had been built to break us. And it was not one meant for repurposing—as poetic as it might have been, the hammer would not yield a crop. It would not nourish our children or give succor to our elderly. And even as Maram became more powerful, gathered more allies, ensured her coming reign, countless people would die. The planet would not survive the time it took for her to take the crown. It would die before Mathis did.

Yet and still—none of the makhzen families had the strength to stand against the regime. Even allied with Maram. Even allied *together*.

The rebels, however, did.

Maram's opposition alongside the rebels could free us once and for all.

I could do this. I could forge a connection between two factions that would save the planet. I thought of my brothers and my parents—they'd suffered for my choice to side with the rebels before. Could I risk their safety a second time? I remembered my brother charging the Garda as they took me. That Husnain would make the same decision in my place should not have comforted me, but it did. My parents had given up on seeing a just world, but it was my responsibility to do this. If I could change the future, then it was an obligation.

I would do what was necessary.

03. Maram

Maram ofttimes wondered if she had a self-destructive quality. That was the only explanation she could find for why she'd wandered into Fatiha's office in the early morning while waiting for Aghraas, and turned on her holovision. It was the only explanation she could find for making sure to tune in to the wedding she'd made sure not to attend as herself. Truly: the only reason for why she would want to see her twin parading around in clothes meant for her.

Amani was a vision in tea and champagne gold, her ears heavy with jewelry, her back straight, head poised. The bridal gown Maram had chosen hung off her as if it were meant *for her,* and the ways her eyes avoided the many camera probes flying about as she walked through the crowd was demure and regal. Maram's fingers twisted angrily at the skin of the inside of her arm as she watched Idris bow over her hand, then guide her to the settee and divan at the center of the room.

What a golden couple they were, she thought angrily.

All her life Maram had known she would marry Idris. It was a contract agreed to before she was born and solidified before her mother's death. She'd never questioned it before, but now watching the two of them she felt an awful twist in her stomach, as if a knife were scraping her insides. Every time she thought of it she felt a rising tide of panic that only grew exponentially when she told herself she would be queen and this was part and parcel of that. Without Idris there was no crown, a thing that had not been true for any of the previous queens of the Kushaila.

It is a question of blood, she'd heard someone say. Idris was meant to temper and dilute her, to return the crown to whom it belonged—half of her did not belong. Her Vathek blood did not belong.

Amani didn't look like her, she thought. Amani looked as a true Kushaila monarch might—the gown and her soft smile and the steel with which she carried herself. She seemed *warm* and alive. Maram's elder half sister Galene was not so, and indeed neither was Maram herself. She rarely smiled so kindly to those she loved, and never to strangers. Nor did she touch Idris as Amani did, hand gently on his arm, shoulder to shoulder—the sort of touching that hinted at an intimacy that only ever bloomed in private.

Her hand pressed against her belly.

The door to Fatiha's office opened, then shut. She expected the soft murmur of voices as Fatiha conversed with yet another page, and instead there was silence.

Maram considered shutting off the holo and didn't. Instead, she turned to face Aghraas, face as blank as she could make it. The falconer was dressed in a modest high-collared coat today, along with her customary trousers and boots. Her braids were bound up at the back of her head in a single clip, and slung over her back was a bag Maram knew was filled with various instruments of her trade.

Aghraas examined her in silence and then lifted her gaze to stare at the holo of Amani and Idris.

"You don't wish to be present at your own wedding?" she said, voice low.

Maram's jaw tightened. "No. I do not."

"Why?"

Aghraas's gaze had returned to Maram, and she fought the urge to squirm. Her gaze was direct and unavoidable. There was no fear, no desire to look away. For the first time Maram had to fight not to look away, not to cast her gaze down.

She wanted to say many things in reply, but the core of her was reliable. Deflection was an old friend.

"You have not earned the right to ask," she said.

Aghraas inclined her head. "Apologies for my tardiness. I didn't count on having such a hard time finding my way out of Shafaqaat."

Maram waved her hand at the holovision, watched it wink out, then turned back to Aghraas.

"Shafaqaat is thirty minutes away at *most,*" she said. "You are three and a half hours late."

"By air car, Your Highness. Few in Shafaqaat want to lease an air car to a woman wearing daan," Aghraas said.

"Don't tell me you *walked?*"

"Normally a family is willing to let me ride on the back of their wagon," Aghraas replied.

"*Wagon?*" Maram could not keep the horror from her voice. "That's . . . two hours?"

"Four," Fatiha interjected from her desk without looking up from the stack of tablets.

"Indeed," Aghraas said with a smile. "Not to worry. Most nights I don't go all the way to Shafaqaat. There's plenty of land outside the estate that's good for camping. The journey most days is much faster."

"*Camping?*"

"Indeed, Your Highness."

"You can't camp outside the estate," Maram said.

"Of course I can. It's perfectly legal."

"I'm not worried about the *legality*. Why should you camp when we have room in the estate?"

Aghraas raised an eyebrow. "Do you suggest that I camp on the estate grounds?"

Maram felt as if she were being strangled. "*No.* We have rooms—why didn't you say something? Are you the child of marauders that you should just endure the elements as a matter of course?" She turned to Fatiha. "Put her up in the master of falcons suite. No one is using it."

"Your Highness—"

Maram spun back around to face the falconer. "This is a royal command," she said firmly. "I will not have you camping on the borders of my property like some vagabond out of antiquity. Bring whatever things you have stashed away in . . . trees or rocks or what have you—Fatiha will install them in your new apartments."

Aghraas bowed, and when she rose and her eyes met Maram's she felt a thrill. She had impressed her or surprised her, she thought.

"You are kind, Your Highness."

"I am practical," she countered, and left the room.

It took no time at all to situate Aghraas into the apartments in the estate, and a little while later they rode out to continue what they'd spent the last two weeks doing. Each day they would ride out into the estate, sometimes alone, sometimes with an escort. Aghraas would take a survey of the land— any creatures they saw, whether in the air, on the ground, or in the lakes and streams that covered the estate. What was indigenous to the region was recorded, what was not was tagged, and anything that hadn't been spotted since before the conquest was similarly tagged.

The day passed quickly. In truth, Maram didn't understand the work. It seemed they were going quadrant by quadrant, but animals relied on no such classification to choose where they ate or bred. Perhaps there was a science to it, but in the meantime, she was happy to tag along. As much as she enjoyed running the estate, she liked riding through it and discovering what lived on it even more. Aghraas was not easy to be with—she was counter to everything Maram knew and understood. And yet she couldn't talk herself out of these excursions. The falconer had been doing her work long before she'd come for this stretch of visit, and she would continue it after she left—

Her mind veered sharply away from thoughts of leaving. It was always hard to leave Dar al-Zahra', but she'd already extended her stay. In truth, it should have been *her* at the wedding. It was not an event open to the public, excepting journalists and their cameras. It was not an event for which she needed a replacement. And yet—

It was a few hours ahead of sunset and the sky was red, the air hot. Fall had well and truly arrived, or so she'd thought until now. Maram reclined on a large rock, her legs crossed, her jacket spread beneath her. Below her was Aghraas, similarly stripped out of her jacket, and leaning over a wide stream. She watched as she splashed water on her arms and throat, then over her face, before taking a large gulp. Her copper skin gleamed with droplets of water and there was something serene about her as she turned her face heavenward and closed her eyes as she absorbed sunlight.

Maram watched her without guile or shame. She'd never seen anyone like her—none among the Vath or Andalaans possessed the surety of movement that she did. Where she chose to go was where she would be, no matter what. She turned her face away from the sky and to Maram and grinned, though Maram didn't know why. She felt an answering grin on her face and a strange warmth in her chest, unweighted by the deep distrust that naturally governed her relationships. She watched her as she climbed the rock easily and collapsed beside her. Wordlessly, she held out a sheepskin to her.

"Drink, Your Highness," she said when Maram stared at it uncomprehending. "It's only water—the freshest on your estate."

Maram took the sheepskin hesitantly and put the opening to her lips. It seemed suddenly important to her that she be able to accomplish this very easy thing to Aghraas's satisfaction. But in the end, she choked on the water and it spilled out of the sheepskin and down her front. Aghraas didn't laugh, only held out her hand to have it back so that she too might drink. When she held it out Aghraas made a sound of curiosity and instead of taking the sheepskin of water, took hold of Maram's wrist.

Maram flinched and dropped the bag between them—Aghraas seemed not to notice, her eyes fixed on the palm of her hand. A flush of shame worked its way up Maram's throat. It was the childish sort of shame she thought she'd left behind when she'd returned to the Ziyaana, churning inside her and upsetting all the old voices that taunted her as a child. Aghraas's thumb traced slowly over the lines of henna stained into the palm of her hand where few people would see or even think to look. The lines meant nothing—they were only meant to be evocative of Kushaila design. And yet by being on her palm at all they meant everything; they were testament to her weakness, her inability to turn away from her Kushaila heritage.

Aghraas held out a second hand silently and Maram, in turn, placed her second hand in it wordlessly. When at last she released her hands Maram didn't know what to do with them. She laid them over her knees and stared at the rock surface between them.

"They would be better hidden on your feet," Aghraas said quietly.

Maram didn't look up. "I cannot see my feet, nor can I routinely take off my slippers to look at them," she replied. She hated that the admission had come out, however lopsided and misshapen. As if she were still a girl fascinated by what her mother had had, by what her mother had worn. By what her grandmother had worn. She was a woman now, a Vathek Imperial Heir of high standing.

"You can make fun," she said stiffly, her eyes fixed now on a spot above Aghraas's head. "I know how it must seem."

"How must it seem?"

Still Maram would not look at her. Inside, the shame had turned to dread and fear and anger. And nursed in its center was grief.

"A half-breed that is hated and reviled equally by all has built for herself a Kushaila retreat where she can pretend," she said.

She jumped when Aghraas's thumb swept over her cheek and turned her head just so. No one touched her—no one ever dared. She hated it, how she craved it—the world blurred momentarily as her eyes filled with tears.

"Do you love your mother?" Aghraas asked.

Maram exhaled a trembling breath but didn't answer. Aghraas's hand remained on her cheek. Maram wanted to— She didn't know what she wanted. The hand wasn't enough and yet was too much at the same time.

"I love mine . . . even when she is angry with me."

Her eyes widened in surprise. "Why is she angry with you?"

Aghraas smiled sadly and withdrew her hand. Maram remained perfectly still as it found hers in her lap.

"She wishes me to come home—I was only here to deliver a message. I became . . . distracted."

She clung to this conversation—anything to take the focus off her. "Isn't . . . isn't this your home?"

Aghraas shook her head. "This is where we're from. But home is elsewhere."

For long moments Maram didn't know what to say. She watched Aghraas, who in turn watched their clasped hands. "Why are you here, Aghraas?" she asked at last.

Her grip tightened around hers. "Where else should I be?"

⊰ IO ⊱

There was one person who would be able to help me contact the rebels.

Tala arranged for Furat and I to meet in a garden adjacent to the royal suite. They were closed to visitors and guarded besides, but Tala promised to make sure Furat could gain entry without being remarked on or remembered. Pathways through the garden were laid with green and white tile, and the whole of it was built around a central gazebo, its structure made of pale wood, its roof tiled in red and silver. From its apex hung a beautiful brass lamp with four glass sides.

Furat stood directly beneath the lamp, her red-brown hair gleaming in the light. I eased the hood from my hair when she turned around, bringing my face out of shadow, and she grinned as she recognized me. Furat, I realized as I hugged her, was one of my few true friends in the Ziyaana. My love of her was uncomplicated—she was a kind woman and a rebel, and I wished that I was not so limited in my ability to see her.

"You look well," I said, pulling back.

"As do you," she replied. "I worried when I heard we'd lost contact with you."

I gave her a wan smile. "After the confirmation ceremony . . . Nadine punished my family. It seemed prudent to cut ties—to destroy any evidence that I was linked to the rebels—lest I be caught in a worse act."

Her face twisted with horror. "I'm so sorry," she said, and squeezed my hand. "They are alive?"

I nodded. "How is the dowager?" I asked.

"In good health," she said. "Asking for you. I told her it was unlikely, now that Maram has married Idris—but I see not?"

"A longer and more complicated story than I wish to tell tonight," I said.

She laughed. "Alright. Then what did you come for tonight?"

"Maybe I came to see you," I protested.

"Come now. We don't live in that world. At least not yet."

I gestured to the bench. "I have a proposition for you and Arinaas."

Her eyebrows rose. "Oh?"

"Idris and I—really, Idris, *Maram*, and I . . . are trying to build an alliance between the houses of the makhzen to secure Maram's rule as queen."

Her eyes widened.

"I think it will work . . . but I don't think either wants to admit that her rule may also need to be secured by force." I looked at Furat. "She needs an army."

"You can't be suggesting—"

"I have done my research. Maram is the only *legal* heir to this planet—the only one who can request galactic aid. The only one the galactic senate will back if we need to push the Vath out by force. If she sides with her father, any galactic alliances will be made in their favor."

"I know that," she said quietly.

"And the rebellion would take that risk, that assassinating her alienates us from outside help?"

She frowned. "There has never been any other option."

"And if she sided with us instead of her father?"

"Has she?"

I resisted the urge to squirm. Therein lay the problem of my request. I couldn't tell Maram that I was requesting an army on her behalf from rebels. Any ground I'd gained with her would be lost; despite saving her life, my connection with them had upset our delicate friendship and pushed her back into Nadine's shadow. But the truth was if she was to have any hope of unifying the planet, she needed them as much as they needed her.

What I'd always believed about Maram remained true—that she would see, given time, that the path of least resistance was also the least just. That removing her father was the only way forward for the planet.

"I'm working on that part," I said at last.

"Arinaas will not pledge the rebellion in support of her without either Maram herself or a powerful enough ally in her stead, Amani," she said. "What about Idris?"

I shook my head. Maram might have feared the rebellion because it endangered her Vathek standing, but Idris's fear was more acute. He'd lost his family to a doomed resistance. Even with 'Adil's abduction he was paralyzed by his fear.

"Perhaps before the wedding," I said. "But since 'Adil's disappearance . . . he is more afraid of the regime than ever, though he will not say it."

"You don't trust him?" she said, dismayed.

"I don't trust his fear," I corrected. "I don't think he would ever . . . report on any of us. But he would refuse to help."

"That's two-thirds of the main continent out—Maram is the last Ziyadi with any pull, and at this point she will not ally. And we cannot ally with you, Amani—it is not enough."

"What about the Banu Ifran?" I said suddenly, my thoughts whirl-ing. Wouldn't it make sense to join Maram's great alliance to the reb-els—to pull the strongest of them into a confederation that would support her?

Furat scoffed. "The collaborators? They wouldn't."

"Rabi'a is new, and by all accounts has great love for her province and its prosperity," I pointed out.

"Prosperity bought because of her mother's collusion."

"She *cares*, and she has been successful in caring for her province. No easy feat. Allow to me to try," I said. "If I can secure her alliance—"

"If Rabi'a will ally with the rebels—if her *house* will ally with the rebels, then yes. She will have our fursa." *Knights.* Dihya.

"I . . . I will need something too."

"I see this was not done altruistically," Furat said, laughing.

"I would not ask if my need was not dire," I said.

"Peace, Amani. I do not judge. We live in difficult times."

"My family . . . they are still on Cadiz. They are still surveilled. If I set a foot out of line—"

"They are always in danger."

I nodded. "It's no easy thing I ask, but if Nadine even suspects that I have risen above my station— If you can—"

"I will make the request and tell Arinaas what you do in the mean-time."

I breathed a sigh of relief. By brokering this alliance, by trying to secure my family's safety, I was taking on Nadine, and she had pun-ished me for less. But if I could secure the Banu Ifran for both Maram and the rebels, their combined forces might be enough to save us. To save our world.

"Thank you, Furat."

"No thanks for what should be done," she replied, and squeezed my hand. "How long do you think you'll need?"

I frowned. "I'd plan on the length of our stay here," I replied. "I haven't even met Rabi'a. I'll be able to tell you how likely it is that she'll turn rebel soon."

"Amani," she said, a warning in her voice. "Don't trust her—whatever love she has for the province, it was bought in blood."

"Her mother—" I protested.

"Her mother raised her," Furat said. "Trained her."

"What dark times," I murmured, "that we have been turned against each other thus."

"And what a rosy memory of our past you have," she laughed. "Don't forget—civil war made us a ripe target. And before that, before we were Andalaan, we were tribes warring against each other. You should know this—half the poems out of antiquity are about war parties."

I smiled sadly. "You're right. It doesn't make it any easier, though."

She hummed in agreement. "I'll secure a communicator for you. In the meantime, be careful. You are one of the few good people on this estate. Don't let the makhzen manipulate you for it."

"Siha, Furat," I said, kissing her on the cheek.

"Baraka," she replied, and was gone.

⊰ II ⊱

The Banu Ifran sisters were not Kushaila like many of the makhzen who had come to the walima, but Zidane like Furat: a tribal confederation as old as the Kushaila, and close to us historically. The elder sister, Rabi'a, was in her early twenties, and had recently inherited leadership of the family from her mother. The younger, Buchra, had never set foot outside Qarmutta or been presented at court. They were a prosperous family, and their province had not suffered the indignities that Idris's province, Ghazlan, had suffered. Their mother had collaborated with the Vath after Najat's marriage to Mathis, and they had been richly rewarded.

Their arrival was heralded by a soft chime ringing throughout the courtyard, and the doors at its north end groaning open.

Idris and I had taken up a game of shatranj in the later hours of the afternoon. The courtyard looked like a scene out of antiquity—

Andalaan nobility reclined beneath trees and gazebos. And it might have been, but for the droids that stood attention at the entrances and the probes that waited attendance on all of us.

I'd improved—or at least, I'd thought I improved. But Idris was still a master, and I found myself locked on my side of the board. I laid a finger on a piece and Idris made a soft sound in the back of his throat.

"That," I said, raising an eyebrow, "is unfair."

The expression on his face could only be termed a smirk. "If you're unsure of your move . . ."

"I hate you," I said with feeling, and moved the piece. A moment later it was captured and Idris had advanced further onto my side of the board.

"You'll get better," he promised.

The Banu Ifran sisters swept in a moment later flanked by estate guards. They wore the colors of their house—green and black. Zidane wear was not so different from Kushaila dress, though the lines often seemed softer. There was just a hint of Vathek gloss in their design, but not enough to obscure where they were from.

The two sisters at last reached our dais and sank to their knees gracefully.

"Your Highness," the elder said. "Thank you for welcoming us into your home. And felicitations on your marriage."

"You are welcome to our hospitality," I said without rising from my seat.

Rabi'a, for she was the elder, lifted her head at last. When her eyes set on the shatranj board between us, they lit up.

"Your Highness plays?"

I could feel the eyes of the court on us, waiting to see how our interaction would unfold.

"I dabble," I said lightly. "My lord husband is the master player."

Rabi'a, I knew, would be the more dangerous of the sisters. Until now, Buchra had said nothing and kept her eyes fixed on the ground. A small idea grew in my mind.

"Why not take my place and see how you fare? Your sister can tell me of your journey."

At that, Buchra looked up, eyes wide in surprise. I didn't bother smiling. Maram would not give the girl assurance that she meant no harm; she would allow her to twist in the wind. Rabi'a eyed me sharply but did not refuse, and when I'd risen from my seat, she took it. I laid a hand on Idris's shoulder for a moment.

"Play nice," he said mildly.

I gave him one of Maram's frosty half smiles. "I'm always nice."

Buchra's hair was brown and curly and she had not bound it up in the court fashion. Instead she used it as a veil and allowed it to fall across her face so that when we walked side by side I could not discern her emotion.

"Do all the girls wear their hair thus in Qarmutta?" I asked.

She nearly flinched; I could see it in the way her body tensed up and the momentary hitch in her step.

"No, Your Highness," she said at last, and tucked some hair behind her ear. "I can't sit still enough for someone to braid it up is all."

"How was your journey?"

She shrugged.

I stopped on the path and held my hands in front of me, waiting for her to realize her mistake. She was fifteen or thereabouts, certainly old enough to know court protocol. Old enough to understand how to communicate with her future queen. She understood her mistake a moment later and sank to her knees.

"Apologies, Your Highness," she said. I waved a hand and she came to her feet once more. "I don't travel often, and I dislike being away from home."

I raised an eyebrow, skeptical. "You are a scion of your house," I said as we began to walk again. "Surely you were prepared to leave it eventually."

"Rabi'a does the traveling and the . . . court things."

"Court things?"

I saw her almost lift a shoulder again, then catch herself. "Making appearances and that sort of thing."

"I see. You hate it that much? You seem quite sullen."

Buchra flushed a deep red and looked away. "Traveling does not agree with me. If you would excuse me, Your Highness?"

I was tempted to keep her, but I needed her on my side. Forcing her to suffer under my eye any longer was counter to that mission.

"Send your sister to me," I said at last, releasing her.

I found a private alcove overlooking the sea and waited. My instructions from the rebellion were clear: find a way to turn the Banu Ifran to our cause. That would be difficult if the younger sister was terrified of Maram, of even being alone with her. Rabi'a presented a different challenge. From the little Idris told me, she was skilled in the games at court. I would have to learn and adapt to the field—my life and the lives of many others depended on my success. I tried to slow my mind and focus on what I had to do today: only make contact. Nothing more.

Rabi'a's quick footsteps heralded her arrival.

"You have frightened my sister," she said by way of greeting.

I turned around slowly but said nothing. Rabi'a was beautiful, I noted. Every inch the Zidane girl as Furat was, with her glistening hair, her heavy earrings, and beautiful dress. But I was the Imperial Heir in this moment, and whether or not she was the scion to a powerful house, Maram would not tolerate being addressed in such a way.

"Your sister seems remarkably ill prepared for court," I said, and raised an eyebrow.

A small muscle twitch in her jaw was the only tell that she might be angry, but she sank to her knees prettily.

"My apologies, Your Highness," she said. "Buchra is the only family I have left. I worry for her."

I flicked my hand lazily, giving her leave to rise.

"It is my understanding that the Banu Ifran clan is large and sprawling in the way most Andalaan clans are."

"She is my mother's only other child," she clarified.

The Vathek conception of family, then. Parents and children, instead of the enormous web of cousins, close friends, and tribal affiliations that an Andalaan would consider family.

"You and your family fascinate me," I said, sitting down. She joined me across the table. "The children of a willing collaborator whose willing defection some say won the war."

"You give us too much credit, Your Highness," she said. I couldn't tell if she seemed pleased or annoyed at the assertion.

"I don't think I do. Your native prefecture is small, to be sure, but it was the crack in the foundation that helped win the war."

"Perhaps."

"But . . . since the crystallizing of power you haven't been seen at court. Your mother rarely made appearances, and you were presented only once. Why?"

"I and my mother before me have had our hands full with the running of our province," she replied. There was a small curl of amusement in her voice. "We have always been and continue to be loyal to our king and his heir."

"You cannot run your province from the capital?" So many of the nobles did, it struck me as a poor reason for her absence.

"My place," she said, inclining her head, "is with my people."

"I would have," I said in Maram's quiet way, "enjoyed having you at court, I think."

The Vath who governed us were concerned with policing and surveillance, not growth and prosperity. I had looked through the history of the province briefly. The Ifranis were diligent about keeping up with technological advances in agriculture, strengthened city infrastructure, and built schools. The Vath, however, did none of these things on our planet. Their collaboration had saved them from the worst of the occupation's effects.

"The empire has its king and has little need of me in the capital,

Your Highness. I remain with those who need me most," she said quietly.

"You are a devoted servant of the people," I replied. "It has been noted. And it is a thing to be admired. I only wish you were in the capital more—others might learn from your success."

She smiled in a way that made me feel young, and I bristled. "They wouldn't," she said. "There is little to learn from a Zidane upstart with no Vathek blood, Your Highness."

"As much as there is to learn from a half breed, I'm sure," I said lightly. I felt uncomfortable using Maram's heritage, but I was building this bridge *for her*.

She let out a soft laugh. "Indeed. I do apologize for Buchra. She will be better behaved in the future."

I inclined my head. "As you say. You are free to go."

She rose to her feet, bowed again, and left. I heard the shuffle of feet and whisper of her skirts as she left and let out a breath. That had gone better than I could have dreamed. I'd made contact and a positive impression. I hoped that I could secure her, both for Maram and for the rebellion.

Our futures depended on it.

❦ 12 ❦

The day was bright and clear as Idris and I, followed by a cadre of guards and handmaidens, made our way to the south end of the estate, beyond the orchard backing our normal meeting place. Beyond it lay the stables, and a large arena where the estate staff trained and broke horses. Idris was nearly bursting with energy, for the day had come when at last he could put the wedding gift the Mas'udi twins had given him to the test.

The estate staff had been hard at work all morning, setting up awnings around the stable yard, and preparing food for the afternoon events. The horse—the prince of stallions—was barely broken and in need of a firm hand. And though the Mas'udi twins loved and respected their prince, what they believed was clear: Idris wasn't capable of keeping his seat, much less training him.

A royal awning had been set up closer to the trees, and so Idris escorted me there. He was eager to be away and among the horses, but I gripped his arm for a moment until he turned to look at me. We were in public and here I was Maram, though all I wanted to do was reach up and kiss his cheek. I could feel the handmaidens pointedly not looking at us, but I couldn't make myself let him go.

There were nights when sleeping in the same room with Idris was impossible, when all I could think of was what it would have been like—what he would have done—if we were married. It was a madness that possessed me, that took hold of my soul, that made it impossible to detach my heart from his.

I remembered— There had been a time when I would have kissed him without worry.

His eyes met mine and I heard the sharp intake of breath, as if my thoughts were writ clear on my face. His eyes fell on the necklace I wore, and he stilled for half an instant before he raised his eyes to meet mine. I knew he thought of the pearls I'd worn on the wedding night, as I now did. My cheeks flushed with warmth, and though I knew I should have lowered my gaze, I could not.

His eyes met mine again, and for a moment I was sure that I wasn't alone in my sleepless nights. But then he smiled and his genial mask slid into place.

"What is it?"

"Be careful," I said, clearing my throat. "I should hate to be short one husband on account of your pride."

He raised my hand to his mouth and pressed a kiss against it, a gesture he would make to Maram. "I promise."

I struggled not to roll my eyes and released him. "Go," I said, a smile teasing the corners of my mouth.

"You are a queen among women," he said, then released my hand and nearly ran toward the stable yard. I watched him clap a hand on 'Imad's shoulder and shed his jacket.

Beside 'Imad was I'timad, who never seemed far from her twin, and beside her were the Nasiris: Khulood and Tariq. Khulood was dressed in a purple-and-gold qaftan, wrapped in her house colors as scion of her tribe, and her hair was braided and wrapped in a crown around her head. I made my way to the collection of couches and cushions set up for spectators.

"Tala," I began as I settled onto a low couch, "summon I'timad and Khulood. Tell them I wish to have tea."

Tala inclined her head and made her way to the two women. The air was cool and the orange trees planted in the orchard at our backs filled it with a citrus scent. I forced my hands to lay easily in my lap as I watched Tala speak to I'timad, and I'timad in turn speak to Khulood. I had made some progress with her, less progress with Rabi'a, but I needed all three women to make the plan Idris, Maram, and I had come up with tenable.

More than that, though I only needed Rabi'a, I wanted to be able to present a complete alliance to Arinaas. Three of the strongest families on the planet, with deep ties to its history, would make an effective symbol to anyone hesitant about raising arms against the Vath.

I hadn't been raised to this, not the way Maram had. I was not a queen's heir. But I had been chosen for this, and I would do it well. Even as I told myself that, I couldn't suppress the frisson of nerves that shivered up my spine. So much depended on my success.

I forgot my nerves when I'timad at last arrived beneath the awning, sank to her knees prettily, then crossed the space between us to press a kiss against my cheek. I froze, my mouth slightly ajar, heart racing. It was not bravery exactly to make such a show of friendship with Maram—but it *was* a show of friendship, a definitive one not required of her.

I let out a strangled, startled laugh.

"Greetings, Your Highness," she said, pulling away.

"Hello," I managed, and shook my head with a faint smile. "Is that the way of greeting here?"

She grinned. "I will say yes, and since you are only recently arrived here, you must believe me."

Her grin was catching, but I was a practiced actress and managed to control my features. I raised an eyebrow as I scanned her mode of dress.

"Is it also the style here to dress like your brother?" I hadn't noticed from far away, but she wore a riding habit identical to her brother's, which was not particularly strange except among the makhzen, who cleaved more closely to gendered clothing.

"I dislike finery most days, Your Highness," she said. "Dressing like my brother is more economical."

I gave her a sidelong glance, then at last turned to Khulood, who had waited patiently at the edge of the awning.

"We have met before, though only briefly," I said at last.

"Of course," she said warmly. "I'timad monopolized all of your attention the last time."

"Khulood, this is Her Royal Highness, Maram vak Mathis, High Princess and Protectress of Andala, of whom you know much," I'timad said, grinning cheekily as she recited introductions according to Vathek protocol. "Your Highness, this is Khulood bint Nasir of the city of Azaghar."

Khulood sank to her knees as prettily as I'timad had and inclined her head.

"It is a pleasure to make your acquaintance again, Your Highness," she said, looking up at me.

I allowed a corner of my mouth to quirk up in a smirk. "Is it?"

Many courtiers would have been put off by such a question, but Khulood was not. She came to her feet and smiled.

"It is," she said.

"You are a rare commodity, then," I replied. The makhzen avoided Maram at all costs, and little had changed in the recent weeks except for my tentative friendship with I'timad, and Maram's marriage to Idris.

Her smile softened, and I felt a bit of Maram's own defensiveness rise up in me. It was not pity exactly, but close enough to it that I did not like it.

"I have known the prince a long time, Your Highness," she said. "And I have not seen him smile so well as the past few days."

I flushed and looked down at the stable yard, where Idris had rolled up his shirtsleeves and was now in the ring with the stallion. I'd known he wouldn't be able to resist the challenge of it, and though I'd cautioned him, most of me had not wanted to talk him out of it. This was a new facet of him I was learning: he was competitive and stubborn. The Idris I'd known in stolen moments and in shadow was sweet and generous and kind. And he remained all those things. But he was also a proud man, a prince of princes. And like most princes, he didn't just like winning; he liked to prove he could win.

"Nor," Khulood said softly, "if I may be so bold, have I seen you ever look so in all my time in the Ziyaana."

My gaze jerked away from him and back to her. Unease churned in my belly. Maram did not love Idris; at least, certainly she did not love him in the way I did. And if the ease and warmth with which both I'timad and Khulood greeted me was predicated on our love for each other—what would happen if they ever found out the truth?

"I hope Khulood hasn't given offense?" I'timad said.

I felt as if I'd tripped over a crack in the ground and could not regain my footing.

"No," I said at last, looking away from them both. I wanted to say something else—that they were wrong, that they had misread the situation. But a new bride protesting love of her husband would not only have seemed strange; they would have marked it an insult. And I had done what I wanted to do, however accidentally—here were the heirs to two of the most ancient houses on the planet beside me, less suspicious than they'd ever been.

"No," I repeated, a little softer. For a moment I wondered what it would be like if I weren't pretending. If I were Idris's bride, if I weren't making alliances on Maram's behalf. But I was not his wife, though the love they'd discerned was real, and it was not me they would make friends with, but Maram.

I'timad must have sensed some of my turmoil, for she touched my hand and came to her feet. "I should like to observe your husband trying to keep his seat a little closer. Khulood?"

"Of course. It was a pleasure meeting you, Your Highness."

And so the day went. It felt strange: because it was a Salihi celebration, there were only Andalaans present. And though Idris and I had focused our efforts on cultivating relationships with three families, many had been invited. I heard cries in Kushaila, Zidane, and Tashfin chiding Idris to keep his seat, watch that step, take firmer hold of the reins. I wondered if this was what M'Gaadir was like before the occupation, if such things had taken place when Houwa reigned as queen. I had never felt so at home, and yet so apart from the whole world.

If I were myself I would be down near the paddock, cheering Idris on. But I was not myself, I was Maram, and she seldom deigned to mingle among courtiers at all. She was practiced at remaining aloof and apart, and it was what had landed her in this situation.

Idris maneuvered the horse over a jumping post, then reined him in and turned him so that he could look at me. He'd shed all his formal outerwear and was now clad in his trousers and a tunic that stuck to his back with sweat. His hair had come loose and clung to the sides of his face. He grinned at me, triumphant, and I felt an answering, irrepressible grin spread over my features.

"Your Highness?"

I pulled my gaze away from Idris and to Rabi'a and Buchra. They stood just outside the limits of my awning. Buchra's eyes were fixed to the ground, her cheeks flushed. Rabi'a, on the other hand, smiled just a little, enough to seem friendly. They sank to their knees together, then rose a moment later.

"We have come to apologize," Rabi'a said.

I waited. Maram would not have let the offense pass unremarked on, and she would make them work for her forgiveness. So I waited, my face empty of the smile I'd shared so freely with Idris, Khulood, and I'timad. I needed them and the rebels needed them, but I could not jeopardize my position in the court as Maram. Rabi'a understood and touched her sister's arm. Buchra looked up at me and if anything her flush deepened, but to her credit she didn't look away. Instead she sank back to her knees.

"I was unforgivably rude to you on our arrival," she said, voice soft. "I have no excuse and I beg your pardon."

"If you are not fit to present yourself at court, then do not come to court," I said, my voice even. "It is a simple lesson to learn, though the price is often high."

Buchra was still on her knees. After a beat I waved a hand, bidding her stand, and gestured to empty spaces among the cushions. They took seats and turned their eyes to the ongoing spectacle. The paddock had been extended for, of all things, a race. I'timad and Khulood made their way back up the hillside just as a series of serving girls appeared with trays of tea and food. Introductions were made and then the five of us sat together and waited while Tala poured tea for us.

The other girls chatted lightly, about the weather and the horses, but Buchra kept her eyes focused on her lap, where her hands clasped each other tightly.

"You have not been at court," Khulood said lightly, tilting her head just a little. "I would have remembered you."

Buchra hunched her shoulders, and her face flushed bright enough that I could see it past the strands of hair she allowed to obscure her features.

"She was not presented," Rabi'a said coolly.

I'timad raised an eyebrow. "Why ever not?"

I hid my expression behind a tea glass. I'timad knew why neither Buchra nor Rabi'a would have been in the Ziyaana in their childhood. Their mother had been a full collaborator with the Vathek government and was richly rewarded for it. There was no need to charge her children with the cost of other people's rebellion. But I was curious how Rabi'a would respond, faced with two girls who had paid that price, along with their parents and their siblings.

"I did not want to go." Four pairs of eyes, including mine, turned to look at Buchra in surprise. She'd tucked her hair behind her ears and lifted her chin despite the persistent flush of embarrassment.

"We've all heard the stories," she continued.

"Buchra," her sister said in warning.

"The stories?" Khulood repeated, voice flat.

"That children of the makhzen go missing without rhyme or reason," Buchra said softly. "That no one is safe. Even the prince's cousin wasn't safe."

"Oh, 'Adil will turn up—" I'timad started, tone jovial.

"The Imperial Garda took him," I interrupted before she could finish. The girls went silent.

I opened my mouth then closed it again. What could Maram say to these girls? What could I? Promises were empty if they weren't kept, but I thought Maram wanted to keep this promise. I knew she did—had we not spoken of it long into the night?

"They took him?" I'timad repeated, voice hoarse. I forced myself to meet her eyes, which were wide, though dry.

"I don't know why—"

"You don't *know*?" I'timad echoed me a second time.

"No, I do not," I said, sharpening my voice. I took a deep breath and softened my voice. "But I don't mean to allow such things to continue."

"You don't?"

"Are you a parrot?" I asked, losing my patience. "No, I don't. We can't rule this world if we don't trust one another. That has to start somewhere, regardless of what our parents have done."

For a moment, no one at the table said anything. We were the children of rebels, collaborators, and a dictator and queen. I'timad and Khulood shared a glance.

"You're right," Khulood said at last. "We couldn't stand together as children—but we aren't children anymore."

No one disagreed with her. In fact, no one spoke as the serving girls returned and laid sweets on the table and refilled our tea glasses.

"He's quite the rider," Rabi'a said when they left. "Do you ride, Your Highness?"

"Not so well as my lord husband, to be sure, nor so recklessly," I replied dryly. I had forgotten he was even riding his horse below amid the tension.

"You don't approve of the theatrics?" she asked with a smile.

I heard a shout from below and stiffened, but it was only a cry of triumph. Idris had won his race.

"I dislike recklessness," I replied at last.

Her smile turned to a grin. "You must ride with us when we go hunting, then. You might see the point in recklessness then."

"You hunt?"

"You don't?" Buchra interrupted, eyes wide.

"I'm a practiced falconer," I replied. "But Walili is surrounded by desert—I rarely have the chance."

"Then you must come to Qarmutta," Rabi'a said, then turned to the rest of the table. "All of you. There is plenty of hunting ground there. We will take you. And the prince, though I think his prize stallion would not be suited to it."

I tried to control the surprise on my face. I had not imagined it would be so easy as that. But Buchra's fear was evidence enough that though her mother had been loyal, they still feared the Vath. An alliance with other Andalaans would do them good, and would protect them in turn. And it might mean that when the time came, they would be willing to extend that alliance to the rebellion.

"I will hold you to that invitation," I said at last, letting out a small smile.

13

The morning dawned early and clear. I'd become used to the quiet bustle of the estate, the murmur of girls as they moved through one room and then another. And they, in turn, had gotten used to me. I didn't have to wait for a hot bath to be drawn, or for breakfast and tea. By the time the sun rose I had broken fast, bathed, and dressed. I stood on the tower balcony, facing the ocean, a heavy mantle about my shoulders.

Idris mounted the stairs to the tower balcony with a heavy gait, and when his head cleared the landing my eyes widened. There were dark circles under his eyes, and his hair was mussed. He looked as if he had stumbled directly out of bed and walked to me. He sank into the chair directly behind me and when I turned laid his head against my ribs and circled his arms around my waist.

"Idris?" I said softly. My hands hovered a breadth above his hair, unsure if I should touch him or not. My heart hammered behind my ribs. "Are you alright?"

"Nightmares," he said hoarsely. His forehead pressed against my ribs as if he might find solace in whatever lay behind them, and for a moment his fingers tightened their grip. My hands settled on his hair and shoulder of their own volition.

"I'm sorry," I said. I should have pushed him away—he was not mine to comfort anymore. But I was not cruel and I loved him and even now he turned his face away and shuddered, as if the nightmares haunted him still.

"It was different, this time," he said, his voice rough. "Normally it's just flashes, but this time—"

One hand tightened around my waist, the other pressed against my back.

"They hid me away—my mother knew what was coming. She could see the desert sand rising on the horizon. Mathis had sent an entire army to subdue the city. You know when I was eight—I was sickly. War does that—you can't keep anything down because you're worried about air raids or— She could pick me up. And that evening she picked me up and fled across the estate and hid me away.

"I promised her I wouldn't leave the hidden room—and I just . . . waited there for hours. But I heard her." I looked down at him but he hadn't looked up. His shoulders were hunched, his back stiff. "She didn't scream when they took her away. Or when they lined everyone up."

"Idris—"

At my voice he looked up. There was no one else in the tower room but us—only us, and his grief, and what we felt for one another. I smoothed a hand over his cheek and tucked a lock of hair behind his ear. His eyes slid closed as if I'd given him solace or benediction.

"You remind me of them," he said, covering my hand with his.

"Them?"

"The freedom fighters," he said. Some of his tension eased as he smiled. "You're fearless and have a sense of justice."

He didn't know what I did in secret, that I had allied with the makhzen and rebels both. Perhaps he sensed it, or perhaps it was simply as he said: that I reminded him of women in that time, and that alone stoked his fear.

"Everyone has a sense of justice—" I protested.

"Don't die as they did," he interrupted me.

"Idris—"

"Please, don't die as they did. As 'Adil did."

My breath caught. "'Adil is dead?" I whispered.

"They sent his body to his parents' estate—it arrived last night."

"Idris—"

I combed my fingers through his hair. "I am not a soothsayer," I said at last. "But I will endeavor to remain alive."

That made him smile. "That is not the same."

"And yet," I said, "it is what you must accept."

His smile softened and his thumb stroked an arc over my spine. We had not been so close since before his marriage, and I was loath to pull away now. For a brief moment in time we were as we'd been before—together and content, unbothered by the outside world. I wanted to kiss him and I saw that same desire reflected in his eyes, in the way his hand tightened over mine.

"Your Highness?"

It was as if someone had doused me in cold water. I withdrew from the circle of his arms quickly and turned to face Tala. Behind me, I heard Idris come to his feet.

"Yes?" I said, breathless.

"She is asking for you," she said quietly.

"Of course. Tell her I'll be there shortly."

I didn't turn back to face Idris as Tala descended the steps back into the main level of the estate. My hand pressed against where his head rested on my ribs, as if he'd branded me there. When I turned around, he was no longer smiling. The air in my lungs seemed to thin as he stepped closer.

"I won't keep you," he said softly.

I fled.

I paused in the hidden corridor outside the double's suite and waited for my hands to stop trembling. It wasn't a surprise that I was still so affected by Idris, but in the last little while the machinations of state had taken over. I hadn't had *time*. I drew in a deep breath, hid my still trembling hands in the folds of my skirt, and entered the double's suite.

Maram was in the suite's tower room, surrounded by dossiers, with one in hand as she paced the length of the room.

I sank to my knees with a murmured greeting.

"Did you approve this?" she asked, and held out a dossier.

My eyes widened as I came to my feet. "I don't *approve* anything, Your Highness." It was a dossier of the servants and handmaidens Tala had collated for hiring. "These are Tala's recommendations for permanent additions to your household."

"But you approve of them?"

She was nervous, I realized. Not angry.

"Yes, Your Highness," I said. "Some are a little chatty, but they're diligent, well trained, and, more importantly, loyal. To you and you alone."

"Why do you like them?" she asked.

I lifted one shoulder. "They're competent and dedicated. Efficient. Self-directed when necessary but prudent enough to know when something should be brought to your attention."

"No, why do you like *them*—you seem fond of them."

I tilted my head to the side as Maram had done many times before. "Truth be told . . . they remind me of my friends on Cadiz."

Maram's eyes widened. "You never talk about it."

"About it?"

"Your home. Your family."

"There is little reason to bring up my elder brothers," I said, trying to keep my voice flat. "Or my friends or life before."

"*Brothers?* I imagined maybe some cousins. Certainly, your parents. You don't act like the youngest."

I grinned. "I'm the only girl. It happens." When she didn't smile back, I sobered. "The girls are trustworthy. If you'd like we can look at others, but—"

"No," she interrupted, then looked over my shoulder. "Ah. And it seems our time together is about to come to a close. Though I didn't expect to see you after—"

Idris climbed the stairs more quietly than he had this morning. In the interim he'd freshened up, and none of the grief I'd seen in the morning remained. He bowed to both of us as one, then straightened and raised an eyebrow.

"After my behavior the last time we spoke?" He inclined his head. "My anger was ill placed. I apologize for my outburst."

From the expression on her face, I don't think he'd ever apologized to her before. I was hard pressed to believe he'd never had such an outburst, but Idris was diplomatic and aware enough that only his cousin's death might have prompted such a thing from him.

"I—" she started. "Thank you. I heard—I'm sorry about 'Adil, though it changes nothing."

He inclined his head again.

"I had another reason for coming," he said, and held up a holosheet. Maram took it first, and I watched her face go blank before she handed it to me. A chill wound its way down my spine as I read. Nadine was only a few hours away. We'd known she would get here eventually—she would be a Vathek royal guest. But I, and no doubt Maram, too, had avoided thinking about it. Maram would have to pit her strength against the stewardess as both a married woman and mistress of her own household. And I could not do it for her. Nadine knew the differences between us too well.

"You will have to meet with the estate stewardess," I said, handing Maram the holosheet. "And Idris can make sure that her servants are monitored so they don't interfere. You will also have to greet her."

"Greet her?" Her eyebrows rose. "Why must I greet her?"

"I can't do it," I replied. "She can tell the difference between us."

"Why must anyone greet her?" she said, one hand on her hip.

"Why does a king greet visiting dignitaries to his home world? Because one is the host and the other is the guest. If only the staff greet her—"

She waved a hand. "Alright."

There was a strange look of nervousness about her, as if she hadn't counted on this. As if, impossibly, she'd forgotten how to be the Imperial Heir. I hesitated, then reached for her and took hold of her hand.

"You are the Imperial Heir and this is your home," I said. "She cannot take power from you if you do not let her."

"Are you . . . rallying me?" she said, on the edge of laughter.

I smiled weakly. "Is it working?"

"No. But good effort."

A passage led from the abandoned suite to a small alcove with a shielded window that overlooked the entryway. It was sequestered from everything, with a single entrance leading back to the rest of the palace. It was there I stood as the estate gates groaned open and Nadine's entourage made their way in.

Maram and Idris stood side by side on an elevated platform, and behind them stood a row of the senior-most staff. They made a striking image. The air had turned sharper and cooler the further into the autumn months we'd gone, and they both wore heavy velvet mantles in complementary shades of teal. Maram's skirt was shot through with white embroidery that looked from one angle like tesleet feathers and from another like the frothing waves of the ocean. She wore a modest crown, but it too bore the sigil of the tesleet in its center. I'd not expected her to take so much comfort in the imagery of her mother's house, but it seemed to steady her as she'd dressed and listened to me summarize the reports on the court that I'd given her.

She would need to be herself today, and likely for many days, a prospect she looked on with little joy. But I did not want to find out what Nadine would think of the role I'd played in shoring up Maram's defenses against her. I'd learned from my loss months ago, and the ease with which she'd turned Maram against me. I would not lose to her again.

Nadine emerged from a self-drawn carriage, her silver hair gleaming in the late-morning sunlight. She surveyed her surroundings. I'd paid little attention to how she was until it was too late, but now I saw. Her eyes roved over the courtyard in a way that showed she was used to being obeyed, and used to the world bending to her will. But she was not the Imperial Heir, and the power she derived from rearing Maram and controlling the palace in which she spent her time would wane.

She stilled, and I felt my heart give a painful thud when at last she saw where Maram and Idris stood. Her walk was not sedate or leisurely; there was something predatory in the way she moved, and I felt my own hands tighten around the folds in my skirt. Maram, for her part, remained perfectly impassive, a half smile on her face as Nadine sank to her knees then rose to her feet.

"Your Highness," Nadine greeted.

"Welcome to M'Gaadir," Maram said. There was no joy or happiness, but a diplomatic neutrality that I marveled at. I could not understand her fear of going into court—she was so practiced at it, in a way I knew I was not. Polished and at ease with power. "I trust your journey was easy."

"It was, Your Highness," she replied. "You need not have troubled yourself to greet me."

Maram's smile grew just a little, and I felt a strange swell of pride. "Of course I did. What sort of host would I be otherwise? We have prepared chambers for you in the eastern corridor."

"I normally stay—"

"Yes," Maram interrupted. "Adjacent to the royal suite. I have ordered them renovated. They will be absorbed into the royal suite by the end of the year."

Nadine seemed at a loss for words. For long moments she stared at Maram, and Maram, to her credit, stared back, one eyebrow raised.

"Have I said something confusing, Nadine?"

"No, Your Highness," she said, and inclined her head. "I am glad you are settling in so well."

Maram gestured to a serving girl behind her. "This is Nahla," she said as she came forward. "She will show you to your rooms and organize your staff so that they don't disrupt the rhythms of the estate."

Nadine knew, of course, what that meant. They would be watched and reported on and prevented from spying on Maram if they attempted it. Her hand did not fist in her gown, but there was something in the air about her that changed.

"I look forward to hearing your news from the capital," Maram finished. Nadine gave her a small bow and that was that. I felt another swell of pride. Maram was royal and I'd always known that. But her self-imposed exile had worried me, that she'd somehow lost her ability to navigate court life, or that she'd given it up like an 'ifrit giving up its magic in exchange for mortality. But now more than ever I felt the possibilities of her future and the future of this planet open up.

O4. Maram

Maram knew it was not the Kushaila way to leave offerings at shrines or images. Graves and tombs, perhaps, but her mother's tomb was in M'Gaadir. She would not go there until the honeymoon and her life was irrevocably tied with Idris's. But it was the Vathek way, and so she'd had a small room built, its ceiling strung with brass lanterns, with a single great stained-glass window within which her mother stood.

For half an instant she'd considered asking Amani how to make bakhoor. It seemed the sort of thing a villager, a farmer's daughter, would have to know how to do. But wherever they were now—*what*ever they were now—she didn't think she could reveal this to her. She couldn't share this with her. And so she'd searched on her own, and soaked the wood chips and found the syrup. When the bakhoor burned it smelled like Najat—jasmine oil and a hint of rose.

Maram found she couldn't move. Her eyes were fixed on the stained glass that made up the folds of her mother's qaftan. She understood that she was a terrible daughter. That she had never made the effort to visit her mother's grave. That she was a terrible successor to her mother's legacy. And that worst of all she was too scared to fix it.

Her hands shook as she unscrewed the top of the jar and moved from brass incense bower to brass incense bower, filling them with wood chips. There were almost thirty altogether, and she'd come home early from a viewing of falcons to do this. The room slowly filled with hazy incense smoke and the fragrance she'd soaked into the chips. Her mother appeared as an apparition through it all, lit by the fading light of the setting sun and the lanterns high above.

The doors to the room creaked open, and still Maram didn't look away from her mother's image. She knew it was Aghraas from her gait and from her silence. Many people would be motivated to make their apologies, to scurry out of the room immediately. But Aghraas stood a few paces behind her and remained quiet as if she were waiting for Maram to choose when to speak.

"Shall I say a prayer?" Aghraas asked at last.

"She can't hear you," Maram scoffed.

"Not *to* her," Aghraas replied. "For her."

"Our prayers help the dead as much as their wishes for the living help us," Maram said quietly, and turned away from the image of her mother. "Which is to say not at all."

Part of her was loath to wash the scent of jasmine and rose oil off her skin, but she was not a child who could linger in her mother's perfumes. So she bathed, and sat still as Fatiha oiled and combed her hair. The sun had set, and the light orbs filled the small estate. She always felt strange after visiting that room, and she felt stranger still now that someone else had been in there with her. There were times when she stood in her mother's shadow and thought she could do the right and necessary thing, that she could uphold her mother's dying wish.

The people depend on us—and us alone—to be their shield. Do not fail them.

The people are almost broken, she wanted to tell her mother. Because I stood by and let him do it.

"There you are," Fatiha said, and draped the heavy braid over her right shoulder.

"You need not do a serving girl's job," she said instead of thanking her.

Fatiha smiled. "It gives me some pleasure," she replied. "You will not believe me, but you remind me very much of your mother."

Maram was too tired to be angry, so she gave her a half smile. "I don't believe you. But I accept the compliment."

"Good night, Your Highness. You know where I am if you need me."

Many of the servants lived on the grounds, and there were times when that showed—a child's laughter, the soft sound of song as they prepared for the evening meal. Maram shrugged into a light robe and slippers and descended from her chambers and into the garden. Aghraas had been at the estate for some time now, and it was moments like these—confronted by her as she was now, haloed by the light of the orbs—that Maram regretted her invitation. Aghraas looked young, as young as her, her braids down around her face and without the martial clothing that made her appear remote. Instead she wore a dressing gown and sat in the grass, her slippers in a pile to her left, with a book open in her lap.

"Your Highness," she said by way of greeting. She did not stand.

"Falconer. You are reading."

"I am, Your Highness."

"What do you read?"

"Poetry, Your Highness."

The Vath had poetry, but they were a society who preferred plays. Maram had grown up watching dramas and tragedies on the Vathek stage—poetry had seemed part of her mother's world and so she'd read little and enjoyed less. But she knew Amani had a love of it, that the Kushaila prided themselves on their poetry possibly more than they did their ability to terraform moons.

"Will you read some?" The words came out more gently than she'd intended. Always, it seemed, Aghraas challenged her and Maram stood her ground. For once she wanted the falconer to be off her guard, to be worried. To—

Aghraas's eyes widened. "Read?"

"You can read, can't you?"

"I can, Your Highness."

Maram gestured toward the book. "Then."

Her pulse thrummed in her fingertips.

Aghraas lifted her chin and met her eyes, and Maram had the sharp realization that she'd made a mistake. That even if she did not understand Kushaila very well, Aghraas's performance would be affecting. And she understood enough—Aghraas spoke with the clarity of ancients, her voice high and pure, her language unadorned with modern flourishes. Maram understood enough for her cheeks to warm and her heart to beat harder in her chest. She understood enough that something inside her recognized itself and clicked into place.

"Shall I translate?" Aghraas said.

Maram couldn't say no. It would be cowardly. It would be admitting defeat. "Yes."

I believe Suhayyah weeps,
And I wish I had been known to her before today.
Before she stopped all speech
And her eyes found mine, stopping me in my path.
She stood exalted over me when my staff fell,
As if she were an idol plied by devoted priests.
Your wealth is yours, and your slaves are yours.
Is your torment for me spent?
Forget my misfortune when the war party comes.
They will swarm like locusts,
They will flee with their saddles wet
with water—ridden by hawks in revolt.
We have struck a great wound in the center
and they pale as they bleed.

There was a long silence after, and Maram had the strange sensation she'd lost feeling in both of her hands. Aghraas's eyes did not waver from her face, and so she didn't look away either. She was surprised at the piercing feeling in her belly when Aghraas's eyes lowered, the sharp pain that bid her take a step forward.

She heard her father's voice. *Control yourself.*

And yet she took a step forward and then another and another. They were measured and unhurried, and yet they were steps, and when she stood over Aghraas she could not keep her hands to herself. She slid a hand beneath Aghraas's chin and raised her face to look at her. Her hands didn't shake and she moved with a surety she didn't feel. Inside, her world had tilted on its axis.

"Why are you still here?" she asked.

Aghraas's eyes widened. "You haven't given me leave—"

"No," Maram interrupted softly. She felt unmoored from herself. "Here. At my estate. With me."

Aghraas's hand wrapped around her wrist, and Maram fought a shudder.

"I serve at your pleasure, Your Highness," she said. "Wherever you are, so too shall I be."

At that Maram could not control the way her hand seized and pulled away from her, nor the sharp intake of breath. It no longer felt as if it were a battle of wills—something she'd lost and won at the same time—but something else entirely. She looked away from Aghraas and pressed her hand against her ribs as if it might relieve her difficulty in breathing.

A shaft of moonlight hit the pool behind them and seemed to illuminate the entire courtyard.

I've stepped into a dream, she thought, and stepped past Aghraas.

"Your Highness?"

There was a feather floating on the surface of the pool. It was night-black and seemed to absorb the silver light around it. She'd heard no bird fly by to drop the feather, no coo to signal one might be nearby. Nor had they stored any falcons in the aviary yet. Maram knew what it was even as she chided herself in believing such a thing.

An extinct bird was extinct. It did not come in times of difficulty or need, did not revive itself as a species for one girl. And yet.

She stepped into the water without thinking and it rippled out around her ankles. The tiles at the bottom of the pool were cool and clean—there was no algae or dirt. She almost didn't pick up the feather. It was light, and when her finger brushed over its curve, color sparked as if following the trail of heat she left behind.

She hadn't asked for a sign or an answer. She didn't even know she had a question. The breath in her lungs thinned and chilled—was the cosmos reminding her of her duty?

"*Maram!*"

Her head jerked up. Aghraas stood over her, her face solemn, her feet as wet as hers, her hands cradling Maram's elbows.

Aghraas was beautiful. That was an easy thing to admit, a thing she'd admitted to herself long ago. And now, haloed by the moonlight, her eyes wide, she seemed more so than before. Maram felt a well of grief rise in her chest, a great spike of pain.

"I'm married," she said hollowly.

And Aghraas did something no one had ever done before. She laid her forehead against hers and sighed. "I know."

14

I could not spend the day traveling abandoned corridors and observing Maram. I returned to the abandoned suite and the tower where I'd found her before Nadine's arrival, and took with me a stack of books to pass the time. This was not the sojourn out into the city that I'd wanted, but it was the respite from court and the strange play my life had become that I needed. The sounds of the city rose as the day progressed, the clamor of carts and carriages, the cries of goats and sheep and donkeys, and the screaming of both merchants and seagulls.

I felt the stress of the last few weeks roll off my shoulders.

When I was small all I'd wanted was to get away from the quiet of our small village. I'd wanted to see the world beyond Cadiz, the cities on Andala, the megatropolises in the Wizaar system, the parliamentary buildings on Maron. And though I hadn't seen half of that, I felt as if I'd seen enough. I would have traded anything to go back to my parents' farm. I would have given anything for my day to start with milking goats and to end in front of a fire with my brothers.

Would I ever return to Cadiz? Would I be able to stomach my old life, given everything I'd endured?

Only Dihya knew, and he gave me no answers. My thoughts were too wound up in it all, and that, I thought, was why I heard no one climb the tower steps.

She stood in the exact center of the room, though how she'd gotten there I couldn't imagine. She was dark-skinned and dressed all in black. Her hair was bound into hundreds of thin braids, and nearly half of those braids wore small gold rings. A collection of them springing from her widow's peak were white. She wore a mantle against the chill, a heavy black velvet; and when the wind caught at its edges and it rippled, it seemed to be made not of velvet but of feathers. Instead of a qaftan she wore a simple blouse and trousers, with leather boots made for walking through the desert. Around her wrists were heavy silver braces, scuffed as if she'd actually been in fights. Most astonishing of all were the marks on her face—on her cheeks and on her forehead, she bore daan similar to Houwa's—sharp, pictographic representations of feathers. One on each cheek, and two crossed like swords on her forehead.

"You look surprised to see me," she said as I rose to my feet. Heat emanated from her as if a furnace burned at her center, but what was perhaps more surprising was the warmth with which she looked at me.

"Have I got the date and time wrong?" she asked.

Dihya, she was tall. As tall as Idris, no doubt.

And she thought I was Maram.

I remained where I was—Maram and I were identical, but I didn't know how well this woman knew her.

"I think," I started in Maram's tone, "that I forgot we were meeting today."

The girl frowned a little. "We've met every day since we've come here. Why should today have been any different?"

"I thought I would have to take my place in the court today. The stewardess has arrived."

I sat back down and she came closer. An ocean wind blew in, and her braids swayed in the breeze, her cloak moved like a living thing about her hips and legs. Where in the world had she acquired such a beautiful thing?

"Has Amani taken your place, then?" she asked, a wry twist in her voice. "Again?"

I did not grin—*Maram* would not grin. But I could not keep the small smile off my face. "You sound critical."

She sat across from me, on the other side of the shatranj board, and shed her cloak. I was hard put not to gawk—every movement of hers was fluid, easy. Idris had the makings of a warrior in him, but this woman *was* a warrior. There was confidence I'd only ever seen in veterans in her body and its limits and capabilities. She sighed.

"I'm not critical, Maram."

That gave me pause, nearly enough to disrupt my stream of thought. Few people called Maram by her given name. In fact, in all the time I'd known her, the only person I'd ever seen refer to her by her name was Idris. Not even Nadine spoke to her without her title.

The woman continued, as if she hadn't crossed a line of decorum, as if she regularly was so comfortable with the Imperial Heir of several star systems.

"Dihya knows I shirk my duties often enough to see you, but . . ."

"But?" I said, raising an eyebrow.

"I don't know," she said, and glanced at me. "Eventually, the world will force you to make a choice."

"Yes," I said softly. "But not yet, it seems."

She smiled. She was entrancing, I thought. There was a flicker in her dark eyes, like flame. And I found myself reaching forward to tilt her face so that I might look at them more closely.

A mistake, of course.

Maram touched no one, if she could help it. The woman's smile, and all the warmth she'd exuded, sloughed off her like water.

"You are not Maram," she said, catching my hand.

I pulled it out of her grasp and smiled.

"You are the answer to a mystery."

She did not smile back. "There is no mystery."

"So Her Royal Highness has not been neglecting her duties to keep a standing shatranj appointment with a very tall and handsome woman?"

There was a shift in her expression, and I remembered the scuffs on her vambrace and stepped back. I could not believe it. It made sense that Maram would wish to avoid her marriage bed if she had a romance of her own—but I would not have imagined it possible. She loathed vulnerability and feared how one might use it against her. To lower her guard enough . . .

"Who are you?" I asked.

She eyed me for long seconds before she spoke. "My name is Aghraas—I am the master of falcons."

"It is bad of you to lie," I replied. "I have the staff roster memorized and there is no master of falcons."

"At another of Her Highness's estates," she clarified.

I didn't believe her. "Then what do you do here?"

"I followed Maram."

The way she said it, plainly, obviously, as if she had nothing to hide, made me believe her. When I said nothing she folded her arms over her chest.

"What?"

"Nothing. But you can't linger here. Maram won't be back today, and there are others who may come through. They can't know you visit her."

She stood over me for a moment, examining me in the way that all people who lived in or near the Ziyaana eventually learned to do. Prying, peeling, as if her silence alone could pry out my secrets.

"I understand why they chose you," she said at last.

My eyes widened, bewildered. "What?"

But she didn't clarify, only gave me a roguish half grin. She bowed and there seemed no mockery in it, and then she left.

The sun had long set when Maram returned to the abandoned suite. I hadn't expected her—the setup Idris and I shared would work for her as well as it worked for me. And yet return she did, just after I'd turned the lanterns low and prepared for bed.

"I can't sleep out there," she said as I turned up a lantern.

"We can switch back," I said, and she shook her head.

"Stay with me awhile," she said. "I'll have to tell you about today."

I called for tea and the two of us found a seat around a small table within the bedchamber. I watched her as she talked and outlined the most important events for me to remember.

"You and Idris have done quick work—I did not expect . . . so much," she said, cradling her glass.

I smiled, thinking of Idris. "He had the lesser challenge. Idris is easy to love, and favored among the makhzen."

"The implication, I take it, being that I am difficult to love," she said dryly. But I could see the small cracks that signaled she was serious.

"No," I said contemplatively. "They don't know you. They don't know—or they didn't know—where you stood."

"Where I stood?"

"Some might imagine that you stood to gain from the destabilization of the makhzen and from the death and kidnapping of their families and allies," I said.

"I would gain from those things—status among the Vath, stability in my claim as heir. Respect from my father." She barked out a short laugh. "But I am not as strong as a High Vath. I cannot stomach it."

"That isn't weakness," I pointed out, frowning. "That is a conscience. Something few in power remember to hold on to."

Maram shook her head, as if she were still undecided. I couldn't undo a lifetime of conditioning at her father's hand. But I would not shy away from the truth, either.

"At any rate," she said, looking at me. "Well done. And they were good choices besides—I'timad is fascinating."

I grinned. "She makes one almost believe that training horses might be a personality trait."

I watched her, Aghraas foremost in my mind. Had a change come over Maram and I simply hadn't noticed? Or was she so practiced an actress that there was no way for me to know?

Did she love the woman I'd met?

It was not hard to imagine that she loved someone or that someone might love her. I knew her well enough to know that. And I could not imagine that she'd turned her back on the duties she'd carried on her entire life and avoided what had been set forth as her destiny since her return to Andala for a new friendship she'd cultivated. No matter how novel that friendship might have been.

"*What?*" she snapped at last. "You've been staring."

I curled both my hands around my tea glass. There was no diplomatic way to say it, and I knew she would have the answer from me one way or another. Worse, if I withheld what I knew and Aghraas told her we'd met, it would go poorly for me.

"I had a visitor today," I said carefully. "She came looking for you."

Maram's hand tightened on her tea glass and she lowered her gaze.

"Who is she to you?" I asked gently.

Her eyes met mine with a flash. "I haven't broken my wedding vows, if that's what you're asking."

"But she prevents you from keeping them?"

I imagined few people had the patience to wait for Maram to open up, and if anything it made Aghraas more intriguing. How deeply must Aghraas have felt for Maram that she'd followed her to M'Gaadir. And how deeply Maram must have felt in turn to have arrived in my suite of rooms panicked at the prospect of carrying out her marital duties.

"It doesn't matter," she whispered. "I'm trapped."

"We could have planned," I said.

"There is no solution," she snapped, and rose to her feet. "By Vathek law I must marry befitting my rank—we are not Kushaila. We do not absorb freely of those below us. We do not marry commoners without noble blood."

My eyes widened. "Is that how you see us?" I asked.

"Furat's mother was a merchant's daughter, wholly unconnected to the makhzen," she said. "And her father was of an ancient and noble house."

"Some might argue that to be a member of a Kushaila tribe is to be of an ancient and noble house," I countered.

"How egalitarian," she said through gritted teeth. "And what a promising world you must occupy to think there is any plan that will rescue me from this."

She stopped in her pacing as understanding washed over her features.

"Khulood made a strange comment about lovers during lunch," she said hoarsely. "She asked me if Idris had upset me that I had withdrawn some of my warmth. You are in love with him."

I didn't look away from her. That would have been cowardly when she had not flinched at my questioning her relationship with Aghraas.

"Yes," I said, voice thick.

Her eyes widened. "You didn't fall in love with him here . . . he *knew*. How long has he known you're my double?"

At that I lowered my gaze. "From the first."

"You were so resistant to taking my place in the marriage bed," she said softly. "I didn't think anything of it. Why did you agree in the end?"

"You were frightened. I was not," I said simply.

She sat down across from me, her gaze distant and focused on the teapot between us. When she at last looked at me, her expression was almost fragile.

"No one else would have done what you did," she said at last. My eyes widened. "No one else would— I know I don't always make it easy for you. I know that I'm not—not loveable—"

"Maram—"

She wasn't crying, but it seemed she was close to it, so I came around the table and laid my hand over hers.

"You don't make it easy," I said, and she laughed, a startled and hoarse sound. "But I am and will always be your friend."

"You said once we were sisters," she said.

"Is that what you want?" I asked her.

She nodded and leaned her head against my shoulder. "I will endeavor to be a sister to you, too. Better than I have been until now," she said quietly, then sighed. "What a pair we make, hm? How unlucky we've been."

"What are we going to do?"

"Do?" She huffed a laugh. "If I dissolved my marriage with Idris, I would lose what little support I have among his people. The peace treaty that legalized my father's occupation of this planet would be in jeopardy, as well as my inheritance. We're stuck, whether we want to admit it or not."

I expected the look of panic I'd seen the day of her bedding night. Instead, she simply looked sad. Her gaze was unfocused, and I wondered if she thought of Aghraas.

"Sometimes," she said quietly, "the state demands horrors of us."

"It shouldn't."

At that, she smiled. "You are remarkably optimistic for someone in your position."

"Because you give me hope," I said with a small smile, trying to disappear the sad air. "You are stronger than I gave you credit for."

"Oh?" she said, an eyebrow raised.

"Aghraas is beautiful. I don't know that I would have been able to resist."

She smirked. "I take it you did not resist my husband," she drawled.

My smile turned into a grin. "You seemed to have little use for him."

Maram threw her head back and laughed.

⇐ 15 ⇒

I had not visited the beach since my outing with Idris, when he had
shown me the mural of Houwa and read my palm. But I stood there
now wrapped in black velvet, a mantle about my shoulders whipping
in the ocean wind. Our excursions out of the estate went from almost never happening to happening regularly. With Nadine in residence and in a foul mood at her expulsion from Maram's inner circle,
Maram and I concocted a strategy where she could both retain the
freedom she'd found in her relationship with Aghraas and not undermine her new position.

This was made easy by the Ifrani sisters, the Mas'udi twins, and
the Banu Nasir siblings. The collection of former Andalaan royalty
and current makhzen, tied loosely together by history and some blood,
numbered almost twenty. Maram complained that they were difficult

to keep track of, but I could tell that they offered a respite she hadn't expected. Every court came with pitfalls and the need to navigate it carefully, but since the event at the races, the core among them showed a distinct warmth toward Maram, and so the rest fell in line.

My mind treaded the same paths it had treaded since the night before, turning over my conversation with Maram. I had never considered the differences in rank between Idris and me—that he was a prince and I was not anything close to that. Or rather I had, but I had never thought of it as a difference that mattered. Kushaila stories were littered with people who found their way to each other despite that sort of gap, and, as Maram pointed out, our nobility was littered with such unions. But there was a large difference between being a wealthy merchant's daughter, from a family that had many galactic trade agreements in hand, and being the daughter of a pair of villagers who worked in a state orchard many months out of the year. Idris had only ever treated me as an equal, but—

I'timad's cheerful cry interrupted my thoughts and I turned away from the sea.

Stable hands had set up a horse paddock on the sand, which struck me as a risky endeavor, but none would be swayed away from it. Many in our entourage meant to race horses on the beach, among them the two Mas'udi scions 'Imad and I'timad. Servants had set up linen awnings a ways from the paddocks and the racing strip, against a cliff that sheltered us from the worst of the wind.

Rabi'a watched the stable hands walk some of the horses through their paces. I joined her and stood to her left, watching Idris's stallion—which he'd named Al-Hays, *the chase*—eye his masters. I had the curious feeling he might bite one at any moment.

"Buchra seems to be settling in much better," I said.

A part of me had worried that Rabi'a and her sister wouldn't join us. Buchra was not so sullen anymore, but it was clear she was out of her element with the boisterous Mas'udi twins and rowdy Nasiris. The inroads I'd made with them so far, however, were not enough. The rebellion needed them and the resources their province would provide to the resistance, and if I didn't secure that soon, I worried where we might stand.

"She dislikes being shut up in an estate—the excursions do her good. Besides—she'd never been away from Qarmutta before," Rabi'a replied. "I commend you, by the way."

"Oh?"

"It is no easy thing to force a raptor like Nadine from her perch. Though I do wonder why you did it. She's a scion of your father's power, after all."

I looked out at the beach and tried to choose my words carefully. I'timad had won a race against her brother, and it sounded like he was accusing her of cheating. She remained astride her horse, her eyes narrowed at her brother as the horse beneath her pranced nervously.

I didn't look away from the race as I answered. "The position of high stewardess affords her access to power. It gives her access to me, whom she hopes to control."

Rabi'a frowned, thoughtful. "You don't think she'll throw you over for your half sister?"

I barked out a laugh. "Galene is a full-blooded High Vath. She wouldn't tolerate Nadine's interference," I said. But Maram, a child of two worlds who feared being rejected by both, would bend to Nadine's wisdom, would listen to the doubts and paranoia she fed her. Through Maram she could one day control the empire.

"And it seems neither will you."

"To Nadine—to everyone, it seems—I'm a compromise. The only way to legitimate rule of this planet is through Najat's heir." I shook my head. "I am not a compromise—I am the rightful heir to this planet, and I will not be undermined by those who believe me to be."

"Strong words," Rabi'a said.

"Too strong for a collaborator's daughter?"

A ghost of a smile passed over her face.

"You have been talking to Idris," she said.

"Does that surprise you?"

"I will remind your lord husband that while his parents resisted, they died and my mother lived—long enough to raise and protect us," she said instead of answering. "As your mother hoped to do. I can bear the slight against her name, because I had her."

"Live to fight another day."

"Fight?" Another ghost of a smile. "Will there be a fight?"

"There are many among the Vath who believe I am unworthy of the throne and who *would* support my half sister over me. So. Perhaps."

"It was your ancestor who formed the first etihad—confederation of tribes. Against an invasion from the north. But the invasion is past, and we lost."

"So you will give over our planet?" I said, trying to control the anger in my voice.

She smiled, this time fully, and this time it did not pass. "I didn't say that, Your Highness."

Our return to the palatial estate did not go unmarked. I insisted that rather than go around the city we must go through it. And the city listened—they turned out, paused in their shopping, forgot that they were meant to be selling wares or going to the zaouia or temple for prayer. Rabi'a was more practiced at such things than I was and raised a hand at a small child with a smile. The little girl grinned and called out, and it only took seconds for others to call out with her. I rode between Idris and 'Imad, and ahead and behind us were standard-bearers holding up flags with the various crests of the houses that had joined us in our outing.

It was a dangerous thing I did, I knew. Tantamount to declaring allegiance with Andala over the empire of the Vath. But it was important that my face, *Maram's* face, be allied with them. That people began to see Najat in her eyes and not Mathis. I could well imagine what we looked like, returning to an ancient palace, bearing ancient crests. Like the confederation Rabi'a had spoken of.

But the city was not the only one that marked our passing. Nadine stood on the parapet over the estate's gate as our horses climbed what little was left of the hill. She struck an imposing figure in her stark Vathek clothes and her silver hair, blinding in the sunlight. But she did not come down to greet us, though I felt her eyes on me as I dismounted and made small talk with the others.

She would not suffer the limitations to her power, and if she ever found out the hand I'd played in it, I would pay dearly. But that, I told myself, was a problem for another time.

❧ 16 ❧

Several days passed as I turned my conversation with Rabi'a over and over in my mind. It had gone well and I knew Rabi'a was firmly a Maram loyalist, who understood the traps and pitfalls of Maram's position, but had allied with her anyway. If Maram could commit to an act of trust, it would solidify the alliance permanently. It would demonstrate to Rabi'a that Maram not only needed her but *valued* her and trusted her enough with a secret only Idris knew.

The afternoon belonged to me—to Maram—since Idris had gone off with the Mas'udi twins to look through the city market. Maram was sitting in the double's suite's tower, curled up beneath a blanket, with fire crackling cheerfully in front of her.

"I didn't expect you," she said without looking up from her tablet.

"Idris is in the city," I replied, still standing.

Something in my voice must have given me away, because she looked up with a raised eyebrow.

"What is it?"

"I think telling Rabi'a that there are two of us will secure her trust completely," I said.

Her face went very still even as she gestured for me to take a seat. "You trust her so much?" she asked quietly.

"Yes," I replied.

Her nails tapped rhythmically against the tablet she still held in her lap.

"It's not fair to you, is it?" she asked. "That you keep shouldering it alone."

"I—"

She smiled. "Don't deny it, Amani. Martyrdom doesn't suit you. And I promised to be a better friend."

"If you think it will endanger you—" I began.

"I fear everything," she said, and her smile turned bitter. "One cannot lead with fear."

"No," I said softly, my eyes wide. "You can't."

Her eyes met mine. "Have I surprised you, Amani?"

I let out a breathless laugh. "Yes," I said. "You have. I thought I would have to convince you."

"Some things are self-evident," she replied. "Have Tala call her in."

"Now?" I said, alarmed.

"Why put it off?" she said.

When at last the suite was clear, I dispatched Tala to Rabi'a with a message to meet Maram in her private garden. Maram was resplendent in seafoam green, her dark hair threaded with pearls, and a chiffon and organza cape of forest green trailing on the ground behind her. She stared down at her reflection in the pool, its surface covered here and there with lily pads, her brows drawn into a small frown.

"Your Highness?" I prompted, and came to stand beside her. Our reflections, side by side, seemed to draw more attention to our differences than our similarities. There was no mistaking who was the princess between us. Even without her pearls and finery, Maram was raised royal and everything about her exuded that. Between the two of us I could admit to myself that I looked vulnerable. Perhaps it was only standing next to Maram that made this apparent. I felt in that moment like the country girl I had been, brought guileless from a backwater moon and suddenly thrust into the center of a dozen royal plots.

It was strange to suddenly feel as if I didn't recognize myself. I was not that girl anymore. I was a royal double and a rebel conspirator. Would Maram guess that more than just our comfort and trust rode on this meeting?

"You're certain this is a good idea?" Maram said at last, looking away from the water.

I smiled. "I have more to worry about than you. You are royal—I am the one who might suffer the consequence of my rank."

Hidden in my rooms, my rebel communicator seemed to burn like a beacon in my mind. Truth be told, if I were ever unmasked, the makhzen who loved me now would turn against me. That I had dared to forge a confederation between rebels and makhzen would seem a betrayal. I would be marked an outsider who didn't understand the stakes or risks of what I'd done. Idris's love or not, his camaraderie or not, they would feel lied to, and that feeling would transform into anger for having been duped by one such as me. One as *common* as I was. Wrapped in velvet and gold, I was one of them. More importantly, I was a daring and hopeful leader. But I was not Maram, and I wondered what would happen to me when I was revealed for what I was: a commoner and a rebel.

Maram stared at me wonderingly. "You truly believe that, don't you? You have no—you don't think that perhaps I might suffer as a matter of who I am. How I am?" She shook her head before I could answer. "If the risk is so large for you, why bother at all? I would have happily continued as we were."

"I should take disdain about my rank," I said ruefully, "if it meant it was about me and not someone else at this point. Do you not want to be known, Your Highness?"

She startled and her gaze turned distant for a moment. "I am known."

"By reputation—but I think few know you well. Myself. Idris. Aghraas. Who else?"

She looked back at our reflection, contemplative.

"We picked Rabi'a for a reason, Your Highness. She has more in common with you than the rest of the makhzen. She's both smart and powerful, a combination in short supply these days." Maram startled out of her contemplation with a laugh. "Friendship is risk. This secret will engender closeness."

"How shrewd you are," she said with a smile. Our conversation was cut short by the click of heeled slippers against marble floor. Maram gestured to me and I lifted the hood of my mantle over my hair and veiled my face.

Friendship is risk. And so, apparently, were alliances. Rabi'a *cared*—she cared about Maram, her sister, her province. It was a gamble to approach her once she knew who I was with a rebellious proposition, but I trusted my instinct.

Rabi'a dressed with the staid elegance of a woman secure in her power. She wore a copper-red qaftan, with the military flourishes favored by Vathek aristocrats at her shoulders and throat. The skirt was slashed with printed brocade, and she wore a single ring—her house sigil imprinted on its surface, to mark official documentation. She frowned when she saw me, and her gaze moved from Tala to myself but she said nothing and sank to her knees.

"I confess . . . I am surprised to be summoned so early and alone, Your Highness."

Maram, I thought as she came closer to Rabi'a, did herself little credit. She retained her regal air, but the Vathek frost she'd worn like armor when I met her had thawed a little.

"I wished to introduce you to someone," she said, and motioned for me to come forward.

The veil and hood I'd only just donned were shed, and Rabia's face went carefully blank as she gazed at me.

"I don't understand," she said at last.

"This is Amani," Maram said, her voice sweet and gentle. "My body double. My shield. My . . . friend."

I came forward then and stood beside Maram. I could have knelt; indeed, etiquette dictated that I should have, for Rabi'a was of a higher rank than I. But I was loath to begin our first true meeting as a servant in relation to her superior.

"It is a pleasure, Lady Rabi'a," I said. "My apologies for the deception."

Rabi'a was still looking back and forth between us. "You are unrelated?" she asked.

"A twist of cosmic fate," I replied, dropping my voice to Maram's register.

She startled visibly, clearly unprepared to see me draw Maram's personality about myself like a second skin.

"Dihya," she marveled, and looked between the two of us again.

"She seems quite taken with you, Amani," Maram said, laughing.

"I am an oddity, Your Highness," I replied with good cheer. "She is likely no more taken with me than she would be by a snake charmer in the souk."

"How long?" Rabi'a asked. Her voice was admirably controlled but for a thread of curiosity.

"Long enough," Maram said. "I trust few people. But Amani made a case for you. She believed revealing myself—that there are two of me—to you would be worth the cost."

"I hope that I have not misled Her Highness," I added.

Rabi'a sank back to her knees. "I am honored by your trust, Your Highness. I will endeavor to be worthy of it."

Eventually Rabi'a did leave, and Maram cried off from her duties for the day. It began to rain in the early afternoon, so I lay in the tower, surrounded by books, interrupted only by serving girls who wished to bring me tea or sweets. It was early in the evening when I sent Tala with a missive to Rabi'a—I was coming to dinner. I knew her curiosity would get the better of her and if not, she couldn't turn down Maram. With Tala's help I dressed in an ivory and white qaftan, with feather printing spilling from my left shoulder and across my chest. Tala found a heavy black mantle with the same design, and pinned a corner to my right shoulder, allowing the rest of it to spill down my back and over the skirt of the gown.

I appeared thus to Rabi'a with an escort in tow, whom I dismissed once she'd greeted me. Dinner was set out in a private room with a balcony, and rain beat against the shield, filling the quiet places between our small talk and the movement of serving girls as they laid out the table.

At last, the room was empty but for the two of us, and I turned to face her.

"I wasn't sure if you expected myself or Maram," I said.

Instead of clarifying, she smiled. "Do you take her place often?"

"Often enough that I know the makhzen quite well."

She took a seat and leaned back. "You didn't grow up in the Ziyaana."

"Neither did you," I countered.

She eyed me and I fought the urge to twist in my seat like a child. I knew what she thought: that I'd taken her ability to offer me a seat was a gross breach of etiquette, but I would not allow her to take any ground I'd gained. I *had* survived, and I would not be condescended to by one who was above me simply through an accident of birth. I hadn't come to where I was by accident either—a confidante to a princess and a rebel besides.

"Does Her Highness know you're a dissident?"

A frisson of fear shot up my spine, but I stilled myself. "I am a royalist," I said firmly.

She smiled and tilted her head just so. "I take it you mean that in the traditional sense, from before the conquest. I would not have guessed but for the conversation on the beach. Coming from Maram it meant one thing. Coming from you, however . . ."

"I am loyal to Maram and Maram alone."

"Ah," she replied. I disliked her tone. "Loyalty to Maram does not require loyalty to the Vath."

It was a show of weakness, I was sure, but I came to my feet and walked to the balcony. Much of the city was obscured by rainfall, but even through it I could see the many lights winding their way around the hill atop which the estate sat. It appeared as a bejeweled skirt, spread just so around us.

"I looked into your province," I said without turning away from the view. "It is quite wealthy, but it wasn't always. At the start of the war the average household was starving. Your family fixed that."

Rabi'a's voice was hard. "That is the social contract we enter into as rulers."

I laughed. "The Vath believe the powerful rule over the weak, and *that* is the social contract we enter into by not being born in the right places. But Maram—she is like you. She wants the planet and its people to prosper."

Rabi'a's jewelry chimed and sang as she came to her feet and stood beside me.

"And that is where a queenmaker comes in," she said. It sounded almost like a question. I eyed her sidelong.

"Is that what you think I am?" I asked, my mouth twisting. "Her Highness has no need of a queenmaker. The throne is her birthright. What she needs are allies who—"

"What she needs," Rabi'a interrupted coldly, "is an army. A war. Maram is no different than the rest of the hostages—a means to control the state before the galactic senate. I will not be party to—"

"To what?" I dared her.

"A rebellion," she said. "I will certainly not be party to a rebellion spearheaded by a rankless girl who has never been to war."

"There is none better than a rankless girl," I replied, "to see the injustice on the ground. Maram can fix much, but she cannot do it from within the machine of empire. And the cost of complacency is too high. Surely you can see that."

Rabi'a walked back to her seat. "There is no hope, Amani," she said quietly. "Any rebellion will fail. You will be wiser when you accept that."

"When I was eight," I said, looking back at the city, "my parents took me and my brothers and marched us through the mountains on Cadiz to a new home. It took six weeks. Six weeks of bitter cold and little food and nonstop walking. I was half my weight when we arrived at the village."

"Why would your parents put you through such an ordeal?"

I remembered so little of it. Eight was not so young that the memories were obscured by time, but I was grateful for this neural trick.

"We lived in a village that was not a village," I said. "It was a kasbah, abandoned by whatever makhzen had held it before the conquest. Nineteen families made their home there. Shortly before we left, the Vath attacked."

"What?" Her voice was hoarse with shock.

"We were defenseless. Most villages have a magistrate, or a surveillance force. We were in truth homeless and trying to eke out an existence. They were slaughtered, looking for someone."

I turned to look at her. Her face was drawn and colorless, as if I'd truly shocked her.

"Do you not know what the Vath are capable of?"

"I do."

"Then don't look so upset," I said. "The dead are gone, and we survived."

She swallowed hard. Her hand gripped the armrest, her back was straight and held away from the chair.

"Everyone imagines that a poor villager has no understanding of the operations of cruelty. That because she is removed from the center of power, she does not experience the way it is used. I know the Vath, Rabi'a, perhaps better than even you. I know what they will do in wartime. There is no survival to be had in this world."

She looked away from me, as if she were embarrassed.

"You are talking about *war*," she said, voice clipped. "A war we can't possibly win."

The problem, I thought, was that each of us had experienced our own particular hurt and thought the other would not understand its consequences. Rabi'a understood the violence she'd been saved from by her mother's duplicity, and yet somehow believed I'd escaped that violence or did not understand its scope. It enraged me—my world until now had been small, and in a way I'd been lucky. Furat and Idris had never underestimated me or my experience.

"I'm talking about the line of succession," I replied. "But she needs the support of an army that will not pledge itself to her without the support of a greater house."

"So, at last we come to it," she said.

Arinaas was coming to the continent—it was the right time, the *best* time, for Rabi'a and Arinaas to meet. For Rabi'a to see how serious I was, how serious the rebellion was. It wasn't just a ragtag group of hungry citizens, but a cause and an army with a chance.

"A high-ranking member of the alliance will be here in two days—meet her, and then make your choice."

"And what would they ask of me?"

"The army will not pledge itself to Maram without the support of a greater house."

She laughed humorlessly. "So without me everything falls apart."

"And the world slides into ruin."

Her mouth twisted as she struggled. "I cannot promise you anything," she said. "I will take the meeting—but if I'm unconvinced of your possibilities for success—"

"That's all I ask."

She came to her feet at last and stood beside me before the opening of the balcony.

"I expect to be impressed, Amani," she said.

"And I expect that you will be."

❧ 17 ❧

Arinaas had at last arrived at M'Gaadir. She would meet Rabi'a herself, and her revelation would cement whether Rabi'a was with us or not.

The allies Idris, Maram, and I had arranged could not do what needed doing alone. They would need the rebels as much as the rebels needed them. They had been demilitarized and disinherited, but the planet remembered them and mourned and wanted them to rise. And so, in giving Rabi'a, the strongest among them, to the rebels, I would forge an unassailable alliance between those held by the empire and those that would break it.

A dangerous risk. But one I knew would pay off.

Tala joined me in the salon with a small lantern and a heavier cloak. The days and nights had turned colder as we'd progressed through autumn. Not so cold as it was this time of year in the mountains, but cold enough.

"Here," she said, and pressed a hand against a wall panel. There was a soft click and it swung toward us, revealing a dark corridor.

"Why is this palace littered with secret passageways?" I asked.

Tala grinned. "You know stories so well—do you not know the story of Kansa's second husband?"

"Are you saying our ancestor was a bigamist?"

She laughed. "No."

I shook my head. "You will have to tell me this story when I get back."

She handed me the lantern and the cloak. "Follow the corridor—it leads directly to Houwa's cave. Good luck."

"Thank you—I will need it."

The corridor was long and cold, and I was glad for both the fur-lined cloak Tala had given me and the lantern to light the way. It dipped down further into the ground, and eventually the ground turned rocky and covered in gravel. I had passed out of the estate's limits entirely and was at the back end of the cave. When at last it opened up into the cave proper, it revealed several Tazalghit women standing guard. A fire was lit just under the mural of Houwa, and standing around it were several women—the one who caught my eye was Arinaas.

I'd forgotten the sort of presence she commanded. She stood across from a woman of height with her, though significantly older and with silver strands in her hair. They were all dressed for the desert, voluminous black and white robes, and loose trousers and blouses bound at the waist with cotton sashes. The woman next to Arinaas wore a black turban, with a silver brooch attached in the shape of a diamond, with a crescent moon piercing its uppermost angle.

"Your spy arrives," she said when she caught sight of me.

Arinaas turned and grinned when she saw me. "Not my spy," she said with a laugh. "A free agent. Perhaps a general."

Like the turbaned woman Arinaas wore black, though her robes were stitched with gold. She seemed, somehow, taller than I remembered, her presence weightier. She put me, strangely enough, in mind of Aghraas. As if the very air would catch fire at her say-so.

She held out a hand—it had been a long time too since anyone asked a soldier's handshake of me. But when I grasped her arm with mine, she drew me in for a hug.

"It is good to see you alive," she said. "I did not like our last meeting."

"It is good to see you at all," I replied. "It is too dangerous for you to be here."

"Your free agent is sensible," the woman said to her, then turned to me. "Would that my daughter would listen to sense."

"Uma." No one in the worlds or in heaven would accuse the rebel leader of whining. But calling her mother came dangerously close. "This is my mother—Tinit, Queen of Queens, leader of the Tazalghit. Uma—Amani. Of whom you know much."

The turban and pin began to make sense.

"Your Grace—"

She shook her head. "Tinit al-Hurra is fine," she replied.

I inclined my head. "Tinit al-Hurra, then—it is good to meet you."

"You look very much like your mother," she said.

My eyes widened. "You know my mother?"

"She is overseeing her relocation," Arinaas said. Tinit said something in Izilghit, and Arinaas replied, but neither let me in on their conversation.

"Are they . . ." I interrupted.

"Yes," Tinit said with a smile. "They are safe. We have a recording, if you would like?"

For a moment it felt as if the whole world stopped. I knew the ocean was just beyond the cavern, and that there were dozens of women in this cave, but I heard none of it. All I heard was the beating of my own heart and the blood rushing in my ears.

"Really?" I gasped. "They're safe?"

"We are women of our word, Amani," Arinaas said. "You kept your end, and we have kept ours."

Tinit held out her wrist and revealed the same gel-like substance that made up my communicator clinging to her skin. It lit up and a moment later an image projected into the air: my family—my mother and father, my brothers Husnain and Aziz—making their way up a mountain path, surrounded by rebels. And rebels they were, to be sure, for they all wore the red flag stitched onto their left sleeves.

I reached out to the screen as if my fingers could pass through it, and break through space to be beside them. They looked tired, but alive and healthy.

For a moment I couldn't speak. Dihya, I missed them like a physical ache in my chest.

"It is not your face," Tinit said to me suddenly, eyeing me. "Though you and your mother certainly have that in common. It is something else that puts me in mind of her."

I didn't know how to reply to that. It seemed she knew my mother well; something about the way she spoke, the surety with which she made her pronouncements, made me think she had not just been surveilling her for extraction.

"Where are they?" I asked, without looking up.

Tinit pulled her sleeve back over her wrist and the image disappeared.

"Is that information you want to risk knowing?" she asked softly.

"No," I said. "The risk if I were captured would be too great."

Tinit nodded, approving.

"Let me talk to her, Uma. You have much else to do."

Tinit, it seemed, was used to her daughter's brusque airs and smiled.

She nodded. "I will see you again, Amani of the Kushaila."

We both watched her walk down further into the cave and collect a bevy of guards around her.

"I see where you get it," I said.

"Get it?" Arinaas asked.

"When I first met you and even now—it feels like being around an unquenchable flame."

She grinned. "Careful. I will grow too flattered."

I smiled back. "So? What would you have of me until the lady arrives?"

Her face grew serious. "Furat says you are quite close with the princess," she began.

"Surely that doesn't surprise you?"

"She is Mathis's daughter—"

"She is Najat's daughter," I interrupted. "She is a direct descendant of an ancient and royal house that has ruled this planet for millennia. But most importantly, she is the *only* ruler the galactic community will recognize as legitimate."

Arinaas looked at me, eyes solemn, hands held behind her back. "I suppose that's why you've allied three of the most powerful families on the planet with her?"

"Should I have left her destiny in the hands of the war? She did not choose the circumstances of her birth, or her father, or her upbringing. She is a scared and lonely girl with the potential of much good in her—and if the rebellion turns on her, we risk creating a worse enemy with a more legitimate claim."

Arinaas sighed. "She is a puppet of the Vath, and your empathy has gotten the better of you."

I resisted the urge to suck my teeth in frustration. "Think better of me than that, Arinaas."

"I think very well of you," she said.

Arinaas appraised me. "She will side with the rebellion?"

"*That* I'm still working on. But in time, yes, I believe so."

Arinaas stared up at the mural of Houwa, then closed her eyes.

"There are few people I would trust in such a thing, Amani," she said at last. "Do not fail in this."

I smiled, relieved. "I won't."

Beyond the berth Arinaas's women had made at the entrance to Houwa's cave was a wider cavern, and it was there that they'd set up a small camp. A few open tents for the night, with lush carpeting, richly embroidered cushions, and low tables. It was clear that this was the queen's retinue—the tables were laden with figs and dates, fragrant pastries, and tea. Hanging from the cloth ceilings were anti-detection probes, though they looked like incense bowers. It was there that Arinaas and I stood, overlooking the entrance to the cavern, and waited.

Rabi'a arrived with a single guard of her own from the same entrance I'd come through. She was dressed simply, with no jewels, though I saw beneath her mantle the shape of a small blaster inside a velvet bag. She paused on the outcrop of the entry ledge with two of the Tazalghit blocking her path.

Arinaas quirked her mouth into a half smile. "She looks Zidane," she murmured.

"What does that mean?" I said.

"The Zidane always look like they're ready to conquer something."

"This from the daughter of a people who have forced tribute from every city on the main continent," I drawled.

She laughed.

We watched as Rabi'a gave the small blaster over with a sigh, then waved her guard back when it seemed he might argue with the Tazalghit escort. I watched her make her way across the cave and then at last up the incline that led to Arinaas and me. Halfway up she paused, staring at Arinaas, her face blank with shock.

I watched Rabi'a take Arinaas in, her eyes going from the crown of Dihya inked into her forehead, to the gold thread sewn into her robe. I remembered seeing Arinaas the first time—the shock of a dead prophetess walking in daylight. I yet recalled the second shock of seeing the holy mark—gold embedded in her skin—and realizing how the rebellion had crystallized around her.

"Well," she said when she reached us. "When you said a high-ranking officer, I did not imagine this."

I gave her a half smile. "What did you imagine?"

"A doddering old patriot with a guerilla army."

"Alas." Arinaas grinned.

"I thought they were rumors," Rabi'a said softly. "But you're real. Cosmetic surgery?"

Arinaas did as she had done when I stared at her in disbelief. She pulled down the collar of her shirt and revealed the gold in her skin.

"*Dihya.*" Her hand made an aborted move, as if she meant to touch the gold in Arinaas's skin but caught herself just in time. "No wonder the rebels are singularly motivated."

"Injustice motivates them," Arinaas said. "I'm the divine coincidence they need to act, that's all. Follow me."

Arinaas led us deeper into the caverns, into a great stone hall where her women had pitched their tents. By the wall was a large case, clearly filled with weapons. She lifted its cover and I drew in a breath of surprise. I'd expected firearms, or side canons—the sort of weaponry the Vath used.

They were bows. Sleek, to be certain, made of light metal, their surfaces engraved with beautiful designs. When she lifted one into her hand its surface lit up, along with a holographic display where the arrow would be loaded.

"The bow can fire with the force of a cannon, and its arrows are essentially small grenades." Her smile was sharp. "But we're nomadic hunters."

"How many?" Rabi'a asked. "The Tazalghit were never counted— you retreated when the war was clearly about to be lost, and the Vath assume your numbers are much reduced. Those who surface are malnourished, their herds thin. But I suspect you could not have built a reliable rebel force with what the Vath believe to be left of you."

"Eighteen thousand mounted cavalry."

I felt a shiver.

"And infantry?"

"Forty-two."

"*Hundred?*" Rabi'a said skeptically.

"Forty-two thousand," Arinaas clarified. "Though that includes guerilla fighters, farmers, and peasants who have joined to swell our ranks."

"Well," Rabi'a murmured, looking at me. "I see you are not delusional. Though that is no guarantee you will win."

I'd taken a gamble on this, trusted my gut instinct that the conversations I'd had with Rabi'a pointed to a person who saw the injustices as we saw them. Who understood that this planet and its people would not survive the Vathek occupation. And who, if given the right push, could help us pull back from the brink of collapse.

"If Maram were crowned," I said, "then she would not only have the combined armies of the rebels and the houses allied with her, but would also be able to call on allies in the senate. We would have a real chance."

"The odds of winning versus the certainty of a slow death is difficult calculus," Arinaas said, her mouth curled.

"Is it?" I said, looking at Rabi'a.

"I dislike the idea of going to war against an enemy we have already lost to," she said, her hand trailing over the box of bows. "But you are right—it is a slow death, a quick one, or victory. I like the odds of the latter over the former."

Our discussion went on for at least an hour. Tayfur province was not only wealthy in material but in men. While many provinces relied on Vathek droids, Arinaas and her mother had cultivated mounted cavalry—afraas—and they numbered in the tens of thousands now.

"It has come with problems," Rabi'a said. "Mathis has installed spies. He will not tolerate a rival military presence. You will have to be careful."

"We need safe houses for now," she said. "Perhaps it will not come to war."

Rabi'a scoffed. "Should we be so lucky."

"We might," Arinaas countered. "I do not utter dreams just to hear them, Rabi'a bint Ifran."

"Well," Rabi'a said, surveying the map. "Whatever you have need of, only ask."

"Said with the brevity of the Zidane," Arinaas replied with a grin, and held out her hand for a warrior's shake.

18

It was not long after that we dispersed. Rabi'a returned with her guard by an alternate route, and after bidding farewell to Arinaas, I made my way back down the cavern path. I made it halfway back before I heard a quiet beeping. I'd only ever heard that sound the night of my majority celebration, standing in line beside the other girls.

I froze, my heart in my throat. Of course security monitored these passages, and if the probe got a scan of me, and the log fell into anyone's hands—I didn't want to imagine the consequences. A hand reached out of the dark and pulled me against the wall.

"Be quiet," Idris whispered. I stared at him, torn between my fear of the probe and the shock of seeing him in the passageway. He had a beacon in one hand that vibrated when he pressed a button.

The probe appeared, emitted a white light, and scanned the space where I'd only just stood. It hovered in place for a minute, then turned around and floated away.

I should have felt relief, watching it drift out of sight and out of range, but a new fear took its place. Why was Idris here, and prepared with a diversion beacon? Had he followed me? What had he seen?

The whirring, beeping sound of the probe faded away completely, and Idris led me back into the main passageway. Neither of us spoke as we made our way back to the hidden entrance in the royal suite. And we remained silent as I led us back to the double's suite I occupied. We made our way to the sitting room. He dropped the beacon on the table, and I closed the doors, then waved a hand. Lanterns ignited around the room, giving his face a garish cast.

"Did you follow me?" I asked softly.

"Yes," he said, and then, "How long?" When I said nothing, he rose to his feet. "You will not answer?"

I lifted my chin. "I do not have to answer."

He swore, angrier than I'd ever heard him, and raked his hands through his hair.

"Do you not understand the cost of what it is you do? Do you not understand what they will do to you if they find out what you are?"

"I know the price of treason," I replied.

"And yet you say it so calmly. I don't think you do."

"Do you suggest that I am stupid?"

"Amani." He said my name on an exhalation of breath, as if all life were being torn from him. "Do not play."

"Long enough," I said at last, conceding defeat.

"You must stop."

"Stop?"

"Stop before you lose your life."

"No. I will not." I remembered and dreamed of the tesleet that had come to me just after the assassination attempt. It carried me through the mornings when I thought I couldn't face another day being someone else. It promised that one day I would be myself again, that when I went out people would know my name.

"No?"

I pulled away from the door and met him in the center of the room. "Would you condemn me to this life?"

"Condemn you?"

"I am a slave, Idris," I said. "I wear jewels and velvet, and I am fed and pampered, but I am a *slave*. I have no future in this world. Is this what you want for me for the rest of my life?"

"No—"

"And your people? The subjects who entrust their health and prosperity to you? What of them? Will you condemn them to this shadow?"

"It is not a shadow," he cried out. "Shadows are benign. It is a cancer, and it has won. It is here to stay."

"Cancers eventually kill the host. I refuse that reality," I said, shaking my head. "We have a chance—"

"We have never had a chance," he interrupted me. "Not when they first came. Not when my family and the Wattasis stood during the last siege."

"So what would you have us do? You have noted it yourself—there is no relief, no help under the Vath. We cannot even keep ourselves fed!"

"You don't understand the cost—"

A cold rage took hold of me, spinning up from the base of my spine and out through the rest of me. It stilled my shaking hands, my trembling voice. It obliterated the fear I felt at his discovery.

"I don't understand the *cost*?" I hissed. "My mother is the last of her siblings. Of her *family*—all of them killed during the war or taken by starvation and disease after. Before I came here—before I was *brought here*—the Vath burned my village's only source of income and food. Every year we worry if they will come and burn our houses or take our boys or our women. I was *taken*"—I was shouting now, and shoving at him so that he stumbled back—"from the only home

I've ever known, my dignity stripped away, beaten and tortured and forced to watch my family pay the price for any dissent.

"Do not tell me I do not know the cost, Idris ibn Salih. I have *paid the cost* three times over." My hands were still on his chest, bent like claws. For a moment I stared at them, then drew them away and covered my face.

"Maybe . . ." I started, then paused and drew in a tremulous breath. "If we cannot agree on this . . . maybe we were a dream."

He sucked in a sharp breath. "This is not about ideology, Amani. This is about your life." His hands came to rest on either side of my face. "I cannot lose you."

"And do you have me now, Idris? Am I yours? Do I live?"

When he laid his forehead against mine, I closed my eyes. I couldn't bear to look at him knowing what would happen in the next minute. All my hopes for the future, the vague uncertain imaginings of what we might be to each other turned to dust.

"Why is this not enough?" he whispered.

For long moments the only sound in the room was our breathing. But I could not give him what he asked. My pride and dignity were all I had left.

"I am half of what I ought to be," I said softly, and drew myself away. "And I would rather be dead than a slave."

❧ 19 ❧

I sobbed myself to sleep. In some ways I'd known this day was coming. Whether open war was upon us or not, the ways I pushed Maram both big and small would have revealed my allegiance to him. Would have revealed the core difference between us: I was not content to sit and watch while the planet slipped into collapse and ruin. We'd both grown up snatching joy and happiness wherever we could, and perhaps he could continue living like that. I could not. Our dream of a future together was always destined for death.

I was roused from slumber violently, with a hand that felt like a claw around my arm, and pulled unceremoniously from the bed. There was no time to understand who pulled me from bed or why. The moment I stood a hand struck me across the face, sharp and hard. Hard enough that I fell again, inches from the fireplace.

Nadine.

My mind was still half-asleep, but it took very little—seeing her silver slippers and the black hem of her gown—to bring it to full wakefulness. Perhaps it was naïve of me to imagine that she would take the severing of her power lying down. Maram, Idris, and I had rooted her power out of the royal household as thoroughly as we were able. And perhaps it was more than naïve to assume that she would not take out her rage on me, the only vulnerable one of the three, when my explicit purpose was to receive the violence and punishment of the masses in Maram's place.

Nadine seemed to have the same thought. She gripped my arm once again and dragged me to my feet.

"Did you think," she hissed, "that I would suffer your meddling? Or did you somehow imagine that I would not put the pieces together?"

She shook me as she spoke and when she finished, threw me once again so that I fell back and tumbled over a divan.

"I . . . I don't know what you're talking about, Your Ladyship."

"*You don't know?*" Her voice was dangerously close to a shout, a loss of composure I had not thought her capable of until this moment. "I was closest in Maram's counsel before her marriage. And now I find that you are deep in counsel with her in the afternoons, that she allows you out among the makhzen, that she *trusts* you. She's pushed me out, fired my servants, watches my movements. Whatever poison you've spewed—"

Nadine rarely lowered herself to brute violence—droids, birds, Maram—they all struck me in her stead. But as I rose to my feet, her anger spurred her further and she struck me across the face a second time. And when I didn't fall, she wrapped a hand around my throat.

I should have felt more terrified than I did, but I knew she couldn't kill me, though she was possessed of a murderous rage. And I had suffered worse—I would not allow Nadine to frighten me.

I met her eyes, my throat still in her grasp. "It isn't my fault she now runs her own house," I rasped.

"I have done things that would turn your blood to ice, village girl," she said. "The Ziyaana, Maram—*the world*—was under my thumb until you. And I will not shy from doing what is necessary to secure what is mine by rights."

"And what is yours?"

Nadine froze and at last released me. "Your Highness," she said, and sank to her knees before Maram.

There was a tightness to the princess's face I had only ever seen once—the day we'd met. She had not undressed after the day's events and looked every inch the Imperial Heir, her chin raised, her eyes ringed in kohl.

"How dare you," Maram said.

"Your Highness—"

"*Be silent!*" Her footsteps rang out in the quiet tower as she came closer to Nadine. I did not forget myself, and sank to my knees, waiting.

"Is that what you have imagined this entire time?" she asked softly, coming to stand before Nadine. "That through me—what was it you said? The world would be under your *thumb*? That in my fear or youth I would give over my inheritance to be ruled by an upstart, a woman of low birth?"

"No—!"

"I thought Amani unfair in her estimation of you," she continued. "I *defended* you."

"My only thought is to serve the crown."

"I *am* the crown," Maram said. "Look at me when I speak to you."

Nadine's face was pale but for two red spots of anger on her cheek. Few people liked to be upbraided, and for Nadine I imagined being upbraided by an eighteen-year-old girl she had raised would sit poorly with her.

"I will never trust you again," Maram said. "Get out of my sight."

Nadine rose slowly to her feet and walked to the staircase. She paused and looked at Maram.

"Beware, Your Highness. I am not the snake the villager has led you to believe."

"No," Maram replied. "You are a foot soldier who believes herself to be a general. Get out."

I didn't move until the sound of the doors to the suite boomed shut.

"Are you alright?" I asked Maram as I came to my feet.

She flashed me a false smile. "I should be asking you."

"I've suffered worse," I assured her. "Though I think she split my lip, and I will have bruises around my throat."

Maram sank onto a divan and put her head in her hands.

"We should call you a physician," she said without raising her head. "Or a medi-droid."

"I'll be fine," I told her. "Just a few bruises. Tala can tend to me. Maram?"

"She raised me. Bandaged my scrapes when I was young. When I was told I had to leave Luna-Vaxor and return to the Ziyaana, she offered to come with me. I had thought her a comfort—" She rubbed her face. "But now . . ."

She rose to her feet and paced, one hand twisted in her gown. I said nothing. *Could say* nothing. I hated Nadine, and my blood sang at her dismissal. I wanted Maram free. I saw the makings of a great queen in her, the traces of her mother's legacy in her blood. She had a shrewdness in her that would aid her, and a kindness that had rarely been given an opportunity to flourish. So I waited.

"Can I trust you, Amani?" she whispered.

I looked up, surprised.

"Or will your rebels supplant me the first chance they get?"

"You are Queen Najat's trueborn daughter," I said. "The rightful heir to this planet. I serve at your will. I will defend you as best as I am able—as I have done in the past."

She sat back down beside me and after a moment, threw her arms around me and drew me close.

"I rely on you," she whispered. "Please do not disappoint me."

"I won't."

20

In light of the bruises I'd suffered at Nadine's hand, I was relegated back to the double's suite. Truth be told, it was a welcome reprieve. I had no desire to spend time with Idris or pick up my role once again as pretend-wife. Nor did I want to wallow in my sadness. But there was little to do in my quarters that didn't remind me of him. I couldn't read poetry without remembering him, or poke at my tapestry of Massinia without being reminded of the mural he'd caught me at all those months ago.

The doors burst open in the midst of my melancholy.

"Amani!" Maram drew short in the room and raised an eyebrow. "What happened?"

My eyes widened. "Nothing. What are you doing here?" I had no desire to share, and I didn't think Maram would commiserate with me or comfort me.

"The king is calling."

A chill shivered up my spine. "He's coming here?"

"No—he's calling."

I raised my eyebrows. "And . . . ?"

"I know you can't always be me," she said. "But can you be there? Hide up in the rafters if you must."

"Why?"

"I feel stronger when you're around," she said, avoiding my eyes.

"Let me dress," I said quietly. "And compose myself. I imagine there is a place for me to hide while you speak?"

She nodded. "It's the diwan chamber."

She waited outside my bedchamber as I rushed through the room, performing ablutions and selecting clothes and jewelry for the day. There was no world, I knew, where I would have been able to spend the day in bed, mourning Idris. Even if I were still a girl living on Cadiz, my mother would have roused me to milk our goat, and then I would have been expected to return to the fields or the village kitchen.

The world never stopped for a single broken heart.

I finished pinning up my hair, then found a mantle with a hood and a veil for my face. Maram stood in the center of the courtyard, face upturned to the dim rays of the rising sun. Sometimes I marveled at how similar we seemed and yet so different, too. Maram was raised among royalty, and despite everything, was told the world would always bow at her feet. That reality was so different from mine, and it poured out of her no matter what she did. Even standing now, with no one to witness, she seemed a queen only in need of her crown.

She caught me staring and raised an eyebrow. "What?"

"Nothing," I said, shaking my head. "You're just—you'll be a fantastic queen someday. You know that, don't you?"

She widened her eyes, bewildered. "Because I can stand still in sunlight?"

I laughed. "Yes. That's what I meant. I assume you have a way for me to reach the gallery that will keep me hidden?"

Maram had thought well ahead, and brought with her not only

a holomap detailing the hidden corridors of the estate, but a beacon much like the one Idris had brought along with him last night. It would allow me to pass unchecked through the passages.

"I don't want the security log to show us both there," she explained. "If people found out—"

"They'd accuse you of needing a crutch." I nodded. "Clever. I'll be close behind. I promise."

I had never been in the diwan chamber when it was empty. I stood on the second-floor gallery level, a little to the left of the throne, and waited. Maram stood before it, her face blank, her hands at her sides. She looked entirely at peace, though I knew she wasn't.

A moment later a sharp beep shot through the room and the air above the throne wavered. Mathis's form came together like an image stilling in rippling water. He sat, back straight, one hand on the arm of whatever seat he was in wherever in the galaxy he was currently situated.

Maram sank to her knees prettily and inclined her head. "Your Eminence." Her voice was strong and clear.

"Maram." Mathis's voice was equally strong and clear, but there was an icy edge to it. I thought of Maram's tone often as one limned in frost, but Mathis seemed to be able to take that to the extreme simply by existing. I felt it sink into my bones, and I marveled at Maram for not reacting at all.

She rose to her feet gracefully and looked him in the eye. "What would you have of me, Your Eminence?"

He rose to his feet and came down the steps so that he was close enough to touch her. He dwarfed her—Mathis was a warrior and he looked the part. Broad-shouldered, tall, large enough that in the days of antiquity he might have wielded a broadsword or a double-headed axe.

"You look well," he said.

"Thank you. I am well."

"We have heard reports," he said.

Maram's face barely moved. "Reports. You are having me watched."

"You're surprised," he replied. "Don't be."

"What do the reports say?" I marveled at her tone—even as far as I was from him, Mathis's voice set a chill in my bones. But Maram sounded as if they were having a polite conversation over tea.

"That you have gathered support among your mother's people." His tone didn't waver toward anger or violence, and yet the air changed. My muscles clenched as if my body prepared to be struck. "That you have allied with the makhzen."

Here lay the difference between Maram and me. She did not shift her footing, nor did her expression break. She betrayed no fear or anxiety. She only folded her hands in front of her and raised an eyebrow.

"It seemed prudent to mitigate what has been a constant threat in my life, especially after the attempt at my coronation," she said. "I did as I have been taught—I found strength. I neutralized those who would be my enemies."

"I didn't know there was such strength among savages." His voice betrayed no emotion. No amusement or rage. There was only the cold.

"I am here because you sent me here," she said. "To live among savages. I have done what is necessary while I abide among them."

I shivered. I knew it wasn't true, that I saw the real Maram and that her father saw a facade, a necessary mask to ensure her survival. And yet her tone chilled me. In what world did a girl learn to lie so easily about her peers?

I almost laughed—the same world I lived in. The world that had taken me from my family, stripped me of my daan, taught me to be Maram. That world demanded a cruel, unforgiving mask. And both Maram and I had learned to wear it well.

"Let's put your . . . *mitigation* . . . to the test," he said. "You will tour the southern provinces with your allies. But you will do it with the Vath in tow, lest you forget you are my daughter and not your mother's. If you survive, then you will have earned the right to determine who are your allies and who are not. If you do not—"

Maram gracefully sank to her knees but did not bow her head. "I think you will find that I am more than equal to the task, Your Eminence."

I could not see his face as he looked down at her, but his body was perfectly still for long seconds. He was not there in truth, it was only a hologram, and yet he reached for her anyway, and swept a finger along her cheek.

"Prove to me that you have risen above your mother's breeding," he said softly. "Do not disappoint me."

Even the mention of her mother elicited no reaction from her. "As you command, Your Eminence."

He did not say goodbye or wish her good health. His image simply rippled away. For a moment the room was silent, and then the diwan doors groaned open. Maram was on her feet, her face hard—I recognized the expression of deep rage, barely leashed. Nadine strode in, then drew up short. There was a tilt to her mouth, as if she'd won a prize.

A frisson of rage ripped through me as I realized what she must have done, how she must have whispered in the king's ear.

"Do you no longer kneel to your future sovereign?" Maram said, her voice dangerously soft.

Nadine bent her knees.

"Lower," Maram said.

Nadine froze, eyes wide, her knees still bent.

"Have you lost your faculty to understand my words," she said, coming closer. "*Lower.*"

The high stewardess sank to her knees. They'd barely touched the ground before she began to rise again.

"I did not give you leave to rise," Maram said. I had forgotten this girl—all rage, bent on someone's humiliation. "Lower."

"Your Highness—"

"I did not give you leave to speak," she said. She waited, perfectly still, as Nadine laid her forehead on the ground. I thought if she'd had a crop in hand she might have whipped it across her face.

She took a deep breath. "I suppose I have you to thank for this," she said.

Nadine raised her head. "I only reported on your success, Your Highness."

"You have set a trap," Maram said softly. "Because you believe me to be the frightened girl you made me. I am not. I am the future queen of this world."

"Allow me to assist you—"

"I would rather suffer the death of my mother a thousand times than accept your help," Maram said. "And I do not need it. *You* should worry what will happen when this trap is sprung."

Something about her tone set a chill in me, and I was not alone. Nadine's face paled, and a pair of red spots rose in her cheeks.

"You forget your roots too often, Nadine cagir Elon," she said softly. "And you forget my father's nature. You have no ancient blood, no family to protect you when he decides to feed you to his wolves. And he will—it is his way."

Maram did not strike her, indeed she never raised a hand, never reached for the high stewardess. But I thought, perhaps, with the guards at the door, and the handmaidens waiting to attend to Maram, that might have been better. She remained on her knees as Maram swept out of the room, the train of her gown billowing out behind her.

Too late, I thought to sink back into the shadows. Nadine looked and found me there, and her face paled yet further with rage. I said nothing, though my heart beat hard enough that my fingertips trembled with its beat. For long seconds she stared up at me, but I did not bow or sink to my knees. I waited, and at last she came to her feet, her eyes glittering with anger, and strode from the diwan.

⇥ 21 ⇤

The rainy season on the coast had at last started, which meant a suspension of the cavalry theatrics we had enjoyed until now. Any other day Maram would have taken her place among her peers, but the level of planning needed for the tour had seen her beg a day of reprieve from me. She could be at two places at once, and so she meant to take advantage of it.

On a day like this most of the estate and its visitors would have found private means to amuse themselves. Rabi'a, however, wanted the collection of princes and princesses who had forged ties to visit in her large salon. In the courtyard where we normally met, any of the other families visiting could join. But in her chambers was a small retreat, closed to everyone else.

Unfortunately for me, however, it meant that I could not escape

Idris. We hadn't seen each other since the night he'd caught me returning from my rebel assignation. In truth I hadn't thought about what it would be like to see him again since then, but when I arrived in the royal suites, anger took hold of me. I grieved what we'd lost, but more than anything I raged—that he, a prince of the realm, could not see why the rebels were necessary was beyond my understanding. Those in power were meant to protect the weak, at any cost. That was the contract they entered into at birth. That he refused, that he saw my choice to step forward as a mistake—it was contrary to everything I knew and loved about him.

I dressed with a steely resolve. When Tala opened the jewelry box, lying on a spread of velvet was the necklace from the bedding night. The emerald, framed by the stack of pearls, gleamed in the early-morning light. I saw Tala flush as though she'd made a mistake, and rush to close the box.

"No," I said. "The necklace."

Let him remember the trade he'd made, I thought. He had lost me in exchange for nothing. When I emerged from the dressing room, robed in green and black, he froze, his eyes fixed on the jewel at my throat. But he said nothing, only offered me his arm. And so away we went.

On an excursion into town or to the beach, he could ride his horse and go to different markets. Rabi'a's salon was large, but not so large as that. And being High Princess and Prince of the Vath meant that we were placed in a position of honor, beside one another. I was spared, however—'Imad was quick to call him over for a game of shatranj.

"Dihya, is there nothing else to do?" Buchra said. She was sprawled on her side among the cushions beside her sister, her head propped up on her hand. "It seems if we are not out of doors, all anyone can think to do is play shatranj."

"What would you have us do instead?" Rabi'a asked dryly. "Play cards?"

"We could have a contest," Buchra said.

Her sister eyed her warily. "What sort of contest?"

"Poetry," I said without thinking. Their eyes all turned to me at once. "What?"

"We did not know you had a poet's ear, Your Highness," said Tariq.

"Perhaps not," I replied. "But I do know the history of my mother's estate. Poetry contests were the norm, were they not?"

"Indeed," Rabi'a said. "Though perhaps few of us have the talent to judge poetry over the language barrier."

"Then we shall raise the stakes," I said with a smile. "A prize to the poet who can move us in their own language and provide an equally moving translation for my ears."

"What is the prize?" Khulood asked, her eyebrows raised.

I considered for a moment, then tapped the emerald, and Idris made a harsh noise in the back of his throat.

"Have you a comment, sayidi?" I asked coolly, raising an eyebrow. The room was quiet. It seemed the state of affairs between us had not gone unnoticed, and they watched us rapt, eyes wide.

His throat moved, as if he were having difficulty swallowing. For long moments he stared at the necklace, and the longer he stared the warmer the flush at my chest seemed to get. When he at last met my eyes I felt as if someone had stolen the breath from my lungs.

"A queenly gift," he said at last, voice harsh. I knew him well enough that I could hear what was not said. Knew myself well enough that the sound of the pearls skating down my chest and into my lap echoed in my ears.

"As you say," I agreed. "Are there none among you who would defend their house's honor, then?"

"I will." Buchra had left unmarked by anyone and returned, a loutar in hand. "Unless my sister would prevent me?"

"No," Rabi'a said, on the edge of laughter. "By all means. Defend us."

In the time she'd spent at the estate, I'd come to like Buchra. To be sure, I loved them both—Buchra was quieter and more reserved, and she approached me with a great deal of suspicion. But she was lively

and clever, and when comfortable, unafraid of making pronouncements or taking risks. She sat elegantly, her feet tucked beneath her,
the loutar balanced carefully in her lap.

The first note hummed through the air and I felt my heart clench
in memory. The notes of this poem had been seared into my mind,
and I was loath to interrupt her and tell her that her poem needed to
be an original. I'd had none of her bravery the first time I'd sung the
poem. She looked not at me or her sister or even her lap, but at Tariq.
And he looked back at her as one possessed.

I'd heard the song many times, but my clearest, sharpest memory
was when Idris played the song on his loutar. It felt as if I'd been called
from a dream, wandering through Ouzdad, hunting down the sound
of the loutar. And there he'd been, still a stranger in some ways, sitting
beneath a fig tree, his hair unbound.

Lamma bada yatathana . . .
When he began to sway . . .
Hubi jamalah fatannah . . .
His beauty seduced my heart . . .

I have the voice of a village girl, I'd told him, and he'd laughed. It
was this moment I remembered, even more than when I'd sung it to
him a second time after Maram's coronation. Because it seemed to
me, in my loneliest moments, that this was what happened between
us. That I'd drifted through a garden and found him, and his beauty
had seduced me.

I was foolish and chanced a look at Idris, only to find him already staring at me. The grief I'd sworn to disavow this morning
rose up in me again, sharp as a knife, twisting in my heart. We had
both made our choices, and they had separated us irrevocably. And yet
and still I wanted to get up and go to him, to tell him that I would
give it up.

I could not.

Aman, aman, aman . . .
Mercy, mercy, mercy . . .

184 ✳ somaiya daud

The last notes of the poem echoed in the quiet of the room, and Buchra's hands flattened against the strings of the loutar. Tariq, for his part, still watched her, his eyes wide and dazed, as if he'd been taken by a thunderstorm.

"Well?" Buchra said at last, grinning brilliantly at me.

The sound of her voice broke whatever spell she'd managed to weave, and Idris and I looked away from each other.

"I think," I said thickly, "your peers will be hard pressed to beat your performance, Buchra."

"Indeed, I think it is unfair to ask the others to do so," Rabi'a drawled, eyeing her sister.

"Unfair," I'timad cried out. "We must all be given a chance for the pearls."

I had not expected a simple contest to have elicited so much feeling in me, and I wanted more than anything to be allowed to retire. But I had suggested it, and so it must continue.

"By all means," I said. "Shall you go next, I'timad?"

It was late in the evening when I returned to the royal quarters. In the end, I'timad, not Buchra, won the competition. Though Buchra was the better performer, I'timad's translation had passed not only my bar, but everyone else's expectations in the room.

The lanterns in the courtyard and connecting chambers burned low. The usual sounds of the household winding down for sleep were absent. I had not been out so long that they should have finished, but then I supposed it didn't matter.

I paused in the parlor that connected Idris and my bath chambers. A single lamp burned in the hallway, but there wasn't a soul to be found.

"Hello?"

Idris. In his bath chamber. The sound of wet footsteps followed, and a second later he was filling up the doorway, sopping wet. He wore a pair of soaking black trousers that hung too low on his hips and nothing else. His valet had yet to shave him, and his hair stuck to the sides of his face and neck. The khitaam on his arm seemed to glisten, covered in droplets of water. And there was, ridiculously, a rose petal stuck to his right shoulder.

I stepped back, struggling against the urge to giggle like a schoolgirl.

"Wh-what happened?"

"They ran a bath and then absconded without leaving me clothes or towels."

"And you tried to wash your pants in the interim?" I said. He did not find my amusement gratifying.

"I misjudged and they fell into the bathwater."

I could not control the grin spreading over my face. It was difficult to forget he was a prince, but with that came limitations. Among those: he did not think to prepare his own clothes before he went to bathe. Dihya, but he was beautiful. He'd spent so much time in the sun that his skin had darkened, and enough time training his stallion that the body I'd known had changed, if only a little. The strum of the loutar echoed in my head, and I felt—Dihya I felt such a need for him. The humor seemed to evaporate in half an instant and I found myself tracing his shape, the droplets of water caught at his throat, the way his eyes darkened when our gazes met.

"Amani," he said darkly.

"Yes?"

"I am cold."

I folded my hands in front of me. "That is hardly a question."

"Do you know where the towels are?"

"I know where mine are kept, yes."

"Please. Surely you will not allow me to suffer like this."

"You will smell like jasmine," I warned him.

"I am cold," he repeated stubbornly and followed me into my bath chamber.

I drew a towel from a wooden chest, and when I turned around Idris was so close the skirts of my gown brushed his toes. We were both quiet as I draped it over his chest and shoulders, then raised on my toes to pat the ends of his hair dry. He watched me carefully, quietly, his eyes fixed on my face. I played a dangerous game, I knew. Fight or no fight, I recognized the way Idris watched me, for it was the way I watched him. And I felt the echo of it deep inside me, shivering over my skin.

His thumb traced the line of my throat—short one necklace—and I went perfectly still. "You gave it to her," he said softly.

"She won it," I replied.

"You did not have to part with it."

I had no desire to reply to that. "Where are all the servants?" I asked instead.

"They have conspired," he said. "Yousef—my valet—said I was being an unkind husband."

My heart gave a lurch, but I managed to speak with some humor. "It is good, at least, that they've decided you are the villain."

My hands had settled on his throat, with the towel keeping skin from skin. I had not been so close to him since the night he'd left. He laid his hands over mine and I froze. His head bent to mine, close enough that a droplet of water slid from a lock of his hair and onto my cheek. His lips were a hair's breadth from mine, and for a moment I closed my eyes and didn't think. Separation had not cooled my desire or my love. If anything it sat now like a dagger in my chest, twisting its way to my heart.

"Amani," he whispered. "Come back to me."

I didn't want to answer. I wanted to kiss him, to draw him as close to me as possible, to feel that he was mine again. But nothing had changed.

"I am not the one who left that night," I said, my voice just as soft. "And my convictions haven't changed. The empire still shadows us all."

I forced myself to release him, to step back.

"Amani—"

"I hope you know where your clothes are," I interrupted, looking at the ground. "Because I cannot help you."

I paused in the doorway. "I will speak to the servants so they don't . . . conspire again."

And with that I left, fleeing to my chambers.

05. Maram

It was a strange thing to be sitting across from a husband she seemed to hardly know anymore. Stranger still to reenter a world which now felt alien and strange. She'd been raised among Vathek royalty, and the gloss and veneer of that court was a different world from the one Amani had built for her. A place of laughter and warmth. And though she was grateful, she itched to return to her estate with its crying hawks and secret poetry. The theory of ruling was easier to stomach than the act itself.

And Aghraas.

There were some nights when Aghraas seemed the shadow of her thoughts, when her whole body seemed wound in heat and her dreams of her were inescapable. The question she'd asked in Dar al-Zahra' echoed in the halls of her mind.

What do you want?

Maram still didn't know how to answer that question. She never had. There was no *wanting* among the Vath. There was your duty to the king. There was the blood he exacted from his subjects. There were the cold eyes that only rarely turned to his youngest daughter.

What do you want?

Today she wanted to throttle the world. She and Amani had organized a tournament for the court and opened it to the city. Aghraas was a stranger here, but it was easy to hide among the masses of people who wanted to show off their skill. Maram watched, caught in the grip of something powerful, forced to remain silent, as Aghraas beat fishermen and princes alike in duels and archery.

The sea wind brought with it an oceanic chill, but the sun shined down and gilded the falconer, marking her apart from the rest. She'd won the longbow competition, and Maram's mind replayed the stillness of her body as she'd aimed, broken only by her swaying braids.

She looked across the table at Idris. They were lunching privately before the tournament resumed. He did not look miserable, but then her husband was practiced at masking how he felt. And she was practiced at seeing the cracks. He had paid little attention during the tournament and had declined to race his horse, which by all accounts was the apple of his eye.

They had been friends for a long time. Not always allies. Not always confidants. But they were the same in more ways than Maram could count. Where they differed was control. She had little control until suddenly she'd been burdened with an abundance. Control stayed her hand and her heart.

"You have been silent most of today," he said. He set a small plate of her favorite pastries in front of her. "What's wrong?"

Since her mother's death, she had held all things close to her chest. Weakness was always exploited. By her sister. By her father. By her cousins.

What do you want?

Help. She wanted help.

"When . . ." She looked away from him and for a moment thought she wouldn't be able to continue. "When you fell in love with Amani . . . how did you know?"

Idris huffed out a laugh. "Has someone displaced me in your affections?"

This time, she forced herself to look at him. "We have known each other long enough, I think, that I am owed the courtesy of not being mocked."

His eyes widened in surprise and for a moment he only stared as she stared back.

"Maram—"

"Answer the question," she cut in. "Or don't."

His throat worked as if he were struggling to pin down his thoughts.

"Dihya," he muttered at last and scrubbed a hand over his face.

"Idris."

He looked around the room as if the vases or the trellis might give him an answer. For the first time she recognized a strange and horrible grief on his face. A part of her felt that she should look away. Idris was not in the habit of sharing his weaknesses, even with her. And to see him so wracked by it twisted in her gut uneasily. They were all fallible to such emotions, but she liked to hope she could protect herself.

Look at yourself now, a voice whispered. *Are you protected?*

"I don't know," he said at last, staring into the middle distance. "I liked her and we became friends and then I wanted her and I told myself no."

"No?"

His eyes flicked to her. "We are both hostages, you and I. And we grew up understanding that loving anyone was a luxury neither of us could afford."

"What changed?"

"It felt like a madness," he said softly. "I dreamed of her. And at Ouzdad we were never far from each other. And then I couldn't . . . justify . . . being apart from her."

"It feels like I'm being strangled," she found herself whispering. "Every moment of every day. Sometimes I look at her and—"

"You don't want it to end," he finished for her. "What you must decide— what all of us who live in the Vath's shadow must decide, Maram, is whose hands you would prefer around your throat."

Maram returned to the double's suite in a daze, Idris's words echoing in her mind. The sun had set and Amani was back at Idris's side yet again. It seemed all her meetings with Aghraas were destined to be dreamlike. She sat in the central tower, haloed by the silver light of the moon, a single brass lantern at her knee. It cast stars and moons as shadows across her face—she looked like a woman out of legend and myth.

Aghraas sat cross-legged on a floor cushion, her cloak draped over the low couch. An unpainted clay bowl sat on the low table at her right elbow, and every few seconds a soft *ping* would sound as a gold ring was pulled from one of her braids and deposited into it. Maram stood perfectly still on the last stair, watching her from the shadows. It was so rare that she was allowed to look her fill—it seemed Aghraas was always aware of her, always knew where she was. Always *caught her* when she tried to observe her quietly. Privately.

You can remain in the shadows, a voice said to her. *Remain beneath the cloud of doubt and fear and loneliness.*

She struggled, her hand pressed against her ribcage, her breath caught in her throat.

Remain shackled to the empire.

Another ring dropped into the clay bowl, and Maram stepped forward. Aghraas did not notice her until she stood over her.

"Maram—"

Maram said nothing, only sat behind her on the couch, and pulled the braid out of her hand. Aghraas went perfectly still under her touch. She did not move as the pile of gold rings in the bowl grew larger.

"Do you do this every night?" Maram asked.

"Yes."

"Alone?"

"At home my mother or a cousin will do it for me," Aghraas said.

"They are so inclined to help you?" Maram was on the last braid, the ring held between her first finger and thumb still on the braid.

"They are," Aghraas replied. "Maram."

When Maram didn't move, Aghraas pulled the braid from her grasp, slipped the ring down its length, and deposited it in the bowl.

"Maram," she said again, and turned around on the cushion to face her. Maram might have looked away, but she didn't. Instead she watched the way moonlight made Aghraas's eyes seem to burn with fire, at the way the lamp-light struck her cheeks. She wanted to reach for her again, to sweep a thumb over her cheek. She wanted to be able to lean close as she'd seen Amani and Idris do over a sheaf of poetry.

She didn't.

"Are you afraid of anything, Aghraas?" she asked, her fingers tightening around the fabric of her skirt.

Aghraas's eyes widened.

"I think I'm afraid of you," Maram continued softly, not waiting for an answer. Her eyes had lowered almost of their own volition, and so it was that she saw Aghraas reach for her hands. Aghraas turned Maram's hand over and traced over the love line cutting through its center.

"Afraid of me?" she whispered. "Or afraid of us?"

⊰ 22 ⊱

The days passed. That was the most I could say of them—one began and then ended and then another and so on. It was difficult to take joy in the successes I'd enjoyed. I'd done the impossible, a thing not done since prior to the civil war that had wracked our planet: united houses against a common enemy, created a confederation. I'd *saved* my family, a thing that had seemed unimaginable to me only a few months ago. And I wanted to believe that my view of the world was not so small that the end—the true end—of Idris and me had so upended it in my mind completely and yet—

The sound of someone clearing their throat roused me out of my melancholy. Tala hovered in the doorway, wringing her hands.

"Her Highness has arrived and awaits you in the tower," she said softly. "She is . . . temperamental."

"Thank you, Tala," I said, and rose to my feet. "I'll handle it."

We had a small kitchen here, and I found and loaded a tray with sweet pastries and a pot of tea, along with two glasses. Maram had gone straight to the tower room, and stood facing the ocean, the pins gone from her hair, her slippers tossed off somewhere to the side. She looked like a young girl, which in theory I knew to be true. But always she seemed to me—or rather, nearly always—to be an unassailable fortress, made of ice and stone. I had only ever seen the walls come down in her worst moments, and this was not one of them.

And yet and still, it seemed she was comfortable enough here and with me to let down her guard.

I set the tray down on the table and Maram did not turn away from her view of the sea, though she smiled.

"Am I a child to be pacified by sweets?" she asked.

"I don't know," I replied archly. "Are you?"

Maram sighed, and threw herself back onto one of the couches. "The machinations never end," she said, and her voice turned sad. "I never thought I would have to move against Nadine, of all people."

"Oh?" I said carefully.

"I know she seems a monster to you—" I snorted, and she ignored me. "She raised me after I was sent to Luna-Vaxor. I thought . . . I thought she loved me." She rubbed a hand over her face. "Maybe no one loves anyone. Maybe all anyone loves is power."

"Your mother loved you," I countered softly.

"And how do you know that?" I could hear the strain in her voice. "Half the time I think she bore me to be a weapon against my father and for no other reason."

"I think you would care less what your mother thought in the grave if she didn't love you. If that wasn't what you remembered."

"Sometimes I think my memory is wrong," she whispered.

I didn't know what to say to that, and so set about dividing up the sweets and pouring out the tea.

"So," I said when I'd handed her a glass. "Shall we begin?"

The work of planning such a tour was enormous.

"We should rely on the others," Maram suggested, surprising me. "They have just as much a stake in its success as I do."

"You're right," I said, staring at her wide-eyed.

"It happens on occasion," she drawled, and I laughed.

"You will need an entirely new wardrobe," I said. "And we will need to invite the press—"

"Why in the worlds would we invite the press?"

"This is your debut as the Imperial Heir," I said. "The support of the galaxy is worthwhile and you should want to cement your place among them."

She grimaced. "I hate the idea of the eyes of the galaxy watching me."

"You will be queen—that is the reality."

We moved on. She came up with a list of Vathek courtiers to invite city by city, and together we winnowed it down.

"You cannot invite the Clodius or Aphelion houses," I said, pausing.

"Why not? They're war heroes!"

I raised an eyebrow. "Because they are war heroes, Your Highness. You want the people's love, not to remind them what they have suffered. And the Clodius and Aphelion sigils were stamped on most flags of conquest. Even I recognize them. Aphelion salted the fields outside of Azaghar. They will recognize the sigil and you will find it very hard to win them over."

"Anyone else I need to worry about?"

"Have you not asked Idris?"

Tala came and set down a second tray with tea and pastries.

"That's a good idea," Maram replied. "I will ask him. But in the meantime, Ofal will meet us in Khenitra. And then one or two in every city after."

I hummed my assent. I'd met Ofal only once at the party Maram's elder sister had thrown in the north. She seemed one of the few family members Maram was truly fond of.

"How did you do it?" she asked. I raised my eyebrows. "The people of this city love me—love the makhzen. They were indifferent to us when we arrived."

"People are simple, and the planet is old, and everyone likes stories. Every society leans on images of antiquity to bolster their claim. Learn the right story, stage it the right way—everything else falls into place."

"Stories?" Maram frowned.

"The pearls," I said. "The horses. The banners. M'Gaadir is the first Kushaila city in all the world. Every time I dress I remember that."

"What in the worlds are you talking about?"

I widened my eyes in surprise. "I thought Aghraas at least would have told you the stories."

"Why would she have told me the stories?"

"Isn't she M'Gaadiri? Her daan are Houwa's daan—the feathers." She stared at me blankly. "The story goes that the Kushaila are descendants of a lost clutch of tesleet eggs. Houwa was the first egg that hatched on the beaches of what would become M'Gaadir. Her feather daan signified her tesleet origins. That is why the Ziyadi crest is the bird—your family draws its line directly from Houwa."

"I thought they were descendants of Kansa," she said.

"Kansa is Houwa's granddaughter. She was known for her pearls. It's why I wore them so often in public. Maram?" Her gaze had turned distant, as if her mind had fled elsewhere. She blinked and focused on me.

"Sorry—yes."

"What is it?"

"Sometimes I think . . . Aghraas is an alien." She said it with a self-deprecating smile. "I don't know where she's from. Or how she came to be where I needed her. One day she was just . . . there, when I needed her most."

"As in . . . from the stars?"

"Sometimes I look at her and—" She shook her head. "It doesn't matter. I can't be Houwa for the whole world."

I resisted the urge to press her on Aghraas. That she had said so much at all seemed a miracle to me.

"Certainly not," I replied. "But sovereigns historically give out gifts and alms. You can do that in every city. Charity leaves a mark. And we can plan to arrive at Azaghar on the Mawlid."

"The what?"

"The birth of Massinia—the whole world isn't Dihyan, but Azaghar is a Dihyan city. And they will be celebrating it. It is custom for the ranking member of court in the city to open the gates of the palace for a celebratory feast."

Some of her old fear passed over her face. "That is dangerous."

"If you keep yourself apart—"

"I know. Try to keep in mind one of them tried to kill me—us—not so long ago."

I smiled. "You will not like the next bit, then."

She waved a hand. "Proceed."

"It is tradition for them to walk from the palace to the zaouia to make a donation."

"No," she said flatly.

"Maram—"

"Let's compromise," she said. "I will hold the feast. I will even be present. I will not traverse the city on foot."

Perhaps the zaouia was too much. Especially in light of her worries about how the Vath would perceive her. She needed to appear to still belong to them for as long as possible. I nodded.

"If you'd told me last year that I would . . . be arguing with my double about what political risks I would take," she drawled, and shook her head.

I smiled. "It is normal to argue with an older sister."

She hadn't sat up from her earlier sprawl and contorted her neck so that she could look at me while remaining on her back. "Do you want to be queen?"

I blinked at her, startled. "What?"

"Do you ever want to be queen?" she repeated.

"No," I said, laughing. "The very idea fills me with dread."

That made her sit up. "Really?"

"Yes," I said. "I was not born to this life. If not—if I were not here, I would be . . . well. I might be married by now. I would certainly not be doing *this*."

She propped her chin on the heel of her hand and watched me. "But you are here, helping me when you don't have to. When . . . in truth, you have every right to let me sink or swim. If not for power, then for what?"

"I love my planet. It has been mistreated in the last decade—" It was Maram's turn to snort and my turn to ignore her. "But I think— No, I *know* that you will be a great queen. That you have the compassion and capability to do better than those who have come before you."

It seemed she did not expect me to say such a thing. She blinked rapidly and looked away.

"What makes you think so, given how I've treated you?"

"Because those who are unfit to rule do not worry about the sins committed by their masters," I replied. "And they make no effort to repair the harm done by them."

She did not look at me when she spoke. "Is it enough to worry when your hands are tied as mine are? I have noticed the ways in which my father's laws chain the people of this planet. I have little recourse against them. And every time I sit at the diwan I notice the silence between words—the hunger that is never spoken of openly. The missing children. What am I to do? What . . . what would you do?"

I swallowed around a lump in my throat. "What would I do?"

"If you were queen. Or going to be queen as I am."

"You know what I would do," I said. "I would expel the Vath."

Her mouth ticked up into a cynical smile. "And how do we decide who is Vathek enough to be expelled? What if I looked like Mathis instead of Najat? What then?"

I opened and then closed my mouth.

"We must face reality," she said.

"And what is the reality?"

"After thirty years, the world is more complicated because of the conquest. Children cannot be held accountable for the sins of their parents."

"Is it so complicated that we must tolerate an occupational government bleeding the planet dry?"

Maram stilled at that. "You of all people understand the cost of dissent against the Vath. I know that. What I don't understand is why you persist in this belief that they can be excised."

"I cannot accept any other world," I said. "You don't understand why I can't give up. I don't understand how you can watch and do nothing."

Her eyes searched my face as if she could divine some secret from my expression. "Amani, listen to me and listen well: whatever conflict with the Vath you choose to enter will never be equal or just. They are not idealists. Their expulsion will be long and difficult, and they will do things you cannot imagine.

"The consequences will rest on your shoulders. And then what will you do with the common Vath who have made their home here? Will they too be punished for their leaders' mistakes?"

I lowered my gaze. I knew what she needed to do; but I knew, too, that to suggest it to her when it had been the thing that nearly broke us apart would do little good.

"How can I be a good queen when I cannot even lead?" *You must engage the Vath,* I wanted to say. But her expression, though calm, was also dangerously still. I could sense the turmoil inside her and I understood that if I pushed too hard too soon she would withdraw.

We had come to a point where *she* would have to decide—I had done all I could to convince her of what was both necessary and just.

"You are leading already," I told her. "And it is early days yet—the problems will not solve themselves overnight."

"They have solved themselves," she said. "It is only that I fear the solution."

❧ 23 ☙

Furat and I arranged to meet a few days later. We met in the same garden where we'd met on her arrival at the palace. She arrived ahead of me and by the time I managed to slip away she was already sitting in the gazebo. Because of Maram's clear position on her I hadn't been able to speak to or see her for the majority of the visit. And because of the friendship I'd engineered with the Banu Ifran she likewise had stayed away. But she smiled when she saw me, rose to her feet and held out her hands.

My sojourn with Maram still lingered in my mind. If she could trust Idris, might there come a day where she would welcome Furat as well? The Wattasis had been close allies of the Ziyadis, and in another world Furat and Maram would have grown up side by side, hand in hand. Fear held my tongue captive whenever I considered bringing it up to the princess, but one day I would have to do it. She was a key member of the rebellion—there was no way for them to keep up the Vathek-instilled feud.

"You have been very busy," she said, kissing my cheeks. "It seems you have the Banu Ifran on your side."

I smiled and nodded. "Rabi'a met Arinaas a few weeks ago."

"And showed you your family, I have heard."

I grinned. The most daunting blade hanging over my neck had at last been neutralized. My family was safe and the Vath could not use them anymore to stay my hand. There was still danger, to be sure— every day under the eye of the Vath was dangerous. But never again could Nadine use their pain against me.

"So," I said, sitting down. "What would you have of me this time?"

"Did Arinaas tell you why she came to this region?"

"The eastern continent is under siege."

"And?"

I frowned. "And what?"

"They are going to assassinate the king."

I felt as if I'd been struck. I found that for a moment I didn't understand what she'd said. That my mind refused to comprehend the sentence.

"Assassinate?" I breathed. It would mean—*Dihya*, it would mean so many things. A rapid ascension to the throne for Maram, the expulsion of the Vath, a return to the world of before.

"Yes. Do you balk at it?"

I swallowed around a lump in my throat. "No," I said. "No. I just didn't think we would take such action so soon."

I remembered Arinaas's comment, that we might avoid war entirely. If Mathis died, Maram would take his place and there would be no need for war. Just an expulsion of the Vath and their power structures. A difficult transition, perhaps, but one with us in power. With the state back in the hands of the people.

"What do you need from me?" I asked her, trying to focus.

"Plans—Arinaas says it will be most expedient if we catch him in transit. Any itineraries for the coming weeks and months. The more recent, the better."

My mind raced with possibilities. The crowning jewel of the planetary tour was its end: the Court of Lions. It was a historic site, and for long ages had been the planet's capital until it was moved to Walili. From it had sprung a hundred empires in our long history. It was where Maram and Idris would conclude the celebrations of their marriage with an enormous parade, peopled by all the major houses on the planet. If Mathis died there—

It would be a symbolic end, and a new beginning before the entire world. The *galaxy*.

"He will join the tour at its very end," I said, voicing my thoughts. "I don't even think he's planetside now—but we know for certain he'll be at the Court of Lions in Qarmutta."

"We need details, Amani. An itinerary. You will need to get one from Nadine."

My jaw went slack. "I've spent the last few weeks doing everything in my power to extract her from Maram's inner circle and have therefore antagonized her completely."

"She's the only one who will have the true route—anything else you secure will be a decoy."

I came to my feet and tried to think. I could not regret what I had done—"forced Nadine from her perch," as Rabi'a had said. It was necessary. For as long as Nadine had cast her shadow, Maram was plagued with doubt about herself, her worth, her ability to succeed her mother. There had to be a way to secure the information we needed without compromising all of my work. Hadn't I spent the last few weeks arming myself with information to better defend against her?

"Did you know that Nadine is not from an ancient and noble house?" I said into the silence. Furat's eyebrows rose. "She was a foot soldier and came to Mathis's attention when she razed a village on Cadiz to the ground. They needed to establish a supply port before they launched the campaign against the planet. The village wouldn't yield, so she burned it and its inhabitants out of existence."

She had made her marks in the ranks by being a ruthless military commander and ascending quickly during the war. But the fact was, the Vath prized blood and lineage over all. And nothing that she did would move her bloodlines from common to ancient and noble. She understood, I knew, the precarious position she occupied.

"A person like that," Furat said, coming to stand beside me, "would do anything to secure her position. Whatever the cost."

"'Cost' being the operative word," I said with a lopsided smile. "Don't worry—one way or another, I'll get the information we need."

Furat smiled back. "I never doubted it. We'll need it three days before the event to plan properly." She held out a small gel-like tab, no bigger than my smallest fingernail. "Place this on any of her networked devices—it will scan for the information and relay it to us." I reached out for it, but she closed her hand over it. "Be careful, Amani. Nadine will always be dangerous."

"I know that better than most," I said. "And yet I'm here."

"Yes. We are lucky to have you," she said, and kissed my cheek.

"Baraka, Furat," I said.

"Siha, Amani."

❧ 24 ❧

I joined Rabi'a for dinner a few nights later. Her dining salon was a small terrace, shielded by a wooden trellis and a plasma shield. A small probe hovered in the corner, beeping at regular intervals, and would emit a single sharp blast if it detected any listening devices. The stone floor was covered in thick carpets and piled in turn with cushions around the low dining table. The spread of food was, to my surprise, not Zidane but Kushaila. I had expected her to serve her own ethnic fare in her quarters, and it was an unnecessary but welcome kindness that instead she'd served mine.

We were quiet as the servants finished laying out the dishes, and my eyes were drawn to the scene outside. At night, the city looked like a strand of pearls winding its way around the hill atop which we sat. My mind wandered as I wound the chain at my waist around my fingers. I heard, distantly, the click of the door shutting behind the last of the servants but couldn't pull myself back. We would leave M'Gaadir in two days. Maram and the makhzen had worked hard to make this a successful endeavor. They'd chosen their Vathek accompaniment carefully, the locations, the public acts—it was all coming together.

Rabi'a rapped a finger on the table, at last drawing my attention back to the present.

"So?" she asked as she reached for the teapot. "What happened? With you and Idris."

I stared at her blankly for a moment. I couldn't tell if this was an olive branch or a barb. Since we'd allied things had been easier between us—since she'd met Arinaas her respect for me had clearly risen. And yet she'd picked the topic I wanted to talk about the least.

"Why does something have to have happened?" I avoided looking her in the eye even as my heart felt as if it were being wrung in my chest. I had talked with no one of what had happened between Idris and I. I had no desire to repeat or retread the events of that night.

"Please don't treat me as if I'm stupid," she replied with a tone of censure. "Up until a week or two ago the two of you seemed like new-lyweds. Now it's as if you want to be together and can't."

"He is not married to me," I said softly. "So it seems we've at last caught up to the reality of our situation."

She caught my hand. "I know you a great deal better than I know Maram, Amani. I even like you—it would help us maintain a friend-ship if you were honest."

She was right. I had become friends with her and gained her trust. The least I could do was repay that trust in kind.

"He followed me to the meeting with Arinaas," I said. "And his discovery of what I did in secret . . ."

Time away from him had not made it any easier. Idris was one of the kindest people I knew—to imagine that he could stand idly by while our whole planet suffered violence and indignity made my stomach turn. I knew the cost was high, but I knew too that if we did nothing, the cost would only grow.

"He could not stomach it," Rabi'a finished for me.

I shook my head. "He won't tell anyone, but—"

"But he would rather you lived than risk your life for freedom."

"You sound like you agree."

"I don't, else-wise I would not be sitting here with you. But I understand the sentiment—such a sentiment kept my mother alive and my family prosperous." She looked at me thoughtfully. "The difficulty is in knowing when you have waited long enough, and when just surviving becomes untenable."

She poured tea in the following silence. I expected her to say something—a criticism or agreement. But nothing came. She uncovered the dishes and set the platter of bread between us, and we began to eat.

"What news, then?" she said a little while later.

I hadn't breathed a word of my next assignment to anyone. I wrapped both hands around my tea glass and fixed my eyes on the way the light played on the tea's gold surface.

"They're going to kill the king," I said, looking up.

She was a practiced courtier, so there was little change—a minute shift, barely noticeable, in the tightness around her mouth.

"You are frightened?" she asked.

"No. And yes. The stakes are high. The cost of failure . . ."

"Is incalculable. But the reward for success . . ." Her voice trailed off as she thought. "It is cleverer than open war."

"Cleverer?"

"No one knows how many cavaliers the Tazalghit have—and with the armies of Tayfur, and the support of the Salihis and their sworn houses, the force would be quite formidable."

"But?"

She sighed. "But we have no armada—the Vath fight among the stars. It is where they are at their strongest. And Mathis is the legal sovereign of this planet. His allies will come to fight for him. Winning a war against him is not impossible—but there is a reason we lost both the initial invasion and the siege of Walili."

"How is it possible we don't have an armada?" I had never thought of it—we were a spacefaring planet. We'd terraformed two moons.

"We were demilitarized after the conquest," she said. "Technically a violation of galactic law, but there was no one to petition on our behalf, so—"

"Then this is our best chance at liberation."

"Yes," Rabi'a said thoughtfully. "Do you know how—"

"In transit to the Court of Lions. Nadine will have the itinerary."

Rabi'a raised an eyebrow. "She is out of your favor."

"But not the king's," I said. "She would have been recalled by now if she were. It's why I continue to have to work around her presence."

Rabi'a looked unconvinced. "And how do you plan to get the information from her? Befriend her?"

I scoffed. "Don't be ridiculous. She will not believe any overture of friendship. But I don't need her to hand me the itinerary. I just need a tablet plugged into her network. I can ask for such a thing under the guise of wanting to see a recording of my family. And I have a device that will extract the information we need."

There would be no current recording, of course. But Nadine could not afford to lose face—not after everything she'd suffered at Maram's hand. She would find an old recording to maintain power over a poor slave girl.

"You're really a farmer's daughter?" she asked.

"We know how to survive," I replied.

"Why would she want to comfort you? She will laugh at your request, Amani."

"You think highly of her," I said with a hard smile. "She would have me beaten for insubordination. The gall of a slave asking for a favor. No—I'll have to think like her."

"Like her?"

I stood up and walked to the trellis. The two moons hung suspended in the sky, one orange, the other a pale green. The light they shed on the ocean water was strange and otherworldly.

"Nadine was a poor girl once, and she has risen high and will not want to lose power." I turned around to face Rabi'a. "It isn't about regaining her favor. Or even offering her Maram's. It's about giving her something that will allow her to reassert power over the royal household."

"How terrifying you are," she said with a laugh.

"But I don't have anything to give her." I sighed. "My position remains the same—I am a slave worth little beyond what I offer Maram. But I *need* access to that tablet."

Rabi'a's eyes lit up. "What if . . . we could take care of two problems at once?"

She came to her feet and walked to a side table. Her hand pressed against its glass surface and a rendering of the planet appeared in the air above it.

"The king has a complicated and global network of spies, a large part of which has cropped up in my province. Some have peeled away to deal with the problems in the east, but . . . It's made up of Andalaans, the Vath, and off-worlders. Journalists, bakers, soldiers—all of them report what they see to the crown."

A web of lines appeared on Andala, spanning the whole of the world, across cities and mountains and through deserts.

"It's quite sophisticated," Rabi'a said. "We have had a hard time tracking those in our province and a harder time still because we cannot kill those we identify. It would be seen as moving against the crown, even though technically and in the archives this network does not exist."

"I don't see how this solves our problem."

"You will have to give her people."

"What—" I began, breathless.

"We can doctor the information so that it looks like Mathis's spies are working against the empire. You give the information to Nadine, and she will do the rest." Rabi'a continued. "If you promise her information—spies she believes she can hand over to Mathis, endearing herself to him—she will likely give you anything you ask."

"She dismantles your spy network and becomes convinced that

she needs the information I have. Now who's terrifying?" I grinned. "Where do we begin?"

Rabi'a's message came at last, two days later. The spy we'd chosen—a minor Vathek lord named Marcus—had been a thorn in Rabi'a's side for years. He paid no taxes to the province, and every year he petitioned to grow his borders. The evidence against him was in place. All I had to do was relay this bit of information to Nadine. Despite the confidence I'd displayed in Rabi'a's parlor, my stomach churned. The last time Nadine and I were alone she'd struck and strangled me. I had no idea how she would react to being summoned, and as ever I was forced to gamble on what I believed would be the most reasonable expectation.

Powerless as she'd become around Maram, I had not forgotten what she did to my family. What she was capable of doing to me. I had not forgotten that she had the king's ear. And what I'd learned of her past only supported what I knew of her—she was ruthless, vicious, and willing to do anything in order to ascend.

I sank to my knees just as the door slid open. Nadine wore her customary black dress with its stiff high collar and sleeves buttoned at the wrist. From her waist hung the silver chain of her office, and her bright silver hair was bound into a single braid that swung between her shoulders.

I chafed at being on my knees and fixing my eyes to the ground. It had been a long time since I'd knelt to anyone—Maram no longer required it, and there was no one outside of Maram who would demand such a thing of me, especially when I *was* her. I had not realized my pride had grown so until this moment. But on my knees I remained, waiting, stomach in knots.

"Have you risen in the household to summon me so?" she asked, her voice dangerously even.

I did not look up. "No, my lady."

"How dare you?" Her voice did not rise, but it took on a cruel edge and her fingers gripped my chin like claws, as if she meant to rip my jaw from my face. I tightened my hold on my skirts. If I took her wrist, if I fought back, I would have lost my chance.

"I had no choice, my lady," I said softly. "I could not summon you as Maram."

A poor choice to rib her so, though I kept myself from saying what it implied. *Nor would she summon you herself.* Her fingers tightened painfully on my face before she shoved me away.

"What do you want?" she snarled.

"I want to see my family," I said, still on my knees. Her eyes were hard and flat as she looked down at me. "I am prepared to pay."

"You have no money."

"I did not think that was a currency you had much interest in, my lady," I said. I cast my eyes down again. "I see how you are left behind. I would help you in exchange for this."

"Why not ask Maram?" she said, coming closer.

"It is not Maram who controls the fate of my family."

I hazarded a glance up at her. Nadine was difficult to read. She was perfectly still, her hands relaxed in her gown, her eyes fixed on me.

"What would you give me?" she said at last.

"Marcus vak Oron," I replied. "He is stealing from the crown."

"In Tayfur?" She looked thoughtful. "Well done."

She stepped close to me and rested a hand on my hair. I resisted the instinct to shudder.

"Discover more information," she murmured. "And you shall have your wish."

06. Maram

Maram's hands shook.

The tour wouldn't start for another week. The gathering was Amani's idea—to invite members of the local college for a feast and celebrate culture and historical preservation in the place many people thought the world had *started*. A first of many college visits, or so the makhzen hoped. The professors and their students had come to the palace for a small feast where Maram believed Amani would have done better. They bantered and laughed about poetry and history, and though Maram had read extensively, she was not a poet, and she did not speak Kushaila.

She left the dinner feeling lost and confused and had returned to her quarters listless and worried. A month of such things—traveling from city to city, speaking to Kushaila and Tashfin and Zidane, balancing all the cultures of the world and their conquerors. She knew at the end, as Amani said, that she would be forced to make a choice. The tightrope she walked now would snap and the world—her world—would come tumbling down. She'd sat down at her writing desk for the fourth time in as many days, trying to write a letter—a request, a plea—and failed. And that failure had seemed to highlight what a dangerous road she walked, how quickly it would crumble under her feet at any moment. All of this, she might have withstood if the eldest professor had not requested a private audience. He was old enough to be her grandfather, though his beard was shorn quite close, as was his hair. He wore a thawb in dove gray, its edges hemmed in gold, which seemed to be the mark of a scholar at the college. His hands, she remembered, had been wrinkled and spotted with age.

"We have kept this in trust for many years," he said, and his voice shook. "But they belong to you."

A sheaf of holosheets sat on the low table between them, along with an old wooden box.

Maram was not predisposed to seem happy or delighted at any occasion, and now particularly, all she could feel was dread.

"Letters penned by your mother. Do . . ." And at last he seemed to wonder if he had made a mistake. "Do you not wish to have them?"

"I didn't know my mother's correspondence had survived," she managed, and then remembered how she had even wound up in this situation. Diplomacy. A public show of faith. She forced a smile. "I'm sorry, sayidi. My mother—"

"Lost parents are hard for all children," he said gently, and she hated him for his sympathy. "By your leave?"

She nodded and he came to his feet. She worried that he would impart some last piece of advice, or that he would try to comfort her. But it seemed that with age had come wisdom, and he bowed deeply and respectfully, then left.

When she was eleven, she'd stood on a cliff in the mountains on Luna-Vaxor. The air so far up was thin and there were moments when she felt as if gravity's hold on her was so little she might jump and simply not come down. That was how she felt now—dizzy, weightless, waiting for the rest of the room to lift off with her.

Her mother's likeness lay in the box on a bed of old frayed velvet, secure in a gilded wooden frame. Not a holofilm, or projection, or even photograph. Someone had painted her mother painstakingly in her youth. It was the smile Maram recognized, sidelong, as if she had a secret and you might know it. You certainly desperately wished to when she looked at you so.

Most of the data in the holosheets was degraded, but enough of it wasn't. Enough to tell they were love letters written by her mother. Enough to see the dates on them—Maram had been five when they were written. Enough to see that her mother had written back, and this person, whoever he was, had kept them.

She braced her hand against the desk. A filial daughter would feel rage on behalf of her father. A dutiful daughter would wipe these holosheets clean and erase any evidence of her mother's affair. But more and more recently she had realized she was neither. The chains of duty and honor tightened momentarily around her heart, then fell away. The weightlessness returned, as if the chains had held weights and now with them gone, her body might float away.

The state does not own my heart, her mother wrote. *This I swore to you in Khenitra, and I renew that oath now.*

The world swam around her. The state. The Vath. Contracts and vows.

"Maram?"

Aghraas stood in the doorway to the receiving chamber. Her braids were bound at the back of her head with her customary silver clip. And hanging from her shoulders was the velvet mantle she always wore. The wind was blowing in through the windows from the ocean, and as the fabric rippled Maram saw the indent of feathers, their edges touched with gold.

"What's wrong?"

What do you want?

She didn't cry often—a sign of weakness that could not be ignored would have served her poorly in all her years at court. But she felt them rise now and one roll down her cheek. Aghraas's eyes widened in alarm and she started forward. Her fingertips were soft as they swept beneath her eye, wiping away tears.

You must decide which hands you prefer around your throat.

"What is it?"

She wanted both. The state and her heart. And if her mother had found it in her to honor both, couldn't she as well?

The control she'd exerted in the last few months over her hands meant that she'd rarely touched Aghraas. She touched no one, and when Aghraas touched her it felt as if every nerve path in her body sparked with lightning. But she stood so close to her now, close enough to see the gold flecks in her eyes, the dark daan inked into her skin clearly, the flutter of her pulse in her throat. Her hands came to rest on Aghraas's face, and she saw the slight widening of her eyes.

"I—" The single word sounded like a croak. How many times had she found herself staring at Aghraas only for her to stare back? How often had Aghraas leaned her forehead against hers and said nothing and waited? How often had she sat beside her and wondered, aching, what it would be like to touch her without worry?

There were days when she was haunted by the little of Idris and Amani she'd glimpsed. Hands linked easily, shoulders bumping, his lips pressed to her forehead. Ease and love—two things Maram had never known.

Aghraas's forehead pressed against hers, and her nose brushed hers, and for a long moment Maram closed her eyes and tried to breathe. But there was no center of contentment to be found in this moment, not with her throat in the grip of something, with her heart and body wound with heat and desire. Aghraas's hands were on her, two firebrands, spread out between the lines of her ribs.

"Maram—" Her name sounded like a prayer, an exhalation. She didn't often pray, but she knew the sounds and rhythms, and this—

Aghraas's mouth was soft and still for less than half a heartbeat. Her fingers tightened around her waist, and Maram pressed back, the line of her shoulders, the length of her body. For half a heartbeat relief roared through Maram, and then a fire caught, as if it had waited all her life in the embers inside her. There was a soft cry—hers or Aghraas's she didn't know—and her hands clung to her shoulders as Aghraas lifted her up onto her lap.

Perhaps it is weakness or stupidity, her mother wrote. *But I cannot sacrifice the needs of my heart for what people perceive to be the needs of the state. I will not.*

The world disappeared and there was only the two of them, the sound of Aghraas's cloak sliding to the floor, the soft chime of the gold pieces in her braids.

What do you want?

This, she thought. *This.*

three

FAKHR: SELF-EXALTATION

⊰ 25 ⊱

We had left M'Gaadir at last.

The caravan was enormous, comprised of two three-level luxury cruisers to house the makhzen and the attendant Vathek courtiers who would join us at various points in our journey, as well as handmaidens, valets, servants, and guards. They had open lawns, and various salons and ballrooms, and from their bellies and their roofs flew the sigils of all the houses on board. Highest and largest among the banners was the sigil for vak Mathis, but alongside it flew the Ziyadi flag. Maram and I had arrived at a way to take advantage of the stories from antiquity, even while making concessions to the Vath: the cruisers would land a mile outside the city the caravan was visiting, and the parade of makhzen, Vathek courtiers, and so on would march into the city led by Maram, Idris, and her chosen court. There were always two

Vathek members in the party, and one of them was always her cousin Ofal, who, of all Maram's Vathek family, she loved best.

Our first stop was the city of the Banu Nasir, Khenitra. It was an ancient and imperial city, the gate between the ocean and the mountains. Rising up behind it like the craggy spine of some ancient beast were the Mountains of Ghufran. Khenitra was one of the few places that had emerged from the war unscathed. For a while, all the children of the makhzen had sheltered here, before it became apparent that we would lose the war. It was a good place, I thought, to test the appearance of the Vath alongside Maram.

I watched the procession into the city on a newsreel from within the palace of Khenitra itself. Maram was dressed in green and gold and astride a beautiful black mare. The new wardrobe had been an excellent decision—all the clothes she'd worn to date had either been wholly Kushaila or wholly Vathek, and the seamstress at M'Gaadir had married the two styles, as they'd done for the wedding. She'd kept the wide belts and flowing skirts, but lowered the necklines on some designs, and forsaken the wide flowing sleeves we favored for the cinched sleeves of the Vath.

She and Idris made quite the pair, she in mostly green and he in mostly black. He disembarked from his stallion first, and a moment later helped her down. She smiled and the corner of his mouth quirked up—the picture of married bliss. Khulood and Tariq waited on a dais at the gates and when they approached the siblings knelt before them. When they rose to their feet, Maram turned and introduced them to the rest of their party, as though they had not spent the last few weeks together. Ofal was the picture of decorum, all smiles and laughs.

Our sojourn in Khenitra lasted four days. During the day Tala and I played newsreels of Maram's engagements. The Nasiris were spectacular hosts, and Khulood and Tariq played their parts well. They dazzled the Vathek courtiers, folded in smaller families who lived in and around the city into engagements, and did what was most important: cemented Maram's ties to the people of the city.

On our final day, Maram visited the city college. The newsreel followed her passage through the impressive entryway, and into the main courtyard where a line of scholars waited to greet her.

"Dihya," Tala said wonderingly, her eyebrows raised. "Never did I imagine you would convince her to interact with us as she is now."

I smiled. "She just needed a push in the right direction."

Though our entrance to Khenitra had been bombastic and loud, our entrance into Azaghar was less so. I'timad and 'Imad had advised that it was better to leave the spectacle to the day of the Mawlid, and to not overshadow it.

I rose early on the second day of our stay, before the sun rose. In the time before the Vath, the Mawlid would have been heralded by the call to prayer from every temple in the city. Such things weren't allowed anymore, and so the day began with the ringing of the bells. On Cadiz I would rise earlier to help my mother cook as we had on my majority night. Everyone wore gold and green, and at midday we would join the village square for an enormous feast.

Despite being unable to participate, I rose early and bathed and dressed well. Tala and I cooked and baked for hours before the sun rose, piling platters with esfenj and briouat, m'hencha, ka'ab ul-ghazaal, and baghrir. When the bells stopped ringing we brought the platters, along with a teapot and glasses, to the central courtyard and settled in around a small projector that would broadcast the festivities.

On the newsreel the people of Azaghar had taken to the streets in the early morning, though they had clearly been hard at work the day before. The streets were decorated in green and white, everywhere a camera-droid flew, streamers waved in the wind. The sound of people was a dull roar of cries, laughter, and singing. The zaouia at the far end of the city was crowded with children as the malawi stood outside handing out sweets, alms, and small gifts.

The newsreel cut to the scene inside the temple beside the zaouia.

It was packed with men and women sitting side by side from the min-bar all the way to the enormous double doors. Atop the minbar a trio of men and two women recited Massinite poetry in harmony. It had been an age since I'd seen anything like this, since I'd *heard* Massinite poetry.

What would my family be doing today, I wondered. Away from home, from their friends and family as I was. The Tazalghit cele-brated the Mawlid just as we did—Massinia had been one of them, after all. Maybe they would celebrate together.

'Imad and I'timad stood on the steps of the zaouia along with the other malawi and handed out gifts—small velvet bags that I knew contained a few coins, some sweets, and a few tiny trinkets. They were clearly well loved in their city, as well loved as Idris was in Al Hoceima.

There was an air to the celebrations—*hope*. I hadn't asked, but I wondered if last year's Mawlid had been as vibrant, as full of cheer. The daughter of their late queen was in the city, preparing to host the feast beside her Kushaila husband. She had brought with her a coterie of important nobles, but it seemed even the presence of the Vath—who salted the fields and burned the farms outside the city during the war to starve them out—could not dampen their joy.

Tala and I worked our way through too much food while the rec-itations wound down and the crowds in the street thinned. At last the newsreels switched to the enormous receiving yard at the front of the Azaghari palace. It had been transformed overnight from a carriage and transport yard to a lush courtyard capable of hosting roy-alty. From the walls hung the banners of the Banu Mas'ud, the Banu Salih, and the Banu Ziyad: blue and gold, red, and green. Singers arrived first and set up in the center of the courtyard.

We didn't have to wait long for the royal members of the house-hold to fill the gallery around the courtyard. 'Imad and I'timad led the procession, with Maram and her Vathek cousin Ofal beside her, and Idris, Tariq, and Khulood behind them.

I felt a swell of pride as Maram took her seat and gestured for the rest of the courtiers to do the same. Here was Maram's court and her power and its love for her. There was the city, grateful for her patronage. There were the children of collaborators and royalists alike, secure in their position in relation to her. Proud and happy and full of hope.

The apartments in Azaghar were much like the apartments I'd been given in Khenitra—two levels facing an open courtyard and a glass ceiling, and from there we could hear the carousing that continued in the city.

Tala and I sat in the open salon facing the courtyard, more food between us.

"You know," she began. "When I first met you, I could not have imagined you capable of all you've done."

I smiled. "What did you think I was capable of?"

She let out a short laugh. "Truthfully? I thought the Ziyaana would break you before you had a chance to do anything at all. And now—"

I remembered the day we'd met—the day my life had changed irrevocably. How long ago was that?

"Truth be told—I didn't think I would survive either," I said softly. "I don't think that girl would recognize herself in me."

There was a certain tragedy in that, wasn't there? If I couldn't recognize myself, would my parents? Would my brothers? It wasn't only that I looked different, I *was* a different person. What I was capable of enduring, what I was capable of committing to—Amani the farmer's daughter had wondered what her trial by fire would be. She could not have imagined this.

"A shadow sovereign," Tala said softly.

"Hardly that," I replied uneasily. "I would need to be a much better shatranj player. And I haven't the aspiration."

Tala laughed again. "Aspiration or not, you are guiding us. Or at least you are guiding her."

"Protecting her—it's different."

She hummed. "Perhaps. The question is: Can you protect yourself?"

"Myself?"

She gestured toward the courtyard. Idris stood by the pool, watching the two of us. He had changed out of festival dress—the feasting outside must have ended and the gates shut while Tala and I talked, though the city still celebrated.

"Did you invite him?" I hissed at her.

"You know I wouldn't dare," she whispered, coming to her feet. "Perhaps he comes to beg."

"Princes do not beg," I snapped.

"When they're wrong, they do," Idris cut in. He'd closed the space between us and now stood in the entryway to the salon.

Tala bowed to him, then squeezed my hand. "I will leave you two alone."

She closed the salon doors behind her as she retreated to the courtyard. For a long time, there was only silence. I could feel Idris's eyes on me, but I couldn't bear to look at him. How well he had done before the people—the doting husband, the beloved prince. A prince who would not commit to doing what was necessary to protect and emancipate his people.

I startled when he sank to his knees in front of me. "I have come to beg."

I struggled against the urge to step away from him. I hadn't been so close to him in a while, and part of me hated the effect he had on me. Nothing, I thought, would erase the memory of him. Nothing would erase the way my heartbeat quickened and my skin prickled when he was near. As if I had an internal sensor keyed to his proximity.

"There is nothing to beg for."

"For your forgiveness."

My eyes widened but I remained silent. My heart ached but my pride stung—and it was my pride that refused to make this easy for him. He had asked me not just to give up the rebellion. It was the implicit belief that I should be made to kneel before the Vath. That life, even in slavery, was better than struggling for something better.

"I was wrong," he continued.

"About what?"

"Before the wedding I returned to Al Hoceima," he started, voice soft. "There was a family who'd come from an oasis close to the city. The Vath poisoned the water to drive them out. They brought their daughter's body—she was five. Maybe six. There was . . . nothing we could do. We could not demand reparations. We couldn't purify the water. *Nothing.*"

The grief twisting his voice was palpable, and I couldn't stop myself from reaching to twine my fingers in his hair. I had never seen him cry, and he did not do so now, but his eyes glimmered.

"I cannot bear the guilt. And yet we are powerless. Paralyzed by fear." He paused and swallowed. "Except you. You are not."

He clasped my hand and rose to his feet. "I regret every day that you must think me a coward. Worse, that I have behaved as one."

"You are not a coward," I told him, bringing his face to mine. "Fear is natural."

"But what I do in the face of fear determines the man I will be," he replied. "And I will not kneel to it anymore."

I searched his face as joy rolled through me. "You mean—"

"I will help you in whatever way you need," he said.

The tentative joy flowered and surged through me.

"Idris—"

"It's not only that I love you, Amani," he said. "I love this world—and I cannot be a prince and stand idly by."

Here then, I thought, was the boy I knew. Kind and brave, stubborn, who understood the weight of the world as it lay on his shoulders. I felt, in that moment, all the love and desire I'd ever experienced with him, churning through me, pressing against my fingertips. The Vath had taken enough from us, I thought as his lips brushed mine.

226 * somaiya daud

They could not have this, too. He was mine as I was his, and we would stand together no matter what.

"Tell me to go," he murmured.

"No," I said, burying my fingers in his hair. His mouth was hard on mine, and his hands tightened around my ribs—I felt as if my breath had been stolen from me.

I could not track our movements between standing and reclining on the divan. I knew only that my heart seemed to beat so hard it would rend itself in two. That my skin felt hot and tight, and that wherever I touched him the fire spread. I had seen such a fire once when I was a child in the mountains. A small ember, barely the size of my littlest finger's nail, blown up by the wind, touched one tree—it took seconds for it to be engulfed in flame. And so too I felt with Idris's shirt first in my hands and then on the floor, and my jacket and gold belt beside it. His lips were on my jaw, beneath my ear, on my throat.

The world narrowed to the two of us, and the expanse of skin spread out over me, and his hands on my calves and then my thighs. The soft murmur of his voice in my ear and his mouth against mine, my fingers wound in his hair. Every moment we'd been together and every moment we'd been apart came to bear on me, and I don't know where we might have gone if not for the bells signaling the end of the Mawlid.

"*Wait*," I gasped. "Wait!" He froze, forehead pressed against my collarbone, shoulders heaving.

"Wait?" he asked, looking down at me.

I felt a new, deeper flush work itself over my still too-warm body. He looked wild, flushed, his hair mussed by my hands. And then he grinned, as if he understood the tenuous grip I had on my control.

"Wait?" he repeated, and pressed a kiss against my shoulder.

"Idris—"

Another kiss where my shoulder met my throat. The curve of my jaw. The corner of my mouth. I struggled to sit up and felt my gown slip from my shoulders. He'd undone the ties on the back.

"*Dihya.*"

"Indeed," he said, still grinning. He sat back, reclined on his hands, easy and beautiful and all too aware of his effect.

"Put on your shirt," I said, coming to my feet. He didn't. Instead he drew me back onto the divan and did up the laces on the back of my dress slowly, as if he relished every time his knuckles brushed against my spine. When he was done he put his arms around me and pressed a kiss into my hair.

"I missed you, Amani," he murmured.

He would have to leave soon. As a concession to the Vathek courtiers there was a ball later in the evening. He would have to be present beside Maram—a united, *married* front. For just a moment I let myself close my eyes and lean back against his chest.

"What are we going to do?" I whispered.

"I didn't want to marry her," he said. "And I don't think she wanted to marry me."

I sighed. "I know. But—"

"But the Vath watch us always," he finished for me.

I turned around in his arms and for a moment I could only stare. He still hadn't put his shirt on, nor had he fixed his hair. He looked, I realized with a start, like a prince out of antiquity. Browned by the sun, too clever for his own good, and well aware of it. He grinned at me as if he knew the progression of my thoughts; as if he were well prepared to take them to their logical conclusion.

"Focus," I said.

"I am focusing."

I raised an eyebrow. "On the wrong things." I continued, softening my voice. "We cannot be together if the cost is other people's lives. The legitimacy of your marriage to Maram secures Vathek rule. *And* it is what has brought many of the makhzen to her side. She needs you." I pulled away from him and came to my feet. "Maram still expects all of that. She needs all of that."

"What if we agreed to not be married?" he said. "Hear me out—I am more than happy to supply her with all of those things, and support her claim to the throne. But we—all three of us—deserve to be happy. Even if we have to hide it from the world for a little while longer."

"You would do that?" I asked. I knew it was a silly question. If our roles had been reversed, I would have done the same.

He came to stand in front of me and rested his hands on my shoulders. "When the new world order rises, Amani, I mean to be with the woman I love."

26

Idris returned to take his place among the makhzen, and I returned to planning. We were only a few days away from Qarmutta and the end of the tour. To that end, I needed to secure the tablet from Nadine, which I had not yet done, despite handing her a second name. I knew what she did—she would take everything she could from me while using the information to assert power over what little of Maram's household she could and keeping me from what I'd asked her for. But I couldn't afford to wait for very much longer, and so I handed Tala a note to give to Nadine and waited.

It took her little time to arrive. Though she would never admit it, being locked out of the princess's circle of power stung a great deal. She relished the little information she could siphon off of me, though I was sure she had an extended network of her own.

The doors to the chambers opened and I sank to my knees, as practiced as ever.

"My lady," I murmured.

For long seconds she said nothing, and at last I looked up and went cold. I'd missed the soft whirring sound the imperial droids made. This one was a model I'd not yet encountered—the distinctive metallic fan spread out over its skull was in place, but it had four arms instead of the regular two. It was not a defense droid—its thin, sharp fingers ended in hooks on one hand, and I could see that one of its arms was denser, as if it hid yet more tools in its hollow tube.

An interrogation droid.

I stared at it, frozen.

"Did you imagine you could outsmart me?" Nadine said softly.

"Outsmart you, my lady?" I said, not bothering to steady my voice. I had to be surprised. I had to be frightened. She could not guess at what I did.

"Are you a mimic, now?" she said, coming closer.

My eyes didn't move from the interrogation droid—the fear of that, at least, was real. I'd heard the stories of what they were capable of; sophisticated enough in their engineering that they could keep you alive even as you suffered excruciating pain.

"My lady . . . why . . . ?" My eyes darted from the droid to Nadine and back again.

"Why?" she repeated. "Because Andalaans, and Kushaila in particular, are vipers. Don't think I trust you."

"I—" I paused and swallowed against a weight in my throat. "I have no desire to deceive you, my lady. I think only of my family."

"Yes," Nadine said thoughtfully, and the droid moved forward. "What would you do for your family, Amani? Is there a limit to it? Would you do anything?"

My eyes widened and I stumbled back. "Please—"

The droid lurched suddenly, the movement too fast for my eyes to follow. Its fingers wrapped around my throat and between one breath and the next I was suspended in midair. My vision filled with spots, my throat ached, my heart pounded. Nadine could not kill me—*she couldn't*. And yet I hadn't counted on her hatred of me and my race outweighing her sense.

It wasn't until the droid released me and I collapsed on the ground that I realized I'd clawed at its fingers around my throat as a matter of survival. I kept my face down as I tried to drag in as much air as possible. If Nadine saw my eyes, she would see hatred instead of fear and all would be lost.

"What have I done," I rasped, "to incur your wrath, my lady?"

"Yes," she said archly. "What *have* you done? Tell me."

"I have given you six men and women—two among them Andalaan—working against the crown," I said, looking up at last. My hand was still around my throat. "Have I not shown deference?"

"Curious that you do not say loyalty."

"Would you believe me?" I asked softly. "I want to see my family. I have debased myself for it. What more would you ask of me?"

"You think yourself very clever, don't you, Amani?"

I trembled and my eyes closed as she trailed a hand over my cheek, her nails gentle against my skin. The threat was clear: she would gouge my skin if provoked. I said nothing, but a tear rolled down my cheek. I had come too close to my end today. My fear was real.

"What do you imagine you have discovered for me today?"

I blinked rapidly and forced myself to focus.

"I want a promise—"

"Remember your place," she snapped. The droid whirred, its two lower arms widening.

"You're threatening to kill me," I said, my voice still low. "I need to be alive if I'm to see my family."

And just like that, some of the tension eked out of her.

She doesn't know, I could see her thinking. *How could she know when she is foolish and young and too Kushaila to be clever?*

"It is impossible to take you to them," she said carefully.

"I only want a recording," I replied, voice soft. Let her see, then, the demure and frightful village girl.

A nod, sharp and hard.

"The information, girl."

"Izaara bint Brahim," I said. "A spy in the hills of Qarmutta."

Every meeting I'd waited with the small gel-like tab pressed against my thumb, waiting to connect it to the tablet. It was not a thing anyone would expect a handmaiden—kidnapped victim of the Vath or not—to have. It was a hacker's tool. As far as Nadine was concerned, there was no reality where I might procure such a thing and use it against her. When she withdrew the tablet from a clip on her waist I remained perfectly still, waiting. She held it out, then pulled it back before I could reach for it.

"You understand," she said, her voice severe. "If your information is wrong, your family will pay for it. *You* will pay for it."

I looked up at her from under my lashes. She wasn't bluffing. I thought perhaps if she found my information to be wrong that she would hunt my family down, no matter the cost. All to make a point to me. And then . . . then the droid would return.

"I understand," I said softly.

"Next time," she said, and my eyes widened.

"*Next* time?" I said, unable to control my rage.

"This is your fault, girl," she said, smiling. "Had you not meddled I would not need to barter. And I will not give you what you want only to lose what *I* need."

Her hand trailed over my cheek.

"Another name, girl," she said. "Who can say what will happen between now and then."

Nadine left and I remained motionless, still on my knees. Fury roiled inside me. At Nadine but at myself, as well. I had counted on every aspect of her personality, except her cruelty. She enjoyed toying with those beneath her as a cat toyed with a mouse. And she had relished my fear and despair as much as she had relished the new and heady power the names I'd given her had bought. She would never give me the recording, and therefore I would never secure the tablet.

Dihya.

I closed my eyes and breathed. I needed it. *We* needed it. There was no new world without it, no dawn for justice. I swore and slammed my fist against the ground. She *had* to give up the tablet. She̅ had to—

My eyes widened. There was someone who could force her to give it up. Someone who didn't need permission and would not be trapped by games or manipulations.

Maram.

She wouldn't agree to taking the tablet unless I told her the truth. And if I told her the truth—what then? The last time she'd learned I was a rebel had destroyed our friendship. But this time, *this* Maram, was changed. She was at the precipice of understanding what was necessary.

She only needed a push.

❧ 27 ❧

We had crossed the Bay of Ghufran and come to its titular port city. Ghufran was a beauty and a wonder with its colorful buildings, and its bright-green-and-gold palace facing the bay. It was not only a seaport but a spaceport as well, and even after the sunset I could hear the whirr and hum of sky-cars and stellar transports landing in the airfields just beyond its walls. The sky was dark but the city itself looked like its own firmament, silver and gold, with lights flickering on the surface of the bay, reflecting the city back to itself.

The good will from the Mawlid celebrations still lingered, and so Maram took a chance and included more Vathek courtiers in her immediate party. In Ghufran they visited the ports, and she and Idris christened a new spacefaring vessel. As the tour progressed, invitations had begun rolling in from makhzen families that, in the past, had done their best to avoid the eyes of the crown. It exhausted

Maram, and so for a day we switched. I'd encouraged her to take her place among the makhzen, for they loved her and now she could see it. But I took the opportunity—I didn't know when I would be able to see Ghufran, or look upon its beautiful bay, or see its crystalline towers again.

I stood now on the royal balcony facing the bay, just as the sun set and lit its surface on fire. One of the men we'd met today said that on the moons of Balor when the sun rose the surface of its oceans caught flame. I did not believe him, but looking at the bay I thought perhaps such an illusion existed.

It was quiet as I left the balcony and returned to the main bed-chamber. The bed was raised on a dais to the left, and the rest of the room was taken up with a sitting area. Serving girls were still pre-paring the room for bed, and all paused and bent their knees when I entered. I waved a hand, allowing them to return to work, and made my way to a seat by the fire.

I was so absorbed in my thoughts I didn't hear the serving girls leave or Idris return. I jumped when he laid a hand on my shoulder.

"Sorry," I said as he sat down beside me. "Where were you?"

He grinned sheepishly and I rolled my eyes. There was hay on his clothes.

"Talking to your horse, I take it?"

"If you rode him—"

"Not even if it were your dying wish," I said with a laugh. "That horse respects one master, and it is you. I won't risk such a thing."

"Maybe." I resisted the urge to roll my eyes a second time. There was no "maybe" to be had about Al-Hays—Idris had barely broken him, and he would tolerate no other rider.

"Why are you so enamored of the horse?"

"Is it silly to say he reminds me of my brother's mount?"

My smile softened and I reached out to touch his hand. "No. That's not silly."

He turned his hand over so that our fingers were linked together, and for a little while neither of us said anything.

"Shall we play a game?" he asked, gesturing to a shatranj board. It was set up in mid-play, on a table on the other side of the room. I nodded and waited while he brought the board over and set it on the cushion between us, then rearranged the pieces.

We were quiet as we began to play and fell into our rhythm. But not even shatranj was enough to distract me from the way my thoughts whirled.

"Amani?"

I looked up from the board, distracted. "Yes?"

"Do you miss your family?"

My eyes widened in surprise. "What?"

"Sorry—I know the answer is yes. You don't talk about them."

I swallowed around a sudden lump in my throat. "It's easier not to. That's all."

"Tell me about them."

For the first time I realized that perhaps Idris would get to meet my family. That brought a surprised grin to my face. "Husnain will probably hate you at first."

His eyebrows flew up in shock and I laughed. "What have I done?"

"Nothing," I assured him. "Although—well, it's different from the last time. Maybe he won't."

"Last time?" he said, his voice choked.

"I was young," I said, voice calm.

"You were young," he repeated in the same tone he'd used when he objected to my offering up the necklace in competition. "You will have to tell me the story from the beginning."

I was still grinning. I *had* been young—or rather, younger. Fifteen, in the first flushes of adolescence, exhilarated at what a smile might yield. And then of course horrified that anyone would take that smile too seriously.

"He worked in a bookshop in the capital," I said, lifting a shoulder dismissively. "I didn't think it was possible he was serious, and then he was, and instead of going to my parents I went to my brother."

"Did your brother kill him?" he asked, his eyes dark.

I felt a strange, bubble-like joy take shape in my chest. Everything lately had felt heavy and difficult, and this felt lighter and easier than anything in the last few months.

"He didn't," I said, and reached over the shatranj board. My fingers tangled in the soft cloth of his shirt and I drew him forward, uncaring that the board was between. "Husnain will love you."

"I'm not worried about him loving me," he said, looking off to the side.

"Aziz, too—he will challenge you to shatranj, probably." I wound my arms around his neck.

He still seemed a little sullen.

"Is it so difficult to imagine that others loved me before you?"

He shook his head.

"I have loved none but you," I told him. "I love no one but you. I will love no one but you."

"I just . . . sometimes I realize you could have your pick of the world, Amani," he murmured, and pressed a kiss to my shoulder.

"I chose you," I replied. "And I have never regretted that choice."

He looked up at me, before reaching for my braid. His fingers were nimble as he pulled pins and clips from it before it unwound and spilled down my back.

"You regretted it a little," he murmured. "Enough to give this away."

He held out his palm between us—nestled in its center was the emerald and pearl necklace I'timad had won from me during the poetry competition. I stared at it for a moment, uncomprehending.

"She gave it to you?" I asked blankly.

"I had to beg," he replied. "And even then, she was not inclined to give it to me."

"Then what did you do to win it back from her?" I asked, suspicious.

He looked away from me. There was, to my shock, a hint of pink in his cheeks.

"Idris?"

He muttered something so quietly I had to ask him to repeat it.

"I had to perform," he said louder, through gritted teeth.

I felt joy bubble up in my chest. "Perform?" I repeated.

"Poetry."

"And you are so skilled, clearly," I said, grinning. "Else-wise you would not have won the necklace back."

"Amani," he groaned.

"You will have to declaim. Fair is fair," I said, leaning my forehead against his.

"I am not half so talented as you," he said, looking up at me beseechingly.

"And yet I require a performance all the same."

"My Kushaila is not— I pieced it together from a performance on a holo."

I combed my fingers through his hair. "Idris . . . I don't tease. It is the performer that matters to me. Not the performance." When he remained silent, my eyebrows raised. "You've recited before—what's the difference now?"

"I did not know what I said then," he said softly. "I did research this time."

Something soft twisted in my heart. Idris had researched poetry for me before, but this he must have done during our separation. I thought too of the difficulty of barely speaking what was meant to be his mother tongue and piecing poetry together. Kushaila was not an easy language; it was one that existed in layers and transformations. There was never a single meaning to anything.

I pressed a kiss against his forehead. I would not force it, as he had not forced me. But I had heard him declaim once, and he had a voice suited to it, a regal manner that conveyed beauty in the telling of the poem. And I imagined that his understanding of the poetry this time would only deepen its beauty.

"Morning came," he started softly in Kushaila, "—the separation— substitute for the love we shared, for the fragrance of our coming together, falling away . . ."

My mouth fell ajar. His Kushaila held just a thread of Vathekaar, but the words rumbled out of him, beautiful, smooth, and clear.

> Our enemies envied us as we drank lovers wine.
> They prayed for it to spoil and the world complied.
> What was bound together was unbound
> And what we held between us withered away.
> Our souls were as one, never to be parted,
> And now there is no world where they can join once more.
> Would that I knew that nothing would satisfy our enemies.
> Has their satisfaction brought us fortune?

For long moments I remained motionless, my hands braced on his shoulders, my eyes fixed on his face. He looked down, at my lap, his hair obscuring his eyes. The first and only other time he'd declaimed had been in Al Hoceima; a later part of this same poem that he hadn't understood but remembered because his father often recited it to his mother. It had been a beautiful recitation, but a blind one.

This—

If he asked me anything, I thought hazily, in the next few moments I would agree to it without thought.

"Amani," he said, voice strangled. "Say something."

I didn't know what to say. That he had chosen this poem, that he had performed it so beautifully, so movingly—

"Was it . . . before Azaghar? That you retrieved the necklace?" I asked, clearing my throat.

He still hadn't looked up. "At M'Gaadir," he said. "Just before we left."

"Idris—"

What I felt I didn't know how to say. Instead I lowered my face to his and kissed him. I heard the necklace strike the carpeted floor as his hands swept along my ribs and over my back. The grief in his recitation had lodged like a shard of glass in my heart, and I never wanted to think on it again. I never wanted to imagine that we would have to grieve one another in such a way, that we would be so irrevocably separated, that we would allow people to drive us apart.

In truth, nothing needed to be said. Eventually we lay entwined before the fire, my head on his heart, his fingers marking a trail over my spine. I remembered what I'd thought in M'Gaadir—that I wanted a lifetime of this. Poetry and politics and passion.

"Amani," Idris said, his hand stilling on my back. "Do not think I am so easily distracted."

I said nothing, though I imagined he could sense the stillness that fell over me.

"What bothers you?" he asked softly.

The problems I'd confronted earlier in the evening reared their heads. Idris had sworn to support me, to support all rebel efforts. But saying so and doing so were two different things, and I'd not yet put it to the test. And something such as this—I didn't know how to explain it to him. I wasn't sure I wanted to.

"I have been given an assignment," I said at last.

He stilled for a moment, then sat up. "Your first?"

I forced myself to meet his gaze. "No," I said softly.

"Then why the reticence?" He frowned.

"It requires Maram's cooperation. It requires her to make a great sacrifice," I said, sitting up beside him. "I don't know— I don't think it's a sacrifice she's ready to make."

His frown was severe. "Amani, I don't think she will. Collaborating with the makhzen is one thing. Making a sacrifice for the rebels— *knowing* that you're a rebel . . ."

"She knew," I said softly, "before you did. That I was a rebel. She's known all along."

His eyes widened. "And yet you live," he said.

"I meant what I said to her at M'Gaadir. She will be a great queen and leader. But waiting—we can't afford it. We don't have time."

"And you would take the risk?"

"The future of the whole world, Idris, against my fear," I said. "What should win?"

He smiled ruefully. "You should bring such audaciousness to your shatranj playing," he said, and I hit him on the arm. A moment later, he sobered. "I understand. And for what it's worth—I think it's a risk worth taking. I think it's time we stopped underestimating our future queen and asked for the courage we expect of her."

07. Maram

Maram had sent the letter.

After days of agonizing, on the eve of their departure from M'Gaadir she'd sent it and had heard nothing. And now they were heading to Qarmutta—they would leave Ghufran in the morning—and her grandmother was nowhere to be found. She wasn't sure what she'd expected. To many she was Mathis's daughter and not Najat's. Perhaps her grandmother thought herself a woman without a granddaughter.

She'd hoped that her grandmother's presence would decide her. That it would lay something awful and devastating inside her to rest. There was a storm inside her. Fear of change. Anger at her marriage. Grief because she had to pretend. She felt as if she would fall apart at any moment.

She donned the gown the serving girls laid out for her—a blue silk qaftan, with a high collar and a feather fan design over her chest. Rimming the hem were crossed scimitars. She'd seen Idris's robes; she knew they were meant to complement him. This is what she would wear at the feast ending her visit in Ghufran. To celebrate her marriage. To a man.

A horrible pain wracked its way through her and she shuddered and turned away from the mirror. She was her mother's daughter, her heir, the rightful inheritor of this planet. She had to do what was necessary.

But she would have given the world to do what made her happy instead.

A knock on the door. "Your Highness?"

"A moment." Her voice was steady, for which she was thankful. The only time she'd felt anything like this was after her mother's death. Gritty eyes and a throat filled with rocks. She hadn't cried; she hadn't dared. But the impulse was there, waiting for her to be weak and give in.

The doors to her dressing room opened as she approached them and all the serving girls bent their knees in greeting. The room was dim; all the lanterns had been turned low, and the room was accented in dark woods and dark reds so that it seemed wreathed in dark shadow.

But the woman sitting in a chair by the window was familiar to her, even if they had not met for more than a year now. She had come. After all this, her grandmother had come.

"Leave," she said to the girls, before her voice cracked.

Maram had dealt with enough emotion in the last week to last her a lifetime. She had no interest in dredging up old wounds or vulnerabilities. She especially had no desire to revert to her child self, though she felt the impulse rise sharply in her chest.

"Yabnati," her grandmother said, and held out a hand.

She almost didn't move.

The thing Maram hated the most about her grandmother was that she imagined her mother would have aged to look the same. Every time she saw her, she imagined her mother, a doting grandmother herself, looking over Maram's children.

But come forward she did, and pressed a kiss against the back of her grandmother's hand, and knelt at her feet. She thought she might retain her composure. She certainly had the strength for it. But her grandmother laid a hand on her cheek, and swept a thumb in an arc beneath her eye, and she felt the tears come.

The dowager sultana said nothing as Maram laid her head in her lap and wept. Her hand was warm on her back, though still.

"I can't do it," she said at last, looking up. "I can't keep doing it."

Her grandmother looked grim as she looked down at her. "Your mother felt much the same. She survived."

"My mother was loved," she rasped. "I am not."

The dowager's eyebrows rose. "Do you think I do not love you?"

Maram hated how her voice wavered when she spoke. "Few people will love the daughter of a monster—even if she is made in their image."

"You are not a monster," the dowager said. "You are my granddaughter. And you will survive this."

Perhaps she was a monster. Every time she looked at Amani she remembered some slight she'd dealt her, some horrible violence. Her life was littered with the evidence of what ran in her blood—the things she was capable of. The things she'd done.

"Did my mother ever give him up?"

The dowager stilled. "What?"

"I was given letters by the scholars in M'Gaadir," she said, and swallowed around the lump in her throat. "Her letters."

Her grandmother leaned back in her seat, her old eyes shrewd. "I will tell you the story of your mother, if you answer me honestly."

Maram nodded.

"Why did you write to me?"

"I—" She blinked rapidly, trying to stem the tears. "I know what I have to do. I know what is expected of me by—by the Andalaans. I know it's the right thing to do. But I can't do it alone. Grandmother—"

"Hush now," her grandmother murmured, and laid a hand on her cheek. "Ruling is difficult beyond imagining. Understand this and you will never be surprised."

"I can't do what my father wants," she whispered.

The dowager smiled only a little. "I know. That is why I have come."

"My mother—"

"During the height of the civil war, Najat believed we would lose. My brother and his daughter Moulouda seemed unstoppable. He'd found a tesleet—or it found him—and they rode to war with its blessing. They'd captured Cadiz, and were moving across the islands, and controlled the Strait of Qurtan and the east continent." She closed her eyes. "She was a foolish girl in love—so she married the boy she loved, thinking we would lose the war and she would never sit on the throne. Thinking that the decision would not have political ramifications."

Maram blinked back her tears, and stared up at her grandmother in disbelief.

"But—"

"Her marriage to Mathis was necessary, but illegal. Neither Andalaan nor Vathek law recognizes bigamy. You must understand—if Mathis could not secure his hold on the planet legally, he would wipe out the makhzen, all our governments—everything. He was willing to make a concession with the understanding that his heir would inherit, and that he would be regent of the planet until her majority. Najat ensured the language of the treaty secured *your* position, not his."

Maram frowned. "I don't understand."

The dowager leaned forward. "The treaty states that Najat was the primary ruler—even if that was not the reality—and that in the event of her untimely death her husband would be regent to her first born. Mathis is not her husband, which renders the occupation illegal. But it's a plan that works only if Najat is alive to enforce it and to plead to the galactic senate for aid."

"He killed her," Maram breathed, stumbling to her feet.

"He poisoned her so that no one could accuse him of killing the rightful ruler of the planet. She died slowly. And her husband was executed on charges of treason. Yabnati—"

"He *killed* my mother," she said again.

She couldn't breathe. Every day of her life had been wracked with guilt—guilt that she wasn't enough for her father. That what she had become would frighten and disgust her mother. She struggled every day between the two—running from one disparate shadow to another. But a dead woman couldn't provide comfort, and her living father had no desire to.

Her head snapped up to look at the dowager. "Is—is Mathis my father?"

Her grandmother smiled sadly. "I don't know. But I do know that his custodianship of this planet is illegal because he never married your mother. And now, with the rebels as strong as they are and you of age—if the world found out . . . If the *galaxy found out*—"

Maram shook her head and closed her eyes. She didn't care about politics, not now. She cared about the legacy she had nursed inside of her, of the promises she'd made because she believed that legacy was real and valid. Of the choices she'd made, believing she could nurture her heart and the state both.

"Maram?"

Her head snapped up.

"Do you understand what I'm saying?" She stared at her grandmother. "Mathis is not the ruler of this planet. You are."

She called a serving girl to escort her grandmother to her chambers, then sank to her knees by the fire.

Her father had killed her mother. She had spent all her life trying to make him proud. Trying to make him love her. Be harder, crueler, more steadfast in the ways of the bloodline. Leave half yourself behind and perhaps they would bestow purity on you.

What, exactly, ran in her blood?

What sort of legacy was she inheriting?

She couldn't stop weeping. She didn't know why she cried. Perhaps for what her mother had endured. For what she had given up in the name of her people. For the death of Najat's optimism and romantic spirit. Everyone remembered her mother as one of the conquered—but Najat had never appeared so to her.

Yabnati'l aziza . . .

Her mother had loved her, though people seemed to doubt it. Would Najat have cared who Maram's father was?

The doors to her balcony rattled, then opened. For a moment she stared at the figure haloed by the lanterns outside, uncomprehending. The metalwork in her hair caught the brassy light of the lantern and seemed to gleam.

"Am I a stranger to you now?"

The cry that left Maram's mouth felt jagged and broken. She lurched to her feet and threw herself at Aghraas, and the solidity of her form shocked her as it always did. Aghraas was a warrior, though she had never said as much. Maram had spent time cataloguing the scars on her arms and on her back. There was one just beneath her ear that had always frightened and perplexed her in what it implied. She felt the rumble of laughter in her chest as she pulled her into her arms.

"You're here?" she whispered.

"Of course I am," Aghraas said, some of the laughter still threaded through her voice. "I have come to take you away."

Maram felt a thrill and a cold fear at the same time and pulled back. "Away? I cannot go *away*. I am the princess."

It was so strange—the image of regality in her head was quite married to the Vathek idea, but whenever Aghraas sat anywhere it put her in mind of a warrior queen from antiquity. Her legs were never crossed, and there was a slouch to her shoulders that made Maram think she was used to being ready to reach for a weapon. She sat thus now, dropping languidly into an open chair without permission, her head tilted just so that their eyes still met.

She'd allowed herself to want for months. She'd shied away from difficult choices. She'd let Amani construct a new world for her and fallen in love. But now that world was calling, and it had demands on her and her blood and her inheritance. Her heart and duty had never been in alignment, but now she felt that disconnect acutely. Like a shard of glass burrowing its way to her center.

"What do you want?" Aghraas said. "Is this what you want?"

Her breath caught in her throat. That was always Aghraas's question. *What do you want?*

"It doesn't matter," she whispered.

"You could leave this war, and this planet, and this rebellion all to Amani. You could come with me and we could go anywhere in the galaxy. You just have to want it enough." Her voice was low and fierce.

She did want it. Dihya, how she wanted it. Sometimes she woke up feeling as if the wanting would choke the life out of her. But this was what she'd been born to. This was what everyone was depending on her for. *This* . . . was her life. It was not the one she'd chosen, but the one she'd been made for.

She wondered if when her mother bore her she'd always meant to pit her against Mathis. If Najat had planned a war from the very beginning. If she had raised Maram she would have turned out differently, a warrior queen preparing for war. Her entire life the choice was between her mother and father.

No one ever suggested there might be a third option. That she might mold a world unlike her mother's, where both justice and love were possible.

"Fate is not real, Maram," Aghraas said, drawing her thoughts back. "Our choices shape our destinies. You have a choice."

Maram walked toward Aghraas, and Aghraas in turn reached for her and laid her hands on her waist. Maram never tired of looking at her, at the strong planes of her face and the spill of her braids and the breadth of her shoulders. It had taken her—she didn't know how long it had taken her to understand poetry. The wellspring from which love and safety spilled forth had been a mystery to her. But whenever her eyes fixed on Aghraas, the whole world seemed to come into focus.

"This is my responsibility," she said, and swept a thumb over Aghraas's cheek. "And if—if I stayed, would you stay with me?"

Aghraas hand came over hers. "Do you remember what I said to you at your estate?"

"Tell me."

She kissed the palm of Maram's hand. "Wherever you are, so too shall I be."

❧ 28 ❧

The morning of our departure from Ghufran dawned and Maram and I met in the double's suite. These meetings had become routine by now; an exchange of clothing, jewelry, and information. While I had taken the first days in Ghufran, she had taken the latter, and now that we were in transit once again, she wished to retire while I handled the makhzen.

I didn't have a courtyard as I'd had in Azaghar and Khenitra. Instead, there was a modest sitting room, with low couches piled with cushions. A table was in the center, and from the ceiling hung several brass lamps. The windows were covered with wooden trellises and Tala had passed through earlier and opened them so that the sounds of the Ghufani harbor poured in, along with the hum of sky-cars and transports. Maram stood framed against one of the windows and its trellis, her hands held in front of her, her gaze distant.

"Your Highness?" My eyes widened in alarm when she looked at me. It didn't look as if she'd slept at all. "What's—is everything alright?"

"My grandmother arrived last night," she said, and gave me a tremulous smile. "It has altered my reality a bit."

I laid a hand on her arm. "In a good way?"

"That remains to be seen," she replied. "I can tell you want to tell me something. Out with it."

I wanted to ask her about her grandmother. She'd avoided meeting the dowager in the summer, and I knew she hadn't been on the official invitation lists. A last-minute addition, done in secret. Perhaps Maram *was* ready to embrace this, to stop fearing her relatives and take control of our planet. But I didn't have time and I hated that the rebellion would have to take precedence over our friendship for the next few minutes.

"I've received an assignment."

Her body, already motionless, took on a preternatural stillness. "What?"

"They're going to kill the king," I said softly.

Her laugh was half hysteria, half the soft, foreboding laugh I'd learned to fear in my earlier days in the Ziyaana. She turned away from me and shielded her eyes with a ringed hand.

"Dihya," she said, walking a few steps away. "Isn't that how the Kushaila swear?"

It wasn't the reaction I'd expected from her, and I was at a loss for what to do. Reach out to her? Comfort her?

"Maram—"

"The cosmos doesn't line up very often," she said. The hysteria hadn't leeched completely from her voice. "Except for the destiny of kings and nations, it seems."

I stared at her, wide-eyed and bewildered. "I don't understand."

"Last night my grandmother told me that Mathis's occupation of Andalaa is illegal. The planet is mine."

I didn't know how to respond to that, either. "What?"

"Insofar as a planet can belong to anyone," she added dryly, and waved her hand.

"I don't understand," I repeated faintly.

"Yes," she said, bemused. "I can see that." Her expression turned more serious. "Amani. What does your little rebel plot mean for me? You're my sister—I expect you don't mean to have me executed beside him."

That snapped me forcibly out of my daze and at last I reached for her hand.

"Do you know what I have spent the last few weeks doing?" She shook her head. "Securing you an army. They will assassinate him to put *you* on the throne."

She looked out at the Ghufrani harbor, though her hand lay in mine. "What do you need from me?"

"Nadine is the only person with a verifiable itinerary of Mathis's flight plans. It will be easier to catch him in transit."

"You need her imperial tablet," Maram murmured. "Easily done. And long overdue, truth be told."

"You can secure it?" I asked, relieved.

She gave me a wry smile. "I am the heir of this planet, Amani. Of course I can. Though the tablet will cost you."

My stomach sank. "Cost me?"

"A meeting with the rebels," she said, and at last pulled her hand free. "If the army is mine, then let it be *mine*."

Maram and I swapped clothes and jewelry and agreed that she would communicate to the tour that our departure from Ghufran would be delayed until the late afternoon. She was gone little more than an hour, but in that time I secured the meeting she required in a place she would not balk at going. My hands trembled. I'd worked so long toward this moment—the joining of the makhzen and the rebels, spearheaded by Maram. That this moment had finally come to pass was almost unimaginable to me.

When at last Maram returned to the double's suite she was grim-faced but had the tablet in hand. She carried something else as well: the medallion that was Nadine's badge of office. My eyes widened.

"Did you think I would suffer her in any era?" she said, raising an eyebrow. "I will not be her stepladder to imperial rule. Now. The rebels."

"I've secured a meeting with them," I said. "In the lower gardens."

"How efficient you are," she replied, and tossed Nadine's medallion onto the couch. "Aghraas will accompany us."

As if summoned, the doors to the suite opened and Aghraas walked through. I hadn't seen her since our first meeting, and I was taken again with how tall she was. She seemed to take up all the space in the room simply by existing. The two of them seemed to conduct an entire conversation with expressions alone. At last, Aghraas's jaw stiffened—an argument, then—and Maram turned to me.

"Shall we?"

The lower gardens in the palace were dilapidated and overgrown. They were built almost directly on top of the harbor, so that quiet conversation was obscured by the roar of waves and the cry of seagulls. Standing by the water, tendrils of her red hair caught up in the breeze, was Furat. When she turned and saw me a smile grew on her face and I didn't resist the hug she drew me into.

"Well," she said, pulling away from me and looking at Maram. "You certainly are a miracle worker. Your Highness."

Maram watched her, eyes hard and flat, as she sank to her knees then rose to her feet.

"I don't know if I should be more surprised that you are a rebel," she ground out, "or that I have survived this long with you at their head."

Furat maintained her pleasant expression as she spoke. "Oh, I'm not in charge. I am Amani's point of contact, that's all. You have been blessed, cousin. Amani's love of you prevailed over the only evidence of your character that we had."

"Evidence?" Maram said. The cold anger in her voice cut through me.

"Your father," Furat replied.

"Enough," I said, and laid a hand on Furat's arm. "We are not here to argue. We're here to at last achieve our goal."

"If my dear cousin is not the leader of the rebellion, who is?" She watched Furat as one might watch a viper, tracking every single movement so that she might cut off its head before it struck. Furat held out a hand and a flat white disc rose up into the air above it, glowed silver, then descended to the spot next to her. A hologram of Arinaas flickered to life.

Maram made a choked noise, half laughter half disbelief.

"Your seduction to the rebellion begins to clarify itself, Amani," she drawled.

Arinaas grinned. "Your Highness. I am told Amani has secured your alliance."

Maram held up the tablet. "Do I have your knights?"

"You have our knights," Arinaas confirmed.

"Good," she said, and handed the tablet to me. "Let us plan, then." Furat's eyebrows raised. "Plan?"

The look Maram leveled at her should have turned her to dust.

"Mathis's assassination will be pointless if the Vathek military takes control of the planet in the ensuing chaos," she said. "We will need to secure the imperial cities: Walili, Palalogea, and Tayfur, along with several others."

"How do you know we have enough fursa for that?" Arinaas asked.

Maram's smile was grim. "Amani is loyal to liberation, but she is also my sister and loyal to me."

For a long tense moment, the two of them stared at one another. And then Arinaas smiled.

"You will make a formidable queen," she said. "What other cities?"

"We will have Qarmutta in hand with Rabi'a's knights," Maram said. "Al Hoceima, Shafaqaat, Rahat, and Ghazlan."

"It will be done," Arinaas said.

"How?" Maram drawled. "By the power of Dihya? I am sending an agent." She stepped aside and Aghraas stepped forward to stand beside her. Arinaas's eyes widened as they fixed on the daan on her face.

"Siha, yakhti," Arinaas said.

"Baraka," Aghraas replied.

"Aghraas will bring you de-armament codes. I do not trust communications enough to send them any other way."

"I dislike leaving you in the middle of an assassination plot," Aghraas said, folding her arms over her chest.

Ah. The argument.

"It's a day's travel. Be back before Qarmutta." Aghraas was silent. "There is no one else, Aghraas."

Aghraas's struggle was visible, and a part of me felt I should look away. In the end, she closed her eyes and nodded. The smile that stole over Maram's face and then was gone seemed too private for me to have seen.

"I will be there soon," Aghraas said, turning to face Arinaas's projection.

"I look forward to making your acquaintance in person," she replied. Her eyes moved to Maram. "I'm glad Amani was right, Your Grace."

Maram's eyes widened and I smiled. "Your Grace?"

"You are queen," Arinaas said. "*Our* queen. You have our knights and our loyalty."

"Yes," she murmured. "I suppose you're right."

"By your leave?"

Maram gestured her assent and Arinaas's holo flickered out.

"And you, cousin?" Maram said, turning to Furat. "Do I have your loyalty?"

Furat sank to her knees and bowed her head. "Until death, Your Grace."

29

Qarmutta was at the heart of Tayfur province and the seat of the Banu Ifran's power. I had been all over the world now, thanks to my duties as Maram's double, but I'd never seen a place that looked like this. It was a world of sandy hills and rocky mesas, dotted with bright green shrubbery, short trees, their branches bowed with fruit, and even brighter flowers. The city itself was spread out over four hills that ringed the mesa at its center, on which was built the pride of the city: the Court of Lions.

Though it was under Zidane rule now, in the era of antiquity Qarmutta had been ruled by the Kushaila. It was a favorite city of an ancient family that no longer existed—a prince had fallen in love with a daughter of the Salihis and built the palace in her honor. A court of lions for his lioness.

It saddened me that Maram could not be here for this—we'd both agreed it was best that I take on this last piece. Before I'd revealed the rebels' plot it was because she felt strange enacting a marriage she had no desire to be a part of. Now—well, I thought now she could not stomach being present when the deed was done. No matter how necessary Mathis's death was, he was still her father.

Despite that, our entry to the city would be a triumphant one. The tour had been a success—we had left each city with more supporters than we'd entered with, with more ties, and with the love of the people. It was clear that they loved Maram. That they had missed the daughter of the queen, and now at last she was returned to them.

But it wasn't just that, I thought, looking at Idris. When the dust cleared, a new world order would rise. And I—and Idris—would be free.

Idris and I stood on the open lawn of the star transport of the wedding caravan: *Heiress-2*. From there, we could see the city on our approach, and the lands spread out around it. We would land outside the city, prepare for the final parade to its center, and be joined by the king. The plan was to feast and celebrate the union of two great families, in the tradition Maram's mother had produced on her own marriage to Mathis.

The hope, however, was that he would be dead before then.

"It's beautiful, isn't it?" Rabi'a said, coming to stand beside us.

"Yes," I replied. "You have done well, keeping it alive."

Rabi'a and her mother had done what many of the Andalaan families in the wake of the conquest could not—they had kept their province alive, and indeed helped it to prosper. And it was its prosperity that had enabled this moment, that would enable our victory.

She smiled. "Do you mind if we unfurl our standard? You will like the results."

I shrugged. "Of course."

The standard of the Banu Ifran was a single tower on a green field, with their words in Zidane beneath it: *Until death*. It unfurled from a flagpole over the ship, and two more flags dropped down over the sides.

"Look," she said softly, gesturing to the ground below. Our caravan was not so high in the sky that I could not pick out the people in the fields, herding livestock, farming, on horseback. It was as if with the unfurling of her sigil the world changed for them. Children cried out, pointing at our transport, boys and girls on horseback raced to keep up with us, waving scarves in our direction. I felt my heart fill with joy. The sigil of the Vath heralded fear. Children fled in the wake of its shadow, mothers worried for those children, and so on. But the children below knew who rode with Rabi'a, saw Idris and me at her side, and yet and still, they waved and laughed. For they knew and loved us.

Idris and I grinned at each other, and waved.

We didn't fly into the city proper. Instead, a camp was set up just beyond its limits. It seemed a city in its own right, a hundred enormous tents erected to house the hundred families who had come to celebrate the marriage. The parade, too, had been a huge undertaking that Maram had handled with grace. It showcased the most important families, both Andalaan and Vathek, though its celebratory air was distinctly Kushaila, to pay respects to her mother's and husband's families. It would enter the city from the south, and wind its way past each of the four hills before climbing the mesa to the palace.

The royal tent was high-ceilinged, its walls draped with Kushaila tapestries, its floor lushly carpeted. The tapestries muffled the chorus of noise outside, and for a moment I let myself breathe. From my left and going around the room, the walls depicted the story of Tayreet, a tesleet who'd come to our world looking for adventure and had fallen in love with a prince. They were beautiful, vibrant. Tayreet in her tesleet form was all blues and greens, jewel-colored and resplendent in every environment.

Idris was in the Salihi tent, so I had the space to myself. Serving girls stood at the entrance, waiting to attend to me, and guards stood just outside. I wore a blue qaftan, embroidered in gold. The skirt was many-layered, its hem embroidered with flowers and vines, crawling their way up the panels of the gown. A testleet was spread out over my chest, its wings unfurled over my arms, its head arched over my right shoulder. Its plumage was bisected by a trail of pearls over the center of my chest. A blue mantle made of organza fell from my shoulders, stitched with ingots of gold and coral, with feathers embroidered throughout. From each shoulder hung three delicate chains, at the end of which floated real feathers: red, green, and blue.

"Your Highness," a serving girl murmured, entering the tent. She bore a cushion, which in turn bore a crown. It was more delicate than the imperial crown I'd worn to Maram's coronation, dotted with emeralds, and at its center a bird rose up, her wings unfurled so that the tips met over her head. I knew it had to be a tesleet, but the design was such that the average viewer would not be able to tell if it was the Andalaan tesleet or Vathek roc. She settled it over my head, then gestured to the mirror at the other end of the room.

I didn't look entirely Kushaila, though I desperately wanted to. There were enough Vathek qualities about the dress—the epaulets, the way the skirt gathered at my hips—that I straddled the line between the two worlds Maram occupied quite well. But if I'd had my daan—I missed all the markings, but the crown of Dihya most of all. It was my link to Massinia, to her poetry, to her life. And the markings on my cheek would have marked me as my parents' daughter, would have preserved all their well-wishes for me.

I had not thought about them in so long, but suddenly, wrapped in wedding finery, I wanted them desperately. It would have been undeniable: who and what I was, my heritage inked into my skin. My fingers tightened in the folds of my gown as I made myself a promise. When all of this was over, when Maram was queen and I was free, I would get them back. I would return to Cadiz and have the tattoo artist remake them on my skin.

I could claim that much of myself back.

I was not prepared for the wall of sound—muffled as it was by the thick cloth walls of the tent—when I emerged from the tent. It wasn't only the parade getting itself back into order. Idris and Maram's marriage had made planetary and galactic news, and journalists, their assist-probes, and cameras all whizzed around, trying to capture the moments leading up to the final wedding feast.

I froze when I saw Idris. I was so used to seeing him wearing clothes that were either entirely Vathek or straddled the line. I don't think in the time I'd known him that I'd ever seen him in entirely Kushaila dress. He wore a black jabadour, with a velvet black jacket embroidered in gold. Along the sleeves and hem were maned lions, their mouths open in a roar. Between the lions were pairs of crossed scimitars. His hair fell down, curling around his ears and at his neck. At his waist was a janbiya dagger, and a scimitar, its sheath bejeweled. The leather gleamed in the noonday sun.

He grinned. "What do you think?"

I let out a strangled laugh. "I've never—" then stopped.

"It was my brother's," he said, taking my hand. "Come on, my family is waiting."

"Waiting?" But he didn't stop to explain, and drew me away from the tent. Guards closed in around us, but even through all the noise of the larger camp, I could hear his family and understanding dawned on me. I could hear the cry of mizmaar horns, a dozen hands striking drums, and the voices of 'Issawa singers, celebrating the marriage. A woman's ululating cry broke out over the music.

The Salihi standard, a maned lion's head with a palm tree cresting over it on a green background, flew from a pennant over the tent, whipping in the breeze. It felt as if there were a border around the Salihis and the moment we crossed over something changed. The voices got louder and the crowd parted when they saw us.

My hand tightened around his. I felt, strangely, as if I'd come home. The music beat in time with my heart, and the cries of his family members were in a language I understood, though I couldn't respond or demonstrate joy or understanding. The silver capsules of rosewater glinted in the sunlight as the women flicked water at us, blessing us. Naima, Idris's eldest aunt, waited for us at the entrance to the tent, sitting on an ornate cushioned chair.

"Khaltou," Idris said, and kissed the back of her hand. She smiled at him. I remembered the last time we'd talked—that she'd spoken to me as Maram. She eyed me, her eyes still as sharp as any bird, then came to her feet.

"You will have to kneel," Idris whispered.

"What?" Maram would not have, ever.

"Do it," he urged.

The music hadn't stopped, but I could feel the eyes of his family on me. If this were truly my wedding feast, I—Amani—wouldn't have hesitated. There was no shame in kneeling to those older than you, to those who commanded and demanded respect. But Maram would chafe at it.

"You will have to help me get up," I hissed at him. "This dress is heavy."

I sank to my knees slowly and waited. A serving girl came forward, a veil of sheer gold cloth draped over her arms.

"This belonged to my niece, I'timad," she said in heavily accented Vathekaar. I froze when she mentioned Idris's mother. "And to my sister, Hijjou, before her. They had long and happy marriages. May you have the same."

My breath caught in my throat. It was not a Kushaila custom—likely something more regional, but the symbolism of it wasn't lost on me. She had no reason to accept me—Maram—into her family. To acknowledge me enthusiastically. But she had. I remained perfectly still as she pinned the veil to the open space behind the crown in my hair and draped it over my shoulders.

I looked up at her, trying to control the emotion in my voice. "Thank you."

She said nothing, but smiled. Idris helped me to my feet, then kissed the back of my hand.

"Ready?" he asked.

"No," I replied honestly. Camera probes flew around us, flashing and clicking as they captured the moment. We made our way through the camp to its head, followed by the Salihis, and picking up stragglers as we moved through. The parade itself would be headed by the Salihi cavaliers, all dressed like Idris, behind them were the drummers and 'Issawa of the Banu Ifran, and then our palanquin. Behind us would be the rest of the families, Vathek and Andalaan. My nerves ricocheted between joy and fear. Mathis would be assassinated soon, sometime while we were en route, and I could not get that out of my head, even as I boarded the palanquin and waited for Idris to join me.

Despite all that, this felt so much different than the last time I'd boarded a Vathek procession. The first wedding rite I'd taken part of had felt like a funeral procession rather than a celebration of marriage. I remembered the heavy mantle of grief that had lain over me. This was not *my* wedding; it was not the culmination of ceremonies meant to consecrate *my* marriage and alliance to Idris. And yet—because I knew one day we would be together, that he would be mine—I felt joy. Even if our festivities were not so large or so loud, they would exist.

This was not an end, but a beginning.

The palanquin rose to its full height smoothly. One moment it seemed the entire camp was in chaos, and then, suddenly, we were moving forward.

The city was joyous. Likely in part, I realized, because the probes had broadcast my moment with the Salihi matriarch to the city. They were loud and waved the flags of their cities and the families in the retinue. Not even the presence of the Vath could take away their joy from seeing Idris and his family, or the Banu Ifran. Or, I realized with some joy, me. They loved Maram, even as she straddled the two worlds. I wished, suddenly, that Maram had come in her own place to see this. Wished that she could experience how much her people had come to love her in a short time. That all they'd needed was a show that she was one of them, a part of them. I heard a chorus of women in the back start crying out, "*S'laat s'laam,*" and grinned.

It seemed to last forever and also be over in an instant. Before I knew it, we reached the foot of the mesa and the palanquin was lowering itself again. The whine of sky-cars roared overhead as Idris helped me disembark, heralding the king's arrival. There was a stone in my chest. Idris and I would climb the mesa with guards and an escort of the makhzen. The rebels would fire on Mathis's vessel as we climbed the mesa. I—we—only had to make it halfway up before the old regime was obliterated.

As we climbed, I tried to keep the smile—soft and distant—affixed to my features. My hand tightened around Idris's the further up the mesa we climbed until at last we cleared the top, and there was King Mathis, alive and well and unharmed.

Something had gone wrong. Something *terrible* had gone wrong.

I maintained my pleasant expression, though my grip on Idris's hand must have been agonizing as we crossed the mesa to meet the king. How had they failed? How had his shuttle evaded the rebels? How could he be here, *now*?

Mathis watched our approach, his eyes cold and hard, his mouth twisted into a small smile. I sank to my knees.

"Your Eminence," I murmured. He watched me sink to my knees, and his smile became more pronounced. Idris knelt behind me, and then the whole escort, as if a wave had rippled through. Mathis's hand slid under my chin.

"I wondered," he said, soft enough that I was the only person who could hear, "whose child you were. Mine or hers. There's some Vathek steel in you." His grip tightened. "But no cleverness, it seems."

I kept my face immobile as he drew me to my feet. I had no way to contact the alliance, to get in touch with Maram, to communicate to anyone the cataclysmic failure unfolding in this moment. When Mathis offered me his arm, I took it. Despite everything, he still couldn't tell the difference between his daughter and her double. Perhaps, I thought, panicked, I could save Maram in all this. Perhaps I could absolve her, and she could live to fight another day.

"Smile for the galaxy," he murmured as the rest stood and followed us toward the palace entrance. He laid a hand over mine and squeezed. "You have started a game for your life. And you will not be able to finish it."

I opened my mouth to respond, though what I might have said I had no idea. Before I could speak, a bird's cry tore through the air. My eyes jerked skyward and I watched in disbelief as the tesleet I'd seen so many weeks ago, its jewel-toned feathers refracting sunlight, streaked across the sky. Seconds later I heard the rapid-fire thud-thud-thud of a fighter's canon. Just beyond the mesa, high in the sky, the Vathek fleet was engaged.

The rebels.

My hand slipped from Mathis's grip as I paused in the archway to the palace and looked up. The Vathek fleet was sleek, all curved edges and bright silver. But on the horizon and closer still I could see more ships; Vathek, older, their hulls streaked in rebel colors.

Mathis's grip tightened painfully on my arm, and drew my focus back. The people on the mesa were silent—among them were dissidents: the makhzen who had allied with Maram.

"*Get them inside*," Mathis snarled. "And I want the ground-to-air cannons up and firing immediately. We will crush this insurrection before it is born."

If the rebels were engaging them in the air it meant Aghraas had gotten the de-armament codes to them successfully. It meant that in at least one of the cities, likely more, they'd not only wrested control of the city, but its defense as well. I turned away from the sky, my face impassive, and met Idris's eyes. He wore the same mask I did, and when I slipped my hand into his, this time his grip was agonizing. He was frightened. So was I. But hope was not lost. Not yet.

Mathis led us into the palace. We were flanked by a full company of guards, and though none of us were bound, we may as well have been. My heart was stuck in my throat. Sometimes we passed a corridor and the echo of fighting would float down toward us. Idris's muscles would seize, and I'd have to tug gently and get him moving again. The Mas'udi twins and the Nasiris were in our escort as well, and they too remained silent. Rabi'a and Buchra had gone ahead with the intention of greeting us in the throne room. Every now and then I would catch Khulood or I'timad's eye. They were terrified. They'd lived through the purge—they knew what was at stake.

The doors to the throne room were enormous—as high as several men stacked on top of one another, made of iron, gilded. There were two guards at the door outfitted in Ifrani regalia, with swords on their left hips and blasters on their right. Their faces were masked, but when I met the eyes of one, my heart went still.

She was Tazalghit and so was her partner.

The spike of adrenaline that followed forced a tremor into my hands, and I tightened my grip on Idris's hand. The two moved as one, turning toward the door, pushing it open. Mathis and our Vathek escort, who had only ever thought of Andalaans as one roiling mass, this tribe indistinguishable from the other, didn't mark their presence and strode into the room. But I understood why they hadn't attacked Mathis on sight when we entered the room.

Nadine stood by the throne, and behind her were the droids she favored so. Lined up along the walls were several directors and generals I recognized from my time in the Ziyaana. It was either an executionary tribunal or a war council. Rabi'a was where she was meant to be, by a side entrance to the room. Her face was pale, her mouth tight, but her chin was raised and her shoulders straight. She was the picture of elegance. Beside her was another Tazalghit in armor.

There was a wide window behind the throne, and I watched as a Vathek vessel, free of rebel colors, hurled itself toward the ground while aflame. Behind me, the doors to the throne room were still open and the sounds of fighting in the palace carried through.

"Now, daughter," Mathis said, standing on the steps. He made a gesture and the droids came to attention behind Nadine. "Call off your troops."

He cast a striking figure. Tall, broad-shouldered, plumes of smoke and fire rising up behind him on the mesas beyond. He was cold, his features hard—a conqueror of the stars. But something was wrong.

I released my hold on Idris's hand and walked to the steps leading up to the throne. The droid's weapons tracked me, but none of them fired. *Where was Maram?*

I tilted my head just as she would have, curious and aloof. "Why haven't you arrested me?"

"You are my daughter," he said, coming down to meet me. "Shall I humiliate you with chains?"

A shadow of Maram's smile tugged at the corners of my mouth. "You have another daughter. But not one with a legitimate and lawful claim to this planet."

"Shall I humiliate you on the battlefield, then?" he asked.

"Who do you think the galactic senate will support?"

His eyes turned cooler still and his mouth flattened. "That assumes you will get off planet."

My mouth rounded into a sarcastic "o" of surprise. "So, I am under arrest."

"Your Highness—" Nadine interrupted. I turned a cool gaze to acknowledge her. She didn't recognize me, I realized with a start. Had she ever been able to tell us apart? She always knew, beforehand, which of us she would be speaking to. Was she like Mathis, unable to discern between us? Or was the Kushaila regalia so obfuscating she couldn't see past it?

"If you would only call your army off and return to us—" she continued.

I walked slowly up the steps toward her, each strike of heel against stone followed by the ongoing sound of the battle raging in the air outside and above us. I was stalling, *hoping* that Maram would arrive. Was she alive? Had she survived the fighting in the palace? Was she coming to take her place?

"You mean: return to *you*. So you can go back to being my puppet master, preying on all my worst fears?"

"I would never presume—" she began.

"You already have," I replied.

The room shook without warning and all eyes turned to the great window behind the throne.

"Heads down!" someone cried just as the glass blew in and a hot gust of wind followed. A shuttle decloaked, its debarking ramp extended into the new hole in place of the window. My knees went weak with relief: *Maram* stepped into the room dressed for battle, with Aghraas at her side and a coterie of Tazalghit behind her. The sound of boots striking against ground filled the corridor leading up to the throne room, and a dozen more Tazalghit warriors poured in through the still open doors. The two guards by the door unmasked, and I watched Rabi'a punch a code into a panel by the wall. A tile lifted away, and she pulled several firearms from within. She passed one to the woman beside her—Arinaas, unmasked—and a few more to the other makhzen in the room.

"I think you will find, Father, that your occupation is at an end," Maram said. She looked like a warrior queen from the days of Houwa or Massinia. Robed in black and gold, shimmering Kushaila script adorned the lapels of her jacket, and she bore a janbiya at her waist and a blaster in her right hand.

Mathis looked from her to me and back. His features were as stone, as cold and hard as they had been when we first entered the room. For a moment I thought he might surrender.

"Kill them all," he said.

The world seemed to slow in my eyes. Nadine's hand wrapped like talons around my arm. Aghraas pulled Maram back and I watched a glittering plasma-mesh barricade rise up from the ground between them and the blaster fire from Nadine's droids. Mathis withdrew with two guards to the other side of the room and Idris climbed the stairs, a firearm braced against his shoulder, its muzzle pointed at Nadine.

"Let her go," he said. He looked calm, dangerously so, though his grip on the weapon was white-knuckled.

Nadine pressed a blaster against my spine.

"The gall," she hissed, "to speak to me thus when you are nothing. *Less* than nothing."

"Nadine, I'm warning you," Idris said.

"Would you risk it?" she asked. My eyes met Idris's. Beneath that calm he was as terrified as he'd been when the first fighters had engaged. I nodded, just a little, even though my hands shook, and my heart beat so hard in my chest I thought the rest of me trembled in the aftershocks.

"Do you trust me?" he asked me.

"With my life," I replied.

We'd never been in a situation like this before and yet I knew: Idris could do this. I waited two heartbeats and then jerked to the left. All sound turned to wind rushing in my ears except for the burst of noise coming out of his firearm. She jerked, her hand still tight around my arm, and then released me and fell back. I didn't wait to see where he'd hit her. Idris took my arm, drew me to his side, and together we walked back until we reached a barricade.

The throne room was large, its ceilings high, and our soldiers were spread throughout, camped behind barricades. Idris and I ended up behind the nearest one, beside Maram and Aghraas, who handed me a blaster. I stared at it, uncomprehending.

"Are you telling me a farmer's daughter doesn't know how to hunt mice and fowl?" Aghraas asked, with a raised eyebrow.

"Mice and fowl are a far sight from droids and men," I replied.

"Pretend," she replied, with a grim smile.

Aghraas and Maram moved as if they'd been in battle together before. I could imagine that I had stepped out of reality any time I watched them and into an old story about a queen and her knight. Aghraas wore black, with a gold-and-green band on her left arm, signifying her allegiance.

"*Jam the doors,*" I heard Maram yell, and looked out to see that Mathis was making his way across the room with a squad of guards. I knew that when this was all over—assuming we survived—I wouldn't be able to stand on my own. The loss of adrenaline would render me inert. But for now, I hefted the rifle Aghraas had given me, braced it against my shoulder, and sighted down its length. The double doors were still open, but there was a blast door mechanism meant to protect royalty in crisis. It could also just as easily trap someone inside.

The recoil of the rifle was gentler than I was used to, but the panel went up in sparks and a great iron grid slammed down between Mathis and his exit. I turned to grin at Maram and found that she'd stood up. My mind seemed to understand what was happening before I did—Aghraas stood beside her, a larger and taller shadow. They were twins in stance, feet braced against the ground, rifles braced against their shoulders, eyes sighting for the same target. They shot at the same time, and the sound seemed to echo through the room, silencing all in its wake. The guards in front of and behind Mathis stiffened, then dropped to either side. Mathis seemed suspended in midair for a long, agonizing moment, then fell to his knees. A moment later, he toppled forward.

Maram lowered her weapon, her eyes hard. "Your king is dead." Her voice rang out, clear as a bell in the ensuing silence. "Lay down your arms and I may show you mercy."

The droids were destroyed, though their mistress—Nadine—had survived with a shot to her shoulder. The Vath had lost two directors and a general, as well as most of Mathis's personal guard. Rabi'a had survived with a shot to the arm and leg, and the rest of the makhzen, who had no combat training, had remained behind the barricades as best they could. Arinaas had lost a handful of women too, and her gaze was somber as she tallied them and made preparations to have their bodies moved.

Maram and Aghraas stood over a gurney that bore Mathis. It floated at hip level, its white medi-light illuminating his features. He seemed as if he were sleeping—gentler than I'd ever had the chance to see him. Maram's face was blank as she looked down at her father.

"I suppose it is only right," she said, voice distant.

"Your Grace?" I prompted.

"He killed his father to secure his throne," she said. "And his daughter has killed him for the same reason."

I thought for a moment she would reach out and touch him. Instead, her hand curled into a fist, and she looked up at the attendants who had born him to her.

"Take him to the crypt below. We'll burn him at sunrise. He deserves that last Vathek rite, at least."

I watched her as his body was borne away. I couldn't imagine what she was experiencing. Her father, dead. Herself now queen. The world waiting for her.

"Your Grace," I said again, and removed her crown from my head and waited. The room stilled. The makhzen who'd been pulled into our uprising without knowing about me had watched me curiously, but not approached. Now they watched us very closely.

Maram sank to her knees, the picture of Kushaila regality, the gold-stitched edges of her robe spread out behind her, her jewel-encrusted braid hanging over her right shoulder. It felt as if every person in the room held their breath as I settled the crown on her head. And then our positions were reversed, and Maram stood over me as I sank to my knees. Aghraas and Idris followed, and then every occupant in the room was on their knees.

"All hail the queen!" Idris cried.

"Hail!" Aghraas said.

"Hail the queen!" we replied.

⚜ 30 ⚜

The main court room Maram had chosen to stage her control of the palace from was wholly Andalaan. Its floors were tiled in green, orange, and blue, its walls covered in beautiful mosaics. The council seating was a ring of low chairs, with engraved wooden backs depicting lions and tesleet alternately. Her throne, a backless divan covered in green-and-gold brocade, sat framed by a wide open window so that she was haloed by light and bracketed by the mesas. She made an impressive figure, regal and crowned.

An Andalaan queen.

Sitting in the council chairs was her court. Not just the makhzen we had recruited, but their own banner houses, the wizaraa' who had joined us on the tour. Nadine was the only Vathek person in the room and she was on her knees, with two of Rabi'a's men bracketing her.

Aghraas stood behind Maram's throne and to the left, and I stood to her right. The makhzen, especially the makhzen I'd befriended on Maram's behalf, continued to watch me closely, but said nothing. It seemed, at least, they knew to show a united front in front of all and any of the Vath. Even one in chains.

"You worked so hard to achieve control over me," Maram said, looking at Nadine. Someone had bandaged the wound Idris inflicted on her. She was pale, with dark circles under her eyes. I imagined that the high stewardess had not conceived of a world within which Mathis lost and she was reduced to this. "Did you imagine I would welcome you back if I had failed? Or that my father would not give me the choice?"

She raised her eyes to look up at her. "I have always been loyal to you, Your Highness."

"I am queen, Nadine," Maram said softly. "You will address me as such."

"Yes, Your Grace," she said. "Please, Your Grace. None of these people can be relied on for advice. I am the only one—"

Maram tilted her head to the left, much as I had when speaking with her father. "How would you advise me? In this moment?" She turned to face me, and circled me slowly. "Should I kill my body double, as you wished to?" She moved to Idris and laid a hand on his arm. "Or should I threaten the scion of the largest tribe on the planet?"

"Your Grace—" Nadine stammered.

"Should I kneel at the feet of your ambition," Maram asked, coming to stand before her, "while sacrificing my own safety and the prosperity of this planet?"

The room was silent.

"Or," Maram continued sweetly. "Will you advise me to let you live so that you may continue to undermine me under the illusion of motherly love while turning my people against me?"

I watched as Nadine began to understand what she had believed to be impossible. To her mind, securing Vathek approval, rising in their ranks—it was all she'd ever wanted. It had not occurred to her that one might turn from that legacy. That Maram, who stood to inherit the highest standing in the empire, might instead choose to side with her mother's people.

"You," she breathed. "You can't."

Maram tilted her head to the side. "What can't I do?"

"I raised you, Your Grace," she insisted, frantic. "Loved you as my own. *Please.*"

The memories of all the things I had suffered under Nadine, that my *family* had suffered under her, surged to the forefront of my mind. I never thought to see her like this—frightened, pale, on the verge of shaking.

Maram gestured to one of the guards, and he stood back then drew his sidearm.

"You Grace, I *beg of you*—"

I remembered another girl, a different girl, on her knees, begging to keep her heritage. And the advice someone had given her.

"Oh," I breathed out. "You should never beg."

Look away, a voice said inside me. But I could not show weakness before the makhzen.

The shot cracked through the air like thunder. Blood pooled down from a hole in the center of her forehead between her eyes and over the bridge of her nose. She was perfectly still, her mouth still open, for a heartbeat, before her body fell backward.

The guard returned his sidearm to its holster and stood at attention once more.

"How long?"

"How long?" Maram echoed.

"Has your body double been among us?" Khulood clarified.

"Amani has been with me for a year," she said. "She has stood in my place when it was too dangerous, or I was—when I believed I was unequal to the task before me."

Her eyes roved across the room, and she laid a hand on my arm.

"Understand this," she said. "I have welcomed Amani into my

family as a Ziyadi. She is, as far as I'm concerned, as a cousin to me. You will treat her as you would treat me."

The makhzen and wizaraa' murmured their ascent.

"You owe her a great debt," Maram said, softening her tone. "Without her we wouldn't be here, together."

My head jerked up and I caught Maram's eye, and her small smile.

"To the future," she cried.

"To the future!"

"Now," Maram continued. "The work begins. Have Nadine's body burned. I want reports from every province and the generals as well. Bring the holocasts in here."

The quiet tension fell away as work was taken up and cities began to check in. I watched as a wall was overtaken by screens, and each screen in turn focused on a city. One by one across the planet, the Vathek flag was cast down and the Andalaan flag raised. There were places, I knew, where the rebels had found more resistance than they'd counted on. And there was the Vathek aristocracy to contend with besides. But Maram was not heir only to Andalaa, but the Vathek empire, and control of the armada was in her hands.

The new world had begun.

It was long into the night before we retired. Rabi'a caught me as my escort of guards prepared to take me to new quarters. She hugged me without warning, startling a laugh out of me.

"This is because of you," she said into my ear. "We are free because of you."

My eyes filled with tears. The exhaustion and emotional roller coaster of the day had finally caught up with me.

"No," I said, hugging her back. "A rebellion is the work of many."

She kissed my cheek. "Go rest. I will see you tomorrow."

Maram had assigned guards to me in the uproar as well as Tala and a coterie of handmaidens. They all followed me as I made my way through the palace and to a new set of quarters. I was no longer a body double in secret. I was, by Maram's royal decree, a Ziyadi. My mind whirled. Did she plan on making that official? Did I *want* her to?

I entered the private sitting room of my new quarters and from there went through the main courtyard. Everywhere serving girls and boys, handmaidens and valets, stepped out of my path and bowed their heads in respect. Dihya. Was this my new reality?

A pair of attendants pulled open the door to the main sitting room.

It was a wide-open area, with high ceilings, and an open vista of the hills beyond the mesa. There was a raised platform before the balcony, and it was there that Idris stood. Our eyes met and an electric shock went through me. There was no one in the room save the two of us, and I forgot sense and decorum and rushed to him. He pulled me into his arms and I felt as if a key turned in its lock and all my fear and terror spilled out. I pressed my face against his shoulder and wept. The euphoria of the day followed by the horror after swept through me and wrung me dry. To be so close to victory and then so close to death and then back to victory again—I could not make sense of it.

"You're alright," he whispered into my hair. "You're here with me."

He settled me against him on the couch and said little, though his hands ran up and down my back and every now and then he would press a kiss into my hair. I thought of the joy I'd felt holding his hand, making our way to the Salihi tent. So secure in my belief that victory was near at hand. Of the terror of realizing we had lost. A loss so cataclysmic it had nearly cost me my life.

At last, it seemed, all emotion had been run from me. I rested my head against his shoulder, and wound my hand in his.

"I will call for food—"

"No," I said, my voice rough, and tightened my grip on his hand. "I do not wish—I couldn't keep it down. Just stay with me."

He settled back down beside me. "Amani."

"Hm?"

"Maram has left me to you."

That made me smile. "Like a family heirloom I must inherit."

He smiled back. "Something like that. Will you have me?"

"Yes," I whispered.

❧ 31 ❧

The next few days passed as if I were dreaming. Fighting continued in some places, but what I found most remarkable was walking through the palace side by side with Maram. On the third day we left the Court of Lions and returned to M'Gaadir. Kushaila custom dictated that Maram spend a month there before proceeding in a caravan to Walili for her coronation. It would be a hard road, I knew. The coronation was symbolic—a gesture to the galaxy that our planet was united behind her. But what had begun in the Court of Lions throne room would not end there. The reconstruction effort would be long and difficult.

And yet, I was grateful to be back by the sea; it felt like a reprieve.

Being back in the palace as *myself* was novel. I dressed how I wished, and after my long sojourn as Maram I found that my tastes had changed. I liked jewelry, when in my life before the Ziyaana such a thing would have been impractical. I liked my hair down, braided, threaded with jewels. Getting up in the morning to select my own clothes, my own rings, to sit patiently while Tala did my hair as I liked instead of in as close an approximation to Maram's preferred hairstyles was strangely delightful. Maram had claimed me as her cousin to protect me from the ire of the makhzen; none of them had liked being tricked, and I didn't like to think how they might have treated me without her protection. I'd understood on some level that it meant I was a Ziyadi, but with it came both responsibilities and freedom. It meant there were days that belonged to the state in its nascent form and days when I could do as I pleased.

It also meant I needed to become used to having an escort wherever I went. I waited now in the courtyard of the palace, flanked by several guards who were assigned to me, and several more who were assigned to Buchra, who stood beside me. At last, I heard the sound of booted feet striking paved stone and a moment later Idris appeared. I groaned when two more guards appeared behind him.

"We will disrupt the souk with so many," I said. "We must be allowed to leave a few."

He smiled ruefully at me. "You are a symbol of the new revolution," he replied. "I won't risk your life so that you can buy spices, instead of having them ordered."

I fought the urge to roll my eyes at him and instead tucked my hand into his elbow.

"I've never gone shopping in a souk," Buchra said from my left.

I smiled as we made our way down. "I miss going out," I said. "I haven't left the palace walls as myself since we've arrived, and I want to—" I cut myself off before forcing myself to continue. "Is it silly that I want to make sure I still know how to do it?"

"Amani," Idris said softly, and I shook my head.

"Most of that girl is gone," I said to Buchra with a half smile. "But hopefully enough of her remains that she can haggle with a spice seller."

Maram had publicly released Idris from his marriage to her before

278 ✳ somaiya daud

we'd arrived at M'Gaadir. I'd read the press release last week, still trying to digest that I'd had a hand in crafting so public a narrative.

Under the tyrannical rule of my father, Amani was pressed into slavery and Idris and I shackled to an imperial machine we could not control. Despite that, Amani and Idris found happiness with one another, and it was against our will that Idris and I were wed.

Our planet, she had written, *is facing a new era. And I would shepherd that era into being with honesty, and so I give my full and complete blessing to my cousin to wed the prince of the Salihis, as she would have done in a fairer and more just world.*

When Idris and I walked together in public now we were the subject of curious stares and romantic sighs. We'd become symbolic of all that had been thwarted under Mathis's rule, and all that was possible despite it. I wasn't sure I enjoyed being part of something so public—my love for Idris had ever been both sacred and private. But we'd needed to usher in the dissolution of his marriage to Maram in a way that did not make her a villain or destabilize the support of the makhzen. As we walked through the marketplace I noted the young girls who watched us with wide eyes and the grandmothers who smiled, as if they were party to a secret about our romance that the very young couldn't hope to comprehend.

Buchra trailed after Idris and me, pausing to sample fruit and spices, drawn here and there by the sparkle of jewelry and brilliant scarves. The guards, I was relieved, were not as intrusive as I'd feared. They were all Zidane and Kushaila, and had, I was sure, grown up running in souks just like this. They remained a respectful distance away and blended into the crowd well. I'd feared they would keep the other souk-goers away, but the people continued to mill about, kept at arm's length by their own awe.

I plucked a jar of saffron threads from a vender shelf and held it up for Idris to sniff.

"It smells . . . good?" he said, and I laughed. "You won't mind it, will you?"

"Mind what?" I asked as we moved to another seller.

"Splitting our time between here, Walili, and Al Hoceima," he clarified.

I frowned. I hadn't thought about it. I hadn't thought about *anything*. Maram wanted our wedding to precede her coronation and I'd agreed, but I also wanted my family to be here and I didn't know when that would be. It felt like betrayal to make plans for my married life without my mother's advice.

"Amani," he said, and touched my arm.

I gave him a reassuring smile. "Ask me again when my parents are here," I said.

"They *will* get here before the wedding," he said. "I promise. The fighting makes it dangerous, but they will get here."

He laid his hand against my cheek, and I was struck by what a miracle that was. All our relationship was spent in shadow. Even when I'd played the new bride, I'd been forced to navigate Maram's personality, and that required a level of reticence in public that limited how we were around one another. I could not have imagined even two months ago that one day I would stand in the souk with Idris beside me as *myself* and be able to look up at him as I did now. That I would be allowed to conduct a conversation with our eyes alone or that he would be allowed to lean down and press a kiss against my forehead in reassurance.

Someone clearing their throat broke into our reverie and we pulled apart. 'Imad stood a few feet away, a wide grin on his face. When our eyes met his grin widened and he swept into a bow.

"Sayidati," he greeted.

"'Imad," I drawled. "What are you doing here?"

"Your wedding and the coronation procession has brought business caravans to town," he replied. "Horse traders from Khemisset have come. I was hoping I could steal Idris away?"

"Of course," I replied, then gripped Idris's arm before he fled. "My future husband will remember that the Mas'udis were kind enough to allow him to keep the wedding gift from his prior marriage and that the stables are *full*."

"Of course," he said, grinning. "I only want to look!"

I waved a hand in dismissal and he and 'Imad shot off like boys half their age, their guards only a few steps behind. When I turned away from them it was to find that I'timad had taken her brother's spot, and with her was Khulood.

We stared at one another, silent. Since my unmasking we had rarely had time to speak. Their provinces had required their immediate attention, and I was likewise occupied with the public-facing duties Maram had assigned to me.

I raised an eyebrow. "Will you stare at me all day or can I shop while you observe?"

I'timad grinned. "I wondered if you had some of Maram's frost or if you were *that* practiced an actor." She came forward and looped her right arm through my left. Khulood came to stand on my right.

"Have you been skulking, waiting for a chance to get me alone?" I asked as we strolled through the souk.

"A little," Khulood said. "We were curious."

"Curious?" I asked. I paused at the fig seller, and Khulood was silent until our transaction was concluded and a bag of figs was passed off to one of the handmaidens.

"How much of the press release was true," I'timad clarified. "If you did love our cousin."

I huffed out a half laugh. "There seems little reason to bind him to me otherwise," I said. "Maram likes him enough that she wouldn't punish him in such a way."

Khulood hummed noncommittally.

"Have I passed your test?" I said, and couldn't keep a little of the sharpness out of my words. The gulf that had opened up between us had stung, though I'd understood it. Rabi'a had known and she had told Buchra. But the rest of the makhzen who'd cultivated close friendships with Maram hadn't known how to treat me, though their friendships with Maram remained unharmed. I was an unknown quantity. What had they said to me and what to Maram, many of them wondered.

"Yes," I'timad said. "You know, we *do* want to be friends. You're marrying our cousin."

"And someone who survived as you did in the Ziyaana," Khulood added, "is not someone to be dismissed."

It was not what I wanted, but what I wanted wasn't realistic. I wanted to slip right back into the friendship I'd formed with them, instead of rebuilding from scratch. But there was no way to pick up the easy threads of conversations we'd had when they believed I was their future queen. And yet, I was a Ziyadi, soon to marry a Salihi, and a rebel. It was enough ground on which to begin.

When I returned to the palace, Maram was waiting for me in the courtyard. She rose to her feet while I instructed the handmaidens carrying my purchases to catalogue everything then store it. Maram watched, bemused, and when at last the girl departed she approached me.

"Your Grace," I greeted her, sinking to my knees.

"Walk with me, cousin."

Unlike I'timad, Maram did not loop her arm with mine. She looked as regal as ever, wrapped in the colors of her house, with a modest coronet settled in her hair. We strolled through wide halls and through gardens and courtyards, until we at last came to a terrace overlooking the horse paddock. I stifled a groan. Idris and 'Imad were below as a trainer walked a new horse through its paces.

"There are worse vices," Maram said with a smile. "I would ask how your time in the souk was, but that is quite evident."

I opened my mouth to reply and was derailed by the subtle shift on her face. Her expression softened and the ever-present sarcastic lilt of her mouth eased. When I followed her gaze, it was back down to the paddock, where Aghraas had emerged in her usual attire, wrapped in a mantle against the cold. Beside her was Arinaas, similarly attired. One of her lieutenants had entered the paddock and dismissed the trainer.

A small portion of the Tazalghit forces had joined us in M'Gaadir to demonstrate the alliance between them and the crown. Arinaas would join us in the procession to the capital for Maram's coronation. I'd been surprised to find that she and Arinaas had become fast friends and that the stoicism she wielded among the makhzen disappeared among the Tazalghit soldiers. Maram had noted that it shouldn't have surprised me at all—Aghraas was a warrior, and the trappings of civil politics frustrated her. Among the warrior women she'd found the same sort of kinship I found with Maram now.

"Do you know, Galene has fled to Luna-Vaxor," she said.

"I cannot imagine what you might have said to her to convince her," I said on the edge of laughter. I liked Galene as little as Maram did, and she was, in truth, the planet's greatest threat. Most of the High Vath had fallen in line, and would remain so as we extricated their claws from the planet. But if Galene chose to rally even a few of the generals to her cause, it would turn to all-out war.

"I asked her if she preferred I take up the Vathek tradition of sororicide," Maram drawled. "She found, suddenly, that she had business interests in Luna-Vaxor and left soon after."

I smiled. "Very well done."

"M'Gaadir is yours," Maram said.

My expression froze, my eyes still fixed on the sight below, before my mind caught up with my hearing and my head swung rapidly to look back at Maram.

"*What?*" I gasped. "You can't be serious. It's the *heir's* seat."

Maram did not look at me and instead continued to watch the events below. Aghraas and Arinaas stood side by side, their arms folded over their chests, as Idris and 'Imad gesticulated wildly. Both of them had, like Aghraas, taken to the Tazalghit if for no other reason than the horse lords had much wisdom to impart. But the military leader of the Tazalghit enjoyed poking fun at them—she'd learned to ride for war, after all, and they rode for leisure.

"Amani, I say this to you because you have endeavored to be honest with me," Maram said. "Aghraas . . . she is my forever. And even with whatever technologies are available, I do not relish the idea of natural heirs. But there must be a line of succession. For the stability of the state."

My mouth gaped open. "Maram—"

"Besides," she said. "Idris's dowry is generous, but you should have something that is yours. *This* is yours."

I didn't know what to say.

"I—"

At last, she looked at me. "I know that it is a gift with much attached to it," she said. "And it may be that the monarchy does not survive me at all. But it's a wealthy estate with a good income. It will allow you to take care of your family without others questioning why such money must come from the crown. More importantly, it is a royal wedding gift—and those cannot be refused."

My eyes remained wide. It was *too much*, I wanted to say. More than I had ever wanted or asked for.

"Say 'thank you,' Amani," Maram said.

I swallowed around a lump in my throat. "Thank you," I said, and reached for her hand. "I will endeavor to be worthy of such a gift."

She smiled. "You already are."

Maram and I walked a little longer, but eventually she departed to a war cabinet meeting and I made my way to my quarters. The page at the door cleared his throat, and I paused.

"Visitors, sayidati," he said. "They would not agree to wait elsewhere."

I sighed and nodded. "Thank you. I will call if I have need."

The doors opened and I felt my world tilt on its axis. My fingertips went numb. I stumbled through the doorway with a cry and threw my arms around my mother. She was shaking and she was thinner, but she was here, *alive*, holding me.

"Yabnati," she murmured, and drew back. "Look at you."

A hand tapped my shoulder and there, too, were my brothers.

I burst into tears. They were both thinner than I remembered, and Husnain's barely there beard had grown out in full in the mountains. Husnain, too, now had a few more inches on me.

"Oh no," Husnain said, and drew me into his arms. "There's no need for that."

"Be quiet," I said through my tears. "I will decide what I have a need of. Where is Baba?"

Husnain turned me bodily, and my father took me into his arms and pressed a kiss into my hair.

"You have been hard at work," he said softly.

"I was so worried you wouldn't be here in time," I said.

"Never," he said, "would we have missed your wedding day."

❧ 32 ❧

With my family safe and in residence at last, plans for the wedding coalesced. It would be a true Kushaila wedding, such that M'Gaadir had not seen in years. I'd insisted on keeping it as small and private as possible—there was no version of myself, I thought, that would submit this private moment to public scrutiny. The crown—for it was not just Maram with which I had to contend, but various makhzen and members of her diwan—and I came to an agreement: one journalist with a single probe who was to be present at the main ceremony, but none of the private family affairs before and after.

I paced the small sitting room, trying to still my mind, to *breathe*. My family and the Salihis were meeting for a small party, where the details of the marriage contract would be hammered out and finalized. And in two days I would be married. I'd spent so much time not thinking about this moment, so fearful was I that my family would never come. And now—I dreaded it. My relationship with Idris had always been a private affair, and it highlighted for me how much my life had changed. I was not only Amani of the Kushaila, Amani of Tanajir, Amani, Tariq's daughter. I was Amani, the queen's councilor, the queen's shield, the queen's liaison. I would never again be a private citizen, and I had opened up my family to public scrutiny as well.

Dihya.

"Amani," Idris said from the doorway, and came forward. "You must stop worrying."

"How can I stop worrying?" I said.

"My aunts and cousins love you," he said, taking my face in his hands. "They will show your family the respect they are due. They will show *you* the respect you are due."

I laid my forehead against his chest.

"What if they hate each other?"

"That is hardly likely," my mother said from the doorway. "Unless the Salihis have changed significantly since I left the planet."

My mother was dressed more regally than I'd ever seen her in a deep blue velvet qaftan. It was simple, with a high collar, and beading from her throat to her navel. She wore a single ring, and her hair was held up by a silver net, studded with pearls.

"Sayida—" Idris cut himself off and froze, his eyes fixed on my mother.

"What is it?"

"*This* is your mother?" he asked, looking between us.

I frowned. "Yes."

My mother, for her part, smiled. "Idris ibn Salihi," she said. "You are the image of your father."

Idris looked as if he'd seen a ghost.

"Oh, don't gape," my mother admonished him. "It is not so easy to kill me, though many have tried."

"What an alarming thing to say to your daughter's future husband," I managed. "On a day when I am already alarmed."

"Your mother," Idris began at last, "is the daughter of Mustafa el-Fatihi, the dowager's exiled brother."

"I am rarely referred to as such," she said, clicking her tongue. "More often I am called Moulouda al-Farisiya."

"Who conquered half the world," Idris continued. "Before the tesleet abandoned her father."

My mouth went slack. "*That's* what the tesleet called jeddou to? *War?*"

My mother slanted me a sad smile. "You can see why I did not like talking about it."

"I don't understand," I said faintly. My dress felt too tight now, and Idris's grip tightened on me as I felt myself sway. I was not some damsel, but I had endured much in the last few weeks, and it seemed that this, here, was where I would break.

I sat and braced my hands on the couch cushions, waiting for my mother to continue.

"You," I started, then stopped. "You're—the dowager's—are you her niece?"

My mother laughed. "Yes. I was not always as you knew me, yabnati."

A princess, I thought wonderingly. I had known many princesses in the last year. My mother reminded me of some. But *general* seemed to fit her very well. It was not a surprise that she'd hidden this—the Ziyadis had been hunted nearly into extinction, until the dowager, Najat, and Maram were all who were left. There was no sense in or reason for telling her children, who in turn might tell someone else.

"I will not tell you all of it," she said, sitting beside me. "We were exiled after my father lost. And then the Vath came, and they hunted us down. I escaped their search by chance. And then they came again and took you away."

My eyes widened. "Maram *knew*," I thought.

"She saw me before you did—apparently Najat kept pictures of the two of us together at her hunting estate. She was here to greet us while you were at the souk and recognized me."

"You conquered half the world?" I said, on the verge of laughter.

"The important thing to remember, Amani," she said, patting my knee, "is I did not conquer all of it."

I tried to still my thoughts. We still had contract negotiations ahead of us—and my mother arriving as the long-lost daughter of the Ziyadis would send a ripple through the palace. *Dihya.*

"Should we cancel—" I began, and Idris knelt in front of me before I could finish.

"Our wedding—our *marriage*—is a new beginning for everyone," he said. "And our elders will behave accordingly."

"My future son-in-law is right," my mother said. "This is a chance to heal old wounds, not take up old wars. It will be good to see my aunt again. Besides—it will be much more fun to extract a city from the Salihis for my daughter, instead of conquering one for my father in war."

The day I married Idris was bright and cold, the sky clear and heralding snow from the north. In the city, celebrations started early. The palace had cooked enough to feed every citizen, and even from my chambers I could see the confetti launched into the air and could hear the cry of mizmar horns. In the palace itself the air was filled with song, the beat of drums, and Kushaila celebrations. I had passed by the gate early in the day and singers were camped on the hillside, announcing our happy news.

The day was half gone when my mother and Maram came to help me get dressed. My arms and feet were wrapped in gauze to preserve the henna designs that were drawn on the night before, and the two of them worked quietly and efficiently to peel them off and help to wash off the dried paste. I bathed and my mother oiled my hair; while my hair dried, I ate.

The qaftan had been delivered early in the morning and hung on the wardrobe door. It was a heavy gown made of sea-green brocade, just shy of true Ziyadi green, embroidered in coral pink. Its bodice was studded with pearls, and a pattern of feathers swept out from the waist and down along the skirt. The collar was high, and from throat to waist were pearl buttons, situated in wound beds of coral thread. My hair was gathered up and wound at the back of my head, and held in place with a white pearl comb, streaked in pink and gray. Tala and my mother helped me into the qaftan and laced up the back, and Maram gestured a handmaiden bearing a velvet box forward. Inside it was a simple gold coronet, patterned with feathers and studded with small jewels.

My breath caught and a lump formed in my throat.

"Please don't cry," Maram said, setting it in my hair. "I wouldn't be able to stand it."

I gave her a tremulous smile. She swept one of my curls behind my ear.

"From villager to princess," she said softly. "Houwa's shadow loosed at last."

Tala set out a pair of bejeweled slippers that I slid into after I stood. My mother draped a sheer coral veil over my head; it was heavy and long, its tail longer than the trail of my gown.

"Ready?" my mother asked.

I nodded.

Outside, singers and well-wishers lined the halls. My mother held one hand, Maram the other, and behind us were my brothers and father. I would have to traverse the length of the palace to the celebration chamber, where only those known to us and the crown would be allowed. I thought of the girl I'd been when I first entered the Ziyaana, the girl I'd become during my time there. I thought of the Amani who had suffered being Maram's proxy to the man she loved, who had walked a similar path laden in someone else's jewels surrounded by strangers. She had not imagined a new world; certainly, she hadn't imagined a world where her marriage would signal the rise of a new age.

The doors to the celebration chamber finally loomed over me and opened. And there was Idris standing on the wedding dais, flanked by his aunt Naima and his cousin Fouad. Our eyes met and he smiled as if a revelation had come down to him. I reached a hand out to him, he took it, and I felt the rest of the world fall away.

Like the first wedding I'd participated in, I didn't remember very much. I remembered Idris, his hand covering mine. I remembered the flash of lights from the journalist's probe and a table being set before us. I remembered signing my name—*mine*, not Maram's—on the wedding contract, and Idris lifting that same hand to his mouth and kissing it in front of all of creation. But eventually the formalities passed and the singing began. Food was brought out to the guests and a space on the floor was cleared. I sat beside Idris in the place of honor, our hands entwined, and looked out over our guests.

We had not passed so far from our time of conquest that their forms of dancing had disappeared too; several couples were on the floor. Buchra and Tariq. 'Imad and a girl from Palalogea. And Maram and Aghraas.

Aghraas cut a handsome figure—taller than most men in the room, robed like one of the Tazalghit in maroon and black, her braids hanging free around her shoulders. She held Maram as if she were the most important person in the world, and her eyes never strayed from her face, nor Maram's from Aghraas's. I saw some of the elders watch them in the same way they had watched Idris and me, content with the understanding of how life could unfold for the truly happy who'd found their other half. Maram, rather than dressing in the Ziyadi colors, had dressed to complement Aghraas, and the image they made as they swept across the dance floor was striking and romantic.

But they were not the only ones who made my heart sing. My mother sat with the dowager and Idris's aunt Naima, laughing as I had never seen her laugh before in my life. She had wept, if only briefly, when she'd seen them again, and I thought of the impossibility of what she'd endured. Civil war, exile, the total destruction of her immediate family and complete separation from the only people who had known her in her first life. Fate, destiny—something had brought her back here, with them. The new world would heal very new and very old wounds.

"Amani," Idris murmured, and I turned my attention to him. He swept a thumb over my cheek.

"To eternity," I said, pressing a kiss against his shoulder.

"To eternity," he echoed.

The carousing continued, but eventually I came to my feet. I waved Idris back into his seat.

"I just want a little air. I'll be back soon."

There was a balcony just to the left of the dais, and it was there I went. The city continued to celebrate. A hundred thousand orbs of light swept through its streets, and music rose up into the air. The snow had at last begun to fall, fat snowflakes drifting down from the sky. The promise of something new and fragile.

The balcony door opened behind me and a wall of sound poured out into the air.

"Sorry," Aghraas said. "I—"

"No," I said, turning to look at her. "There's enough space for both of us."

She hesitated on the threshold, then at last came to join me at the balustrade.

"The noise is a little overwhelming," she admitted.

I smiled. "I agree."

She looked out over the city. "Maram would be horrified to hear me admit it, but I'm more comfortable sleeping under the stars. Closed spaces wear on me after a while."

In the half light Aghraas's face took on an otherworldly aspect. There was a glow to her, an iridescence that seemed inhuman. I did as I had done the first time I met her and reached for her cheek to trace her daan.

And from His first creatures He made stars, glowing hot with their fire and warmth.

All may see the stars, but few will see their forebears. And to those whose eyes see golden fire We say heed Us and listen.

"For we have sent unto you a Sign. See it and take heed," I said in Kushaila.

Her face stilled.

"Who were you sent for?"

Her throat moved, as if she were nervous. "You."

"And why did you stay?"

"For her."

I drew in a shuddering breath. "You said to me once that you understood why they chose me," I said softly, searching her face. "I understand why you chose her."

Her eyes widened. "You do?"

"I know her better than most," I replied. "I have had to. And I am glad to."

I saw, too, what Maram saw in Aghraas. There was a sweetness to her in this moment, and a warmth that would have drawn Maram to her like a moth to a flame. At last she inclined her head.

"Get some rest, sayidati," she said. "The new world requires a great deal of work."

Coda: Maram

Maram stood in front of the image of her mother, grandmother, and herself. There was still much to do, and in truth taking this short reprieve at her estate was a selfish luxury. She'd wanted three days to herself, away from the planning and celebrations and reconstruction efforts. She wanted to *breathe*—Mathis's assassination had thrust the world into motion and there never seemed a moment for her to stop. But they had come here—Maram, Aghraas, and her grandmother—without wizaraa' or cabinet members or makhzen. Her small and very immediate family.

For the first time in many years she wished her mother were alive to see her. To see the world she so loved struggling back toward freedom. The daughter she had borne trying to shepherd it out of tyranny and decay. The mother she'd been forced to exile returned to the planet of her birth.

Aghraas's feet made no sound on the stone and yet Maram knew the moment she'd crossed the courtyard to her. She slid her hand into Maram's and drew her to her side.

"She would be proud," Aghraas said.

"Do you speak to the dead now?" Maram asked without looking away from the portrait of her mother.

Aghraas squeezed her hand. "I don't need to speak to the dead to know the truth."

Maram turned at last to look at her. She wore a sleeveless brown tunic and loose trousers, and a heavy robe over it. Her braids were down and un-adorned and her feet bare. Maram thought very few people ever saw Aghraas thus—she presented to the world as a warrior, implacable and unapproach-able. But dressed thus and in the light of brass lanterns and the moon, she was closer to the falconer who'd first startled her on the estate. Before Aghraas could catch her watching, she lowered her gaze and turned Aghraas's hand over in hers. Aghraas was still as Maram traced the tendons on her wrist and the love line bisecting her palm. She was patient as Maram contemplated the way her hand fit in hers.

She had done many difficult things in the past months. She could do one more.

"I don't read very much Kushaila literature," she said, voice hoarse. "But in Vathek literature, in the old stories, when marriage must be deferred people—lovers—plight their troth."

"Oh?" Aghraas said. She lifted a hand and twined a curl of Maram's hair around her finger. "Why would marriage be deferred?"

"Sometimes," she began, then cleared her throat. "Sometimes, one wishes to wait. Or—there are too many ceremonies. Or—"

"Maram."

Maram looked up at her, eyes wide. Aghraas's expression had softened as if she'd seen something in Maram's face or heard something in her voice and it had moved her. *Vulnerability.* Maram would only ever stumble as she was doing now with Aghraas.

She pulled her hands from Aghraas and walked to the table where they'd dined. A handmaiden had brought the small wooden box from her room a little while ago, and Maram laid her hands on it now.

"When reconstruction is well under way," she said, looking down. "And it won't be seen as an exorbitant—"

"Maram," Aghraas said again. "What is in the box?"

She'd come forward as she said it and now stood beside Maram. Maram lifted the lid of the box and waited.

Inside were two rings—simple, silver, from her mother's collection. She'd had them smelted down and reshaped, one enlarged for Aghraas, both set with one half of a single gem each. A yellow stone, flecked with red. The sound Aghraas made—Maram could not look up.

The falconer pulled one ring from the box—the smaller one—and held out her palm until Maram laid a trembling hand in it. Neither spoke as Aghraas slid the ring onto her fourth finger.

"A promise," Aghraas said, and Maram retrieved the larger ring from the box and slid it over Aghraas's finger.

"A promise," she repeated, and her voice broke. So few people made promises to her worth keeping. It seemed foolish to hope, even in this new world order, but she wanted to believe so very desperately that she could trust in this. That she could be worthy of it.

Aghraas bent her head to Maram's and her arms came around her waist and her mouth met hers. She never ceased to be surprised by her warmth or the frisson of pleasure that shot through her from a single touch.

"One heart, one home," Aghraas murmured against her cheek.

And Maram looked over Aghraas's shoulder at the image of her mother and felt for the first time that her mother's dream had been realized. That she had found a world, had begun to shape one, in which justice and love could be one and the same.

POLITICAL FACTIONS

The Vath: an invading race of humanoids who have thus far conquered four planets, the most recent being Andala. They are ruled by a council of High Directors, and their king, Mathis.

The Kushaila: one of three main ethnic-tribal federations on the planet Andala bound by common language, traditions, and the first woman: Houwa. Largely based in the northern section of the main continent.

Banu Ziyad: the ruling tribe of the Kushaila who, before the conquest of the Vath, ruled the entire planet. They were decimated in the conquest and are now survived by Itou, the Dowager Sultana, and Maram vak Mathis, the Vathek king's half-Kushaila daughter and Imperial

Heir. Based out of the Walili province on the main continent. Their colors are green and gold, and their crest is a tesleet bird in flight.

Banu Salih: a ruling tribe almost as large and powerful as the Ziyadis, they were long allied with them before the conquest. In 4380 they attempted a coup against the Vath and failed. Idris ibn Salih is the only survivor of Vathek retribution from the main tribal branch. Their colors are green and red, and their crest is a lion's head with a palm tree cresting over it.

Banu Mas'ud: a banner family to the Banu Salih, led by the twins 'Imad and I'timad. Their colors are dark blue and gold, and their crest is a moon in sun.

Banu Nasir: a banner family to the Banu Salih, led by Khulood an-Nassiriya. Their colors are purple and white, and their crest is a dagger and coin.

The Zidane: an ethnic-tribal confederation much like the Kushaila, though they differ in their native tongue. Based largely out of the southern cities on the main continent.

Banu Wattasi: the largest tribe of the Zidane who aided in the coup led by the Salihis in 4380. Were largely obliterated by Vathek retribution. Furat al-Wattasia is the only survivor and is out of favor with the current royal court.

Banu Ifran: a small Zidane tribe who collaborated with the Vathek conquest and were in turn rewarded with wealth and lands. Now a power on the main continent. Their colors are red and gold, and their crest is a tower and palm frond.

The Tashfin: a tribal confederation based largely on the eastern continent and along the coast.

The Tazalghit: a nomadic pastoral tribal confederation known for their horses and cavalrywomen. Historically demanded tribute from city-states on the main continent, and later allied with the Ziyadis first in conquest and then in colonial resistance against the Vath. Many believe their numbers much diminished postwar, though they lead the rebellion in its current form.

THE VATHEK CONQUEST

YEAR 4356: Mathis commits patricide and takes over ruling the Vath.

YEAR 4359: The Vath begin conquest of the Outer Rim, with a young Mathis at their head. (The conquest includes Shlou and Rifa, and Moran-Andala is the final planet.)

YEAR 4363: The Seige of Andala begins.

YEAR 4364: Cadiz is seized and a base is established.

YEAR 4364: Vathek forces land on northern landmass, campaign lasts nine months.

YEAR 4367: The Vath take the south-southeast landmass.

YEAR 4369: The Seige of Walili begins, the loyalists buckle down and push Vathek forces out of Greater Walili and off the south-southwest landmass.

YEAR 4373: The Vath are now entrenched on the coastline, mass starvation and famine are rampant throughout the planet, and the planet is under imperial blockade.

YEAR 4374: A peace treaty is signed between Queen Najat and Emperor Mathis. They are married and the blockade is lifted. Maram and Amani are conceived this year. Idris is two years old.

YEAR 4380: The Bani Salihi, Wattasis, key members of the Banu Ziyad, the Masmuda, and others withdraw from the capital and assemble forces against the Vath. (Maram and Amani are five, Idris is seven.)

YEAR 4381: The loyalist forces begin negotiations. Najat dies suddenly. Itou is expelled from the Ziyaana to Gibra after a coup is attempted by Furat's family. They are all put to the sword. (Maram and Amani are six, Idris is eight.)

YEAR 4384: Loyalists surrender.

YEAR 4385: Many of the loyalist elders and supporters are executed without warning, including the leading members of the Bani Salih, what remain of the Wattasis, and the dissidents among the Banu Ziyad. (Maram and Amani are eight, Idris is ten.)

YEAR 4393: Amani is kidnapped to the Ziyaana. Our story begins.

KEY TERMS

Cagir: a term that denotes common or low status among the Vath as part of the last name; always precedes the person's father's name.

Daan: tattoos signifying lineage and faith, a practice common among the tribal confederations of the main continent. Largely outlawed among the makhzen.

Dihya: the god of the majority religion on Andala, most commonly practiced by the aforementioned ethnic groups.

Makhzen: the upper echelons of indigenous Andalaan nobility, largely absorbed into the Vathek imperial structure. Many of the makhzen coming of age now were hostages of the Vathek regime in the early days of its rule and expected to be loyal servants of the state.

Tesleet: a holy bird and the servant and messenger of Dihya. Long thought extinct.

Vak: a term that denotes high and pureblooded status among the Vath as part of the last name; always precedes the person's father's name.

Ziyaana: the imperial palace in the capital city of Andala.

WANT MORE?

If you enjoyed this and would like to find out about similar books we publish, we'd love you to join our online Sci-Fi, Fantasy and Horror community, Hodderscape.

Visit hodderscape.co.uk for exclusive content form our authors, news, competitions and general musings, and feel free to comment, contribute or just keep an eye on what we are up to.

See you there!